HER TOUCH—INNOCENT AND HONEST—
RIPPED THROUGH HIS BODY

. . . tightening Mick's gut and creating an unexpected and unwanted reaction.

She had brushed the tips of her fingers across his bruise. And from the tremble of her fingers, Caterina clearly had experienced something intense as well.

He rose from the chair and the motion brought him close to her. Too close. Her eyes were that intense dark blue once more, the pupils wide. The blush even stronger across the high slashes of her cheekbones. She licked her lips.

Very human lips.

Very luscious womanly lips.

He dipped his head down, hesitating when he was about an inch away. Warning himself that if he took a taste . . .

Praise for
SINS OF THE FLESH

"Captured my full attention with its too-human characters and its too-real plot. A fascinating, adrenaline-fueled read! I could not stop turning pages!"

—Debra Webb, national bestselling
author of *Everywhere She Turns*

more . . .

SINS
OF THE
FLESH

CARIDAD PIÑEIRO

FOREVER

NEW YORK   BOSTON

Copyright © 2009 by Caridad Piñeiro Scordato
Excerpt from *Stronger Than Sin* copyright © 2009 by Caridad Piñeiro Scordato. All rights reserved. Except as permitted under the U.S. Copyright Act of 1976, no part of this publication may be reproduced, distributed, or transmitted in any form or by any means, or stored in a database or retrieval system, without the prior written permission of the publisher.

Book design by TexTech
Cover design by Diane Luger
Cover art by Herman Estevez

Forever
Hachette Book Group
237 Park Avenue
New York, NY 10017
Visit our website at www.HachetteBookGroup.com.

Forever is an imprint of Grand Central Publishing. The Forever name and logo is a trademark of Hachette Book Group, Inc.

Printed in the United States of America
First Printing: November 2009

10 9 8 7 6 5 4 3 2 1

ATTENTION CORPORATIONS AND ORGANIZATIONS:
Most HACHETTE BOOK GROUP books are available at quantity discounts with bulk purchase for educational, business, or sales promotional use. For information, please call or write:

Special Markets Department, Hachette Book Group
237 Park Avenue, New York, NY 10017
Telephone: 1-800-222-6747 Fax: 1-800-477-5925

*This book is dedicated to Anne Frazier Walradt,
Gail Freeman, Kathye Quick, Lois Winston, Melinda
Leigh, Michele Richter, and Rayna Vause for being an
amazing group of friends and for all their hard work and
dedication in helping found the Liberty States Fiction
Writers. You all rock!*

*To my wonderful agent, Kevan Lyon, and my amazing
editor, Selina McLemore, who believed in this series from
day one and helped make it possible.*

*To Michele Maughan for enduring my many questions
about gene expression and the "what ifs…" Any and all
scientific errors are solely my fault and no reflection on this
very bright and understanding Graduate Student Senate
president and PhD graduate student.*

*Finally, to Colleen, Gretchen, Irene, Jamie, and Tami
for helping me while I struggled to find a new title for
SINS OF THE FLESH. Your help was truly appreciated!*

PROLOGUE

The day the music died, Caterina Shaw did as well.

Not physically, although she understood the death of her body was inevitable. She had come to terms with that reality some time ago. She had even managed to deal with the blindness caused by the tumor eating away at her brain. But then the pain had become so great that it had silenced the music, stealing away the only thing that had made life worth the anguish.

"You understand this treatment is new and uncertain," Dr. Rudy Wells explained, his voice smooth and comforting. The touch of his hand, warm and reassuring, came against hers as it rested on her thigh.

"I understand," she said and faced the direction of that calming voice.

Another person abruptly chimed in, his tones as strident and grating as a badly played oboe. "We'll begin with laser surgery to remove the bulk of the tumor followed by two different courses of gene therapy."

Two? she wondered and sensed Dr. Wells's hesitation as well from the tremble that skated across his fingers. He removed his hand from hers and said, "Dr. Edwards believes that we can not only shut down the tumor growing in your brain, but possibly regrow the portions of your optic nerve that the tumor damaged."

Caterina's only wish when considering the experimental treatment had been to stop the pain so that she could play her cello once again. So that her last months would be filled with the vitality her music provided.

It was through her music that she lived. That her mother lived, Caterina thought, recalling the passion she had felt as a small child when her mother had played the piano for her; the way her mother's fingers had coaxed life from the keys much like she now did with a stroke of her bow and the deft touch of her fingers on the strings of her cello.

Or at least like she had up until the cancer had put an end to her music, bringing her life to a close. Except now she was being told something different.

Caterina had never thought about eliminating the tumor. Every prognosis so far had been that she was terminal. Now these new doctors told her not only that she might live, but that she might actually see again, too. She didn't dare believe that she would be able to get her old life back completely, as well as her sight, but...

"You think I'll be able to recover? To see again?" Caterina asked, needing to be sure she had understood correctly.

"The risks are great, my dear," Dr. Wells urged gently.

"But you qualify for the human trials because of the advanced state of your illness, Ms. Shaw," Dr. Edwards added, annoyance at his partner evident in the staccato beats of his voice.

Her advanced state, which could possibly bring death even with this treatment, Caterina thought. Not that she feared her end. What she did fear was letting the pain in

her head rob her of the one thing she could not live without: her music.

She knew without hesitation that it was worth any risk
to regain that part of her. To drive back the illness so she
could play her cello once more and reanimate her heart
for as long as she had left if the treatments couldn't stop
the tumor.

"What do you need me to do?"

CHAPTER 1

Six months later

Mick Carrera understood what kind of man he was.

Ruthless.

Determined.

Skilled in the art of killing.

People came to him when no one else could handle their problems because Mick either solved them or eliminated them—if Mick thought elimination was justified. Some scruples remained buried in his soul, a secret he closely guarded. In his line of work, having scruples equated to weakness.

Dr. Raymond Edwards had presented him with the kind of job that possibly ended with elimination, although Edwards hadn't come right out and said so during their short telephone conversation. The doctor had skirted around the subject with the skill of a ballroom dancer, insisting time and time again that all he required were the services of a security specialist to assist with a problem at their facility.

Mick's initial misgivings made him wonder why he had even come to the doctor's office for this additional discussion. His typical clientele preferred meeting places that were much less visible, but then again, maybe such transparency meant that the doctor had been truthful about the nature of this assignment.

He scoped out the office as he entered, taking note of the fact that there was only one entrance in and out. Not good for a quick escape. As he passed a credenza located beneath a wall filled with diplomas, framed news articles, and photos, he noticed a small bronze statue of a horse mounted on a heavy marble base.

The size and weight of the statue would make it a handy weapon for either cracking open a man's skull or breaking through the plate glass windows which lined one long wall of the office. The clear windows were now darkening, the color becoming as deep and dense as squid ink and likely for the same reason—concealment.

Mick had noticed all the high-tech security on his way through the entrance of the building. He had expected it even while worrying about it. He knew his image would end up saved on a hard drive somewhere from the assorted cameras positioned throughout the offices, but if Dr. Edwards was on the up-and-up, this was one job that was too good not to consider.

"I thought you might like some privacy," the man behind the desk said as he rose and offered his hand.

"Dr. Raymond Edwards," the man said.

Mick shook his hand and with a nod said, "Mick Carrera."

As Mick sat, he caught a glimpse of another security camera behind the desk, aimed directly at his chair. When Edwards tracked his gaze, he said, "Don't worry, Mr. Carrera. I'll make sure all traces of you are erased from our systems."

"I appreciate your understanding," Mick replied, even

while wondering again why a supposedly distinguished scientist like Raymond Edwards had sought out the services of a man like him. What else had the good doctor erased from the company's security videos?

Dragging his attention back to the man seated behind the desk, he listened as Edwards offered a rather lengthy introduction about the work that his biotech company did and their many accomplishments. Edwards's manner was outwardly confident and businesslike, but Mick couldn't help noticing how the doctor kept his right hand on the face of the file on his desk and fiddled with one corner of the thick folder, thumbing it again and again. The curled corner of the papers confirmed that Edwards had opened up that file more times than the good doctor wanted Mick to know.

When Edwards paused for a breath, Mick seized the opportunity. "Your mission is clear, Dr. Edwards. Your company specializes in developing gene therapies for the terminally ill."

The man stiffened and immediately corrected him. "Our present group of patients is terminally ill, but we hope that what we learn from our current research—"

"Will help all of mankind in the future. So why do you require my services?"

Edwards thumbed the edge of the folder again before lacing his hands together on the face of the file. He leaned forward slightly, as if he was about to share something intimate. A furrow of worry developed over the bridge of his nose, but the rest of his thin face remained passive.

"I've been told your specialties are corporate security and discreet investigations," he said.

The dance has commenced, Mick thought. He was almost amused by the way the man was twirling his way around the true nature of Mick's work. "My experience—"

"Is rather extensive. Army Ranger. EMT. Security consultant for one of the nation's top companies before you decided to go out on your own."

It hadn't really been a voluntary decision, but in the end it had worked out well for all involved—except the two civilians who had been killed during his last assignment.

Mick pressed on. "Your background check seems to have been quite thorough, Dr. Edwards, which makes me wonder just why you need my . . . special skills."

A sly smile slinked across Edwards's face as he finally pushed the folder across the desk, but another thicker file still remained beneath the doctor's manicured fingers.

Mick opened the slim manila folder. On one side were copies of preliminary police reports on a murder that had occurred in the company's labs. He recalled hearing about it on the early morning Philadelphia news a few days before and had immediately made the connection last night when Edwards had telephoned.

Dr. Rudy Wells, a top researcher and co-owner of the biotech company, had died a grisly death. Both the officers' notes and photos detailed the many injuries he had suffered.

Wells had been ripped apart. One arm and leg had been torn from his torso. The sharp point of a broken chair leg had been jammed through the *foramen magnum* at the base of his skull.

Mick flipped through all the pictures, imagining the kind of strength it would take to do that to another human being. Gauging the apparent rage, Mick reasoned it must have been a personal attack, since no professional would have done such a messy job.

The bruises visible on Wells's body in the photos would likely yield prints of some kind, and with the battle that probably went on between Wells and his assailant, a treasure trove of DNA, fibers, and other evidence had likely been transferred to the dead scientist or left behind in the lab.

As he finished reviewing the last of the photos, he risked a quick glance at Edwards to study his reaction. The other man's lips had stiffened with displeasure, but there was nothing else to give away what Edwards was thinking.

"This is the problem you wouldn't discuss last night on the phone? Aren't the police already investigating this murder?" With a quick flip of his wrist, he tossed the file back onto Edwards's desk.

The clear grey of the other man's eyes chilled at Mick's dismissal. Tight lines bracketed Edwards's thin lips before he said, "If the police get wind of what actually happened here, everything we do could be in jeopardy. That's why we need a man of your caliber for this assignment."

Mick motioned to the file. "Let me get this straight. You don't want the police to solve this crime—"

"There's nothing to solve."

Edwards finally handed him the second, thicker file. "We know who the murderer is—Caterina Shaw. One of our patients."

As he opened the file, Caterina Shaw's engaging smile and intense blue-eyed gaze peered at him from the photo within the folder. A beautiful woman, he thought. A wealth of midnight-black hair contrasted nicely with her perfect, creamy skin and surrounded a delicate face with a pouty pair of lips.

The photo was clearly intended for business purposes, as Ms. Shaw was dressed in what looked like a sedate black gown. A motherly string of pearls lay at the long elegant line of her throat. Mick couldn't help but notice that the low cut of her gown provided a delicious glimpse of her other endowments as well.

It took all his willpower to battle the very visceral response that the photo created. He definitely had been without a woman for too long, and with good reason.

Women seemed to find him physically attractive, but he always felt it was the aura of danger surrounding him which really drew them. Either reason did not generally lead to anything of lasting value, since relationships based on such shallow motives lacked the kind of trust necessary for permanence.

Reviewing the short bio on Caterina Shaw, Mick realized that permanence was something to which she was accustomed. Caterina had been born in the Philadelphia area and had stayed there for most of her life. The only breaks from the city had been for schooling, but each time she had returned home to Philly. Even her employment record screamed of stability. She had been with the local orchestra for several years.

He gazed at her picture one last time before turning his attention to the final entry in what appeared to be a lengthy medical history.

Patient has recently developed uncontrollable seizures leading to episodes of memory loss and rage combined with full expression of the implanted gene sequence.

Medical mumbo jumbo, Mick thought, for *she's a raving psycho.*

As Mick flipped back to the photograph of the woman, he was struck again by her beauty—not that beauty wasn't capable of the kind of violence perpetrated on Dr. Wells.

"Why is Ms. Shaw one of your patients?" he asked as he closed the file and returned it with greater care than he had the previous folder.

Edwards flipped open the file and removed the photo, glancing at it almost wistfully before he said, "She was beautiful, wasn't she?"

"Why is she here, Dr. Edwards?" Mick pressed, annoyed by the man's almost staged theatrics and his use of the past tense for a woman who was still very much alive, as far as Mick knew.

"Sad, sad story," the physician said with a *tsk* and dramatic shake of his head. "About three years ago, Ms. Shaw was diagnosed with an inoperable brain tumor. Slow-growing at first, but then some switch flipped and the tumor became more aggressive."

"So she came to you?" he asked, wondering just what state the young woman had been in when she arrived at Edwards's facility.

"Not at first. The only patients we are allowed to admit are those with no other recourse."

"Which means?"

"Ms. Shaw went blind when the tumor invaded her optic nerve, but she managed to deal with that. Some laser treatments kept the growth confined for about another year, but then—"

"It spread and she came to you for help." A note of

disdain escaped with the comment, obviously irritating the man across from him.

Edwards jerked Caterina Shaw's photo into Mick's line of sight. He jabbed at the image of the woman. "Just twenty-eight and already at the height of her career. Her brain was rapidly being destroyed. Even if our treatments were untried, Ms. Shaw understood the possible reward. Wouldn't you do the same?"

Mick thought he would have probably put a gun in his mouth and blown what little brains remained out the back of his skull, but suspected the doctor sitting across from him wouldn't appreciate hearing that solution.

"What do you want from me?"

Edwards picked up both files and thrust them across the width of the desk. "After killing my partner, Caterina escaped the confines of our facility. Find her. If you can, bring her back so that we can get her under control before we turn her over to the authorities."

Something about the tone of Edwards's voice didn't ring true.

As Mick met the other man's icy stare, he got the sense that the seemingly proper physician was much like he was.

Determined.

Ruthless.

And possibly not above breaking a few rules to accomplish his goals.

"What if I can't bring her back? What if—"

"Caterina resists? Chances are she will. She's quite dangerous in her current state. My partner found that out the hard way."

Mick glanced at the files in his hands, debating if he

would take the assignment. As if sensing his hesitation, Edwards leaned forward once again and passed him a check with too many zeroes to refuse.

He examined the check for only a second before slipping it into the pocket of his black leather jacket. As he rose, Edwards held out his hand to seal the deal.

Mick ignored the man and walked to the door, certain of one thing as he exited.

If Edwards wasn't telling the truth, what happened to his buddy Wells would seem like a cakewalk compared to what Mick would do to him.

CHAPTER 2

Caterina struggled to contain the thoughts rampaging through her brain. Scattered ideas and images collided there, creating a convoluted maze which kept her a prisoner of her own mind. The images surprised her, prompting other vague memories of unending darkness.

Unwelcome darkness that had lasted for too long. That had been accompanied by pain only...

Little pain remained anymore and the darkness was gone, replaced by bright images swirling around in her brain, a weird melding of colors reminiscent of a Peter Max painting.

Peter Max.

She forced herself to focus, remembering other pictures and artists. Lots and lots of paintings and artists while people milled about.

Had she been an artist as well? she wondered, confused about who and what she was as she gazed around again at the multihued shapes surrounding her. As unnatural as the colors were, she was grateful she could see, suddenly aware that she hadn't been able to do so in some time.

Trees.

Bushes.

Birds twittered overhead. A tiny flash of brown and white scurried into the underbrush.

She was outdoors, which meant...

She was free.

She had escaped.

Escaped, she realized, honing in on that idea as she tried to make sense of the thoughts and memories creating havoc in her brain. Finally a picture formed in her mind of a hospital.

No, not a hospital. An office maybe? Or a lab? Yes, a lab.

At some point she had escaped from one of the cells in the lab. The day before or maybe the day before that. She couldn't remember. And now she was in the woods, she realized as she skirted the edge of a stand of scraggly pines, their fragrant needles soft beneath her feet.

A step later, Caterina stubbed her toe on an exposed root.

Fearful of discovery, she contained her cry of pain and examined her foot. Like everything around her, the colors were off.

Bright yellow-green blood at the tip of her stubbed toe glowed against the darker browns of dirt and leaves along the rest of her foot.

Caterina forced herself to focus on that appendage, gathering her thoughts. Reality momentarily returned, restoring with it the peachy hues of her healthy human skin, although something else was odd.

The nasty stub at the end of her toe was already healing.

The only thing that remained from the injury was a bit of phosphorescent yellow-green on the ragged wood of the root where she had stubbed her toe.

Yellow-green blood?

Impossibly wrong. Her toe should still hurt. And her blood should be red.

Try as she might to connect her thoughts to understand, whatever was happening to her—within her—made no sense.

A sudden loud thumping noise came at her, like the insistent beat of a timpani drum. At first it beat at a regular pace but soon became a rapid roll as the sound came closer.

Wump, wump, wump, quickly and persistently. Over and over as the sound approached, battering the air viciously. The noise was strong enough to become a physical pulse against her body.

She had to avoid the noise.

Caterina hunkered down beneath the lower branches of one of the more thickly needled evergreens in the Pine Barrens. The sound intensified as did the wind, which whirled fallen leaves and needles around and around the base of the tree. The helicopter making the din paused overhead and the branches of the pine whipped wildly against her naked body. Caterina remained immobile, hugging the trunk of the tree, digging her fingers into the wood to hold on.

The tree trunk gave easily beneath her fingers, surprising her, but providing her with a firm grasp as she tried to blend in beneath the branches of the evergreen.

Danger was near.

Danger from the helicopter kicking up the air and foliage around her.

Closing her eyes and letting out a soft mewl of fear, she burrowed deeper against the thick trunk of the pine, hoping she wouldn't be seen.

She couldn't go back to the lab.

After long minutes, the helicopter moved on with a loud screaming whir, but Caterina remained in her protective squat, waiting. Her fingers dug as deep as her knuckles into the tree trunk until she extracted them, sticky with sap.

It would be night again soon, she realized as she looked around.

She glanced at her fingers—tacky from pine sap, with an odd cast to the skin. She tried to make sense of her actions and the strange color but couldn't.

Immediately after came the vision of those fingers rapidly shifting against strings. Pressing against smoothly shaped wood, producing sensually rich sound.

Producing music.

Her music.

She grabbed hold of those ideas, hoping the fragmented ideas would finally come together to make sense. She didn't know how long she remained there, rooted to the spot, trying to collect her thoughts, but the strain in her legs grew steadily until her muscles screamed in agony.

Caterina finally gave into the call of her body, rose, and stepped away from the protective embrace of the evergreen. But even as she did so, the deep green of the pine needles remained wrapped around her skin as she stepped out into the open.

She studied her hands and feet. Her skin had assumed the color of the verdant woods around her.

I'm human, but my skin isn't normal, she thought as the full impact of her condition hit her.

Shaking her head to clear the illogical vision, she then noticed something familiar, despite the odd colors that

had returned to her vision, creating almost a kaleido-
scopic blur. As she locked her gaze on one spot in the
distance, the images sharpened.

Lights.

Those were lights up ahead. And lights meant something good. Something better than the woods around her.

That recollection triggered a string of other ideas
which finally coalesced into a more complex understanding about herself.

She had been at the lab because she was sick, but had
escaped to be safe.

With that realization immediately came another.

She was naked.

Or at least she thought she was, gazing down at
herself.

Her skin had that odd cast to it. When she touched her
stomach, the sap-sticky pads of her fingers met the softer
skin of her midsection. The deep green of the pine tree
covered most of her body, but near her ankles the tone of
her skin blended to the color of the earth at her feet.

Impossibly wrong, she thought again.

As wrong as the now fully healed stub of her toe and
the way she had been able to shove her fingers into the
trunk of the evergreen.

She had to hide until reason returned and provided
some answers as to what was happening, but she couldn't
walk around naked.

She should have grabbed some clothes when she had
made her escape, only . . .

Visions battered her brain, driving her to her knees.

So much blood.

On the floor and walls.

All over her hands.

All over Dr. Wells.

She wrapped her arms around herself and rocked back and forth for a moment as she forced away the disturbing memories and marshaled her thoughts.

She would have to find some clothes once she went...

Where am I going? she asked herself, standing and examining the bloodstains on her body.

The realization rushed through her, surprising her with its clarity and bringing immense joy.

I'm going home.

CHAPTER 3

The whole thing stank, and not even the possibility of becoming a rich man could make the smell go away.

Mick refused to think about why after two days he still had not cashed the check tucked into his wallet. A job was a job, he told himself, and this assignment was paying way better than most. He had opted for this way of life years earlier because of the money, needing to help his family. A fire had nearly destroyed the restaurant which had been their livelihood since their arrival from Mexico over twenty years ago. The money the insurance company had provided as a settlement had not been enough to repair the damage, and without his assistance it would have been impossible to reopen the restaurant and allow his siblings to finish their schooling.

But they don't need your help anymore, the voice in his head challenged, urging him that there were other jobs he could do. Jobs that were not as risky and where he could use his skills to help and not hurt.

The way he might have to hurt Caterina Shaw if he couldn't control her.

Images of the destruction wrought on Edwards's dead partner came to mind, warning him about what Caterina had supposedly done. But apprehension suffused him as he stared at the nervous young woman seated across from him, Caterina's best friend.

"I appreciate you taking the time to speak with me, Ms. Rogers," he said in an attempt to alleviate the woman's obvious distress.

"At the door you said you were hired by—"

"Wardwell Biotech," he said, providing her with the name of Edwards's and Wells's company, much as he had when she had been shutting the door in his face. It had been his warning about her friend being hurt and his big booted foot in the door which had gained him access to the tony Rittenhouse Square townhouse.

She nodded, but continued to wring her hands over and over as she said, "I was so worried when Cat told me about the treatment, only..."

"She would have died without it."

After a precise nod of her head, Ms. Rogers finally stilled the motion of her hands, splaying her fingers against the legs of her tailored navy blue slacks. "Cat knew she might die even with the treatment, but she had to have her music back."

Mick recalled the video he had watched the day before and which had been taken months before Caterina had signed onto Dr. Edwards's little science experiment. Anyone viewing the performance would have been hard pressed to realize that the vibrant young woman creating such wondrous music was terminally ill.

Caterina's legs had been wrapped around the cello as she fingered the strings and her bow stroked the profoundly rich tones from the instrument. Every movement seduced yet more from the musical piece, imbuing each note with emotion and passion.

The music had clearly been her life.

With a curt nod, Mick reached into the pocket of his leather jacket and removed a small pad and pen. Flipping through his notes, he continued with his questioning.

"I've spoken to a number of Caterina's acquaintances in the past two days. Everyone says she was pleasant and caring. Dedicated to friends, family, and career. Would you say it was in that order?"

A confused look danced across Elizabeth Rogers's flawless features. "Meaning?"

"Which was more important to Caterina? Her career or her family or—"

"Cat didn't have any family. She lost her mother when she was six, although there were some distant cousins in Mexico. She and her father were estranged. He never really approved of her chosen profession. He died when Cat was in college."

"So her father never knew about her success?"

"No, not that it mattered to Cat. She wasn't about being a celebrity."

Caterina had come across as humble, even possibly shy in the interviews Mick had seen. But he wondered how it must feel to be one of the world's premier cellists and perform for kings, presidents, and other dignitaries and have no one with whom to share that success.

"What about men?" he said. Caterina had been elegant. Refined. Passionate. Physically beautiful.

Elizabeth shook her head and her blond ponytail swished back and forth. "Cat was too involved with her friends and career. In that order," she clarified. "There was an occasional man every now and then, but nothing significant. Especially not in the last several years, thanks to the cancer."

He nodded, imagining that the illness might have made relationships difficult.

Had that made her resentful? Had the loss of her parents angered her? he wondered as he flipped the pages in his notepad.

It would take a lot of rage to cold-bloodedly rip a man apart and pith him the way one might a mouse before vivisection.

"Did that bother her? Was she upset—"

Elizabeth's rough laugh stopped him. "Upset? On the contrary. Cat never let it get to her. With each setback, she found a way to continue. When she went blind, she learned to play the pieces by ear."

He sensed something behind her words. Disapproval? "You were her best friend."

"I *am* Cat's best friend," she immediately clarified.

Mick leaned back in the delicate wing chair and it creaked under the weight of his body. Considering the other woman as she nervously fingered the thick gold chain at her neck, he said, "You're angry. Jealousy, maybe? She was first chair and yet she relied on you—"

Elizabeth's voice escalated with each word. "To help her prepare her pieces after she went blind? While playing second fiddle, literally."

He shrugged, prompting her to rise elegantly from the sofa, her hands clasped tightly before her. "Cat and I are best friends. I'd do anything for her and she would do anything for me."

He rose from the chair as well, understanding that she

was done with his questioning, but he pressed on. "Including giving her a place to hide?"

"I don't believe what they said about Cat on the news," she answered, reaching for the thick gold chain again with a trembling hand.

"Your friend is the main suspect in a gruesome murder, Elizabeth. These treatments—"

"Wouldn't change Cat. This is all a lie," she said and walked out of the parlor and down the short hall to the door of her townhouse, clearly intending him to follow.

At the door, he paused and handed her his business card. She wouldn't take it, so he leaned over and left it on a carved mahogany table near the entrance. "In case you have something else to tell me," he said and walked out.

The door slammed shut behind him, the sound like a gunshot in the quiet of the night.

A block away lay Rittenhouse Square. It would be nearly empty at this time of night. A good place to think.

Mick shoved his hands in his pockets and walked down 18th Street to Walnut, crossed over, and at the corner strolled down the diagonal path to the center of the square. He stopped to listen to the sounds of the fountain, assembling his thoughts, and then sauntered to a bench located close to a streetlight.

He sat and considered what he had learned about Caterina Shaw. Worried because he had let all that he had discovered about Caterina's background influence him, something he rarely did. Usually all that information just amounted to raw data used to track his target. Determine its strengths and weaknesses. Prepare for the capture or kill.

During the course of his brief investigations, it had become difficult to be so clinical about Caterina Shaw.

He could kid himself and say that he didn't know why, but it would be a lie. He knew precisely why.

His search had revealed Caterina's painful past as well as her tragic present. Neither had kept her from what she had wanted to do.

He admired courage and perseverance. Traits he had relied on more than once to keep himself safe. To keep safe the men in the Army Ranger unit he had once commanded.

Although he didn't know Caterina in the real sense of the word, Mick had gotten to know more about her than was good for him if he wanted to complete his assignment. He forced himself to remember that whatever she had been before, she was now a dangerous murderer.

Or at least that's what Edwards wanted him to believe.

He was having trouble buying into that, but then the last entry on her medical history played through his brain for what had to be the hundredth time since his meeting with Edwards.

Patient has recently developed uncontrollable seizures leading to episodes of rage combined with full expression of the implanted gene sequence.

Mick's early life hadn't allowed for extensive schooling, but he had more than made up for that during his time as an Army Ranger. He had devoured whatever manuals the Army had tossed at him, in addition to finally not only obtaining his college degree but also his EMT certification.

The medical information in Caterina's file was therefore clear. Coupled with the information he had gathered on the good doctors Edwards and Wells, he once again tried to imagine the real-life results that could occur based upon the last statement in her medical history.

Uncontrollable seizures...episodes of rage...full expression...; he repeated these phrases to himself before turning to the notes he had made from her medical history and his own research.

Apparently, Edwards and Wells had been able to identify beneficial gene sequences in nearly half a dozen creatures. Using modern cloning techniques, they had isolated those sequences and replicated them in sufficient quantities to be able to combine them with viral carriers.

Although the idea of intentionally letting a live virus loose in someone's body made him nervous, apparently it was common practice to use simple viruses, such as the ones that caused colds, to become transport mechanisms. Once those carriers were injected into the subject, the natural viral process took over, replicating and insinuating the DNA into the subject's genes.

As Mick reviewed his scribbling by the light of the streetlamp, he realized that Edwards and Wells also appeared to have found a way not only to target where the recombination occurred, but to control the replication process and the expression of the implanted gene sequence.

Or at least they'd *thought* they had learned to control the replication and expression.

The seizures from which Caterina had supposedly been suffering, together with the aberrant activity caused by the gene, clearly meant their control wasn't all it was cracked up to be.

If that entry in her medical history was even true. The entry could be the start of groundwork for framing Caterina for Wells's murder.

He put aside his pad and leaned back against the stone balustrade which surrounded the center of the square and formed a backrest of sorts for the nearby cement bench. He laced his fingers behind his head while he imagined what kinds of behavior the foreign genes might cause, as well as how desperate someone might need to be to try such a risky procedure.

Once again it occurred to him that he would have rather chosen to blow out his brains, but...

He surged forward and pulled out Caterina's photo from his jacket pocket. Ran the pads of his fingers across the glossy surface, intrigued not only by her beauty, but also by her tenacity.

Such strength.

Passion.

Intelligence.

Hard traits to resist, he thought, and recalled the check he had folded and slipped into his wallet.

Quite a bounty.

Enough to make him set for a couple of years. Maybe even allow him to leave this rather treacherous and troublesome life for a more rational one.

Possibly even an honorable one, with simpler demands and easier decisions to make.

He risked another glimpse at Caterina's photo. It was a damn shame that the sole decision he would have to make about her was whether to take her in dead or alive.

As soon as it was dark again, Caterina moved from the safety of the Pine Barrens and slipped through an unlocked door into one of the buildings along the edges of Camden.

Inside she kept close to the outside wall, plastering

herself to its rough cinder block. When she heard a sound, she paused and held her breath.

Someone coming her way. The footsteps soft, regular as a metronome as the person approached.

A night watchman?

A flashlight beam swung back and forth, back and forth in a determined arc. Swept across the unlocked door and then in her direction. For one heart-pounding moment, the light tracked across her midsection, but then moved on.

Why hadn't the guard seen her?

The light had been directly on her. She glanced down at her stomach, recalling where the beam from his flashlight had hit her body.

Grey mottled with specks of black had blossomed across not only her midsection, but all of her torso, making her nearly invisible against the cinder-block wall.

She picked up her hand and stared at it. She couldn't understand the current color of her skin any more than she could the forest hues which had covered her flesh the day before.

She focused on her hand until slowly the mottled color faded away, leaving behind the tones of normal human skin. But almost immediately after that, the odd vibrant colors reappeared, painting everything around her with a bold impressionistic brush.

She didn't understand the colors on her skin, in her vision.

They weren't right. She wasn't right, she remembered.

She was sick. Only a sick person would hurt...

The memories pounded at her brain again, creating a crater of pain in the center of her skull.

So much blood on the floor and walls.

All over her and the pieces of Dr. Wells.

Soft wet pieces beneath her fingers.

Control, she urged and leaned back against the wall to stabilize herself. Her fingertips sank into the cinder block, grounding her as she tried to focus.

Focus. Focus. Focus.

She repeated the word like a mantra until the reminders of blood and death receded, replaced by scattered recollections of people and pictures and music.

Music, she thought, imagining the black and white of notes on a page. The rough bite of metal strings beneath her fingers. Smooth wood and cold varnish.

She loved music, she recalled, and with that came the picture of a building in her mind's eye.

A building filled with welcome.

She had to get to that structure. The music would be there. Music and happiness.

Retracting her fingers from the cinder block, she carefully kept to the outside wall, following it around the edge of the building until she came to some lockers. Slightly rusty and battered, they nevertheless might hold what she needed.

She quickly found a grey T-shirt in one open compartment and slipped it on. It hung on her, overly large on her slender body. A musty smell clung to the thin cotton.

All the other lockers had locks dangling from their handles, sealing in their contents.

With a sharp twist of one lock, however, it sprang free. Inside she found a pair of men's jeans and shoes. Both were immense. She effortlessly opened the other combination locks, the metal bending like putty beneath her fingers.

Within a short time she had scrounged together more clothing and a pair of sneakers she could wear. A candy bar as well. Her stomach had grumbled noisily, since Caterina couldn't remember the last time she had eaten. Dressed, and with her hunger temporarily sated, she hurried toward the open back door, ever vigilant for the presence of others. She listened for a hint of any approach, the sounds of the night exceptionally loud.

No one came.

At the exit, she paused, hesitant. She felt surprisingly strong and energized, but still unfocused. Her vision drifted from the surreal colors which came unbidden to those familiar hues of reality.

A reality which she had struggled to maintain since escaping the lab. A reality which seemed to elude her more often than she cared.

As she escaped into the night, she knew she still had some distance to go until she reached anything familiar. Until she got to the building with the music, certain that once she arrived there, things would make more sense. Maybe even go back to normal, but more importantly . . .

Instinctively she knew that once she got there she would be safe.

CHAPTER 4

Mick stared at the bright yellow police tape and evidence seal on the door of Caterina's townhome, which was located a block off trendy South Street. No matter how much Edwards wanted to avoid police involvement, they were clearly already on the job. Mick would have to hurry and locate her in order to curtail any further investigation. He wouldn't try to guess why Edwards didn't want the police poking around. His job wasn't to question; only to acquire his target.

Or so Mick told himself, hating that the scruples he still possessed insisted that he had to find out why Edwards wanted Caterina so badly before turning her over.

As he examined the evidence seal, he realized that someone had carefully slit it open. The razor-fine cut wouldn't be visible to a casual observer, but upon a more thorough examination someone would discover the break-in.

With a quick look down the street to make sure no one was watching, he easily turned the knob, slipped beneath the caution tape, and entered the townhouse.

He stopped short at the mess within.

Someone had knocked over bookshelves, tables, and

chairs, and knifed open the sofa and cushions. In the upstairs bedrooms, drawers and closets had been rifled, the contents strewn carelessly on the polished wood floors. The linens were tossed and the mattresses slashed.

The deception with the evidence seal and the devastation in the home were not the kind of action he expected from an everyday burglar. Damage of this nature was intended to deliver a personal message, a message that warned about either evening a score or scaring someone off.

He would put his money on the latter, he thought as he glanced out through the front windows to check the street outside before exiting into the night.

Shoulders hunched and head tucked down to conceal his face, he walked at a brisk pace toward South Street, where it would be more populated and he could get lost in the crowd just in case anyone was tracking him.

As he considered the wreckage of Caterina's home, it was clear that someone didn't want her to stay there—not that she would anyway if she had a lick of sense remaining in what was left of her tumor-laden, gene-invaded brain.

A common criminal would avoid any places they regularly visited, knowing that the police would look for them there first. But someone like Caterina might head to familiar things where she likely felt safe and would know where to hide. Maybe even to people she could trust, like her best friend, Elizabeth Rogers.

He contemplated immediately heading back to the Rogers residence, but didn't believe Rogers was covering for her friend. She had let him into her home too quickly and there had been nothing suspicious in her manner, only concern.

If Rogers was not hiding her friend and Caterina had

already come by her home and seen the destruction, she would either head toward Rogers or another safe haven.

The Rogers home was a far walk from Caterina's townhouse while his second targets were closer—the Kimmel Center and nearby Music Academy.

At the corner, he turned onto South and walked toward Broad, all the time keeping an eye out for either a tail or anyone who fit Caterina's general physical description, since she might have had the sense to try and disguise herself.

In the shiny windows of the Whole Foods Market on South Street, he thought he caught a reflection of unusual activity behind him and paused, seemingly to peruse the sign listing their specials. Instead, he focused on the reflection of the few people walking by, trying to pinpoint what had snagged his attention.

A minute or so passed, but whatever he had seen was long gone.

Or maybe he had only imagined it.

He continued onward, hurrying down past the more residential section of South Street until he hit Broad.

It was close to ten and a fair amount of vehicular traffic still traveled along the street, as well as some stray pedestrians, mostly twentysomething students by the University of the Arts. Heading down Broad, he crossed the street and hustled toward the Kimmel Center. The rounded arches of the center's vaulted glass ceiling radiated shards of light into the murkiness of the night sky.

The marquee by the ticket office indicated there had been a performance of the philharmonic that night, but now only a few people lingered in and around the periphery of the building.

He had calculated that Caterina might return here because she would know where to hide within the performing arts complex. However, given the event that night, there would be too many people around for her to enter undetected.

He wouldn't find his target here, but he also suspected she would not be far away.

He continued down the section of Broad known as the Avenue of the Arts until he stood in front of the plain red-brick facade of the Academy of Music.

The building was quiet tonight. Only the muted glow of the gas lanterns cast glimmering light onto the empty sidewalks surrounding the building.

The gated entrance near the front of the building was too conspicuous, even though the recessed stage door lay in the shadows, providing some protection from prying eyes.

Mick had downloaded the blueprints for the building from the Internet and knew just where to go. Turning onto Locust, he proceeded to a narrow alley behind the building. The light from the streetlamps illuminated the mouth of the alley, but beyond that only darkness lingered.

He looked around.

The cobblestoned street was empty of any pedestrians, so he slipped into the narrow alley and paused a few steps in to allow his eyes to adjust to the lack of light and to check for signs of anyone else.

The long slender alley was also empty.

Time for him to move in.

He stole down the alley while hugging the wall, the ground uneven beneath his feet, the area lit only by the small beam from a flashlight he pulled from his pocket.

He moved quickly, every action efficiently cautious, until he located the entrance shown on the blueprints.

Pointing the flashlight at the door, he prepared to jimmy the lock but found that someone had beaten him to it. And rather inexpertly at that. Large sharp gouges along the seam of the door and at the lock gleamed silvery bright in the beam from his flashlight.

He reached behind him, withdrew his 9-mm Glock from beneath his leather jacket and released the safety. With a gloved hand, he slowly opened the door and risked but a sharp glance inside before he cleared the entrance.

The interior was almost as gloomy as the night outside, but since his eyes had adjusted already, he could make out the tangle of shapes before him.

Large lockers and an assortment of equipment lined the edges of a hallway, but a fairly wide and navigable path existed down the center. Slowly he inched along, pausing well before the low light cast by an illuminated exit sign so that he would remain hidden.

He recalled from the building plans where the stairs would be that led to the manager's office and dressing rooms, as well as the stairs to the basement level and trapdoor area. Crouching, he rushed past the dim circle of light cast by the exit sign.

As he did so, his foot brushed against a cable housing on the ground. It slithered and shook like an angry rattlesnake. The rattle bounced loudly off the walls in the quiet of the hall and he stilled, waiting to see if anyone would respond to the sound.

Only silence answered.

Mick released a low grateful sigh and proceeded, decidedly more careful of the objects littering the floor and sides of the hall. More cables. A klieg light. A box brimming with colored gels for the spotlights.

Muscles tense, every inch of him on alert, he skirted all these items until he neared the stairs to the basement level. Pausing, he peered down the darkened stairway, vigilant for any signs of life. As before, the space was empty and the area down below was deadly quiet. He took the first step down the stairs.

A muffled thud sounded behind him.

He whirled on the stair, stepped back up, and took cover behind one of the large grey metal lockers lining the hall, his hand tight on his pistol grip.

Listening, he heard the squeak of a sneaker against the tiled floor. Soft footfalls immediately came, followed by the thud of heavier steps.

Two people.

Somewhere dead ahead in the dark.

Coming toward him as he hid by the stairway.

He picked up his gun, trained it on the area. Waited patiently for any additional movement. A sudden flash of muzzle fire erupted in the dark followed by the familiar pop from a silencer.

Cautiously he eased from behind the locker and made his way closer to the spot where he thought he had seen the flash, ducking in and out from behind the equipment along the hall for protection. He was several feet away from the location when he heard the sound of light footsteps racing away again, followed quickly by the flat-footed pounding of the heavier body.

Another silenced shot rang out and the shooter carelessly stepped into the dim light from the exit sign Mick had avoided earlier, giving him a clear view.

"Stop or I'll fire," he called out while sizing up the man in the illumination from the sign.

The shooter was middle-aged and dark-haired, with a pronounced scar above one brow. Tall and thickly muscled, the man was fairly fit, but with a midsection that was starting to turn to flab. His easy stance with the gun spoke of training, and the silencer on the weapon confirmed he was a professional. But he had made a totally careless mistake by exposing himself in the light from the sign.

The man peered into the darkness toward Mick, searching for him in the shadows. His face was flush with embarrassment—or maybe from the red of the sign—and gleaming with sweat.

From a chase? Mick wondered.

"Identify yourself," Mick said, but then shifted farther back behind the protection of the locker and closer to the wall so that the shooter couldn't place him based on the sound of his voice.

"This is none of your business. Stay out of it," the man called out and moved as if to shift away from the light, but Mick shouted out a warning.

"Move another step and you're dead."

At that command, the man finally did as he was told, remaining in place, but still ready to fire.

"Shaw is my capture," the other man threatened while peering into the dark for any sign of Mick.

The big metal locker provided great cover, and Mick took advantage of that. Reaching down, he picked up a heavy metal hook wrapped with rope. With his free hand, he tossed the hook up ahead of him and toward the wall opposite both him and the shooter. The hook landed with a noisy clatter against a pile of lighting equipment.

The other man turned and shot in the direction of the sound, exposing his gun hand as he did so.

Mick fired, the reverberation of the gunshot loud as it echoed along the hallway.

The shooter grunted in pain and dropped his weapon, but he was already reaching for it with his uninjured hand when Mick charged him. With a strong shove of his shoulder into the man's thickening midsection, Mick sent him careening into the far wall where he collapsed to the ground in a heap.

While keeping his gun trained on the shooter, Mick bent and retrieved the other man's dropped weapon, tucking it into his waistband at the small of his back.

"Who sent you?" Mick asked.

"Like I would tell you," the gunman said as he cradled his bleeding forearm against his chest.

"Get on your stomach." He urged the man on with a wave of his gun. When the man complied, he placed his knee in the middle of his back.

Working quickly, he grabbed some cable ties from his jacket pocket, pulled the man's arms back one at a time and trussed them together with the ties. When he was done, he stood and nudged the man with his foot.

The man rolled over and there was no mistaking his anger.

Mick bent and grabbed the front of the shooter's drab olive military jacket, lifting him off the ground a bit. Not an easy thing to do, since the man had a good bit of bulk in his physique. He gave him a rough shake.

"You're too stupid to be working on your own. Who sent you?" To stress his point, he brought his weapon to the man's temple and repeated his earlier question.

"Franklin Pierce," the man finally replied, unable to hide the quiver of fear on his lips. His eyes jumped back and forth from Mick's face to the gun pointed at his head.

Franklin Pierce, Mick's ex-Ranger buddy who now ran his own private security firm. It had been years since he had talked to his old friend. He would definitely have to pay Franklin a visit and find out what was up, but first...

"Tell Franklin that I don't appreciate him sending in the second string. That he needs to stay out of this."

The flush along the man's face deepened and he stuttered with indignation as he tried to sit up. "You d-d-didn't have t-t-to shoot me, man."

Mick had no doubt that if the situation had been reversed, the gunman wouldn't have hesitated to kill him. He seemed like the kind to shoot first to avoid asking questions later, which was why he had made sure to tie him up. Wanting the man to have no doubt about his earlier warning, he pointed his gun at the man's groin.

"If there is a next time, I'll shoot something you'll really regret losing."

For good measure, he once again grabbed hold of the man's jacket and shoved him away forcefully. The other man rebounded against the wall with a thud, and then lay there, moaning but relatively uninjured.

Mick raced in the direction in which he thought the gunman had been shooting.

Nothing but empty hallway greeted him.

He hoped that the time spent interrogating Franklin's goon hadn't allowed his target to escape.

Gun drawn, he crept along the edges of the hall, the narrow beam of his compact flashlight sweeping the area in front of him and along the walls as he searched.

Just the shadows and equipment.

He advanced, continuing his hunt, and suddenly something gleamed back at him from the ground before him.

He trained the flashlight on the floor.

Bright droplets of yellow-green phosphoresced into luminous life. Bending, he inspected them for a moment.

Memories came speeding back of hot summer days and the twinkling of hundreds of lightning bugs in the woods behind his home. His cousin Ramon used to trap dozens of the flashing bugs in a rusty-topped Mason jar. When Ramon tired of watching the insects crawling around the inside of the jar, their asses shining light against the glass, he would spill out some of the insects and squish them against the sidewalk.

The drops on the ground reminded him of those squashed bugs, their guts glistening in the night.

He removed his glove and stuck his index finger into one small glob. The phosphorescent yellow-green liquid was warm and grew sticky on his finger as it slowly dried. Bringing his finger up to his nose, he inhaled.

Shock filled him as he smelled blood.

Human blood.

He rose slowly, examining the area around him. Flashing the light more closely into the equipment to try and find what had left such blood behind.

The shadows were devoid of life.

With one eye on the ground and what he now realized was a trail of blood, he kept on the lookout for his buddy Franklin or any other unwelcome visitors and proceeded down the hall, constantly swinging the beam of light and the muzzle of his weapon along the hall, ready to fire.

The trail of blood droplets brought him to a stairway

leading to the areas beneath the trapdoor in the stage. On the jamb by the stairs a bigger splotch of lightning bug color gleamed as he shone his light on it.

Had Franklin's man hit something?

Make that *someone*, he thought as he neared and realized the splotch looked like a partial human palm print.

Too weird, Mick thought as he headed to the lower level. Much like the floor above, scattered bits of equipment lined the hall. Gun ready, he examined the floor for any telltale signs. A few steps from the stairs, the iridescent droplet trail stopped.

Mick paused, his movements cautious as he considered what he might find at the end of the trail. The words from Caterina's medical report flashed through his brain, suddenly becoming more urgent.

Full expression of the gene.

Could that be the weird-looking blood? He wondered as he slowly panned the flashlight along one wall, finding nothing.

Seizures, he recalled a second after something fell behind him and landed with a faint thud.

Rage. Rage. *Rage*, he warned himself as he swung the beam of the flashlight to the opposite wall and trained his gun on the space.

An even bigger blotch of firefly green caught his eye. The bright radiant color stained a large area on a commonplace grey T-shirt. What wasn't routine was how the shirt seemed to be suspended against the wall and above a pair of jeans.

A jolt of adrenaline raced through him. What he was seeing was illogical. Something beyond belief was staring him in the face.

Steadying the flashlight and gun on the glowing green, he took a step closer.

Sneakers peeked from the legs of the jeans, which possessed too much shape and bulk to be empty.

A body? Mick thought; except, as he trained the flashlight above the neckline of the shirt, he saw nothing but the duller grey-painted brick of the basement walls until...

A pair of startlingly blue eyes popped open suddenly and glared back at him in the midst of all that dim, deceiving grey.

Human eyes.

Caterina Shaw's eyes.

Just the sight of them made him catch his breath, and he jumped back before reason returned.

This wasn't possible, he thought.

With a hand that now had a bit of a waver, he targeted a spot smack between those amazingly human, but haunting, eyes.

"Don't move," he said and kneeled beside one of the legs of the jeans. Laid his hand on the denim to confirm that what he was seeing was actually real.

Beneath his fingers came the feel of a human body, but he was still having trouble believing his eyes when a hand of that indeterminate grey stained with yellow-green covered his.

A woman's hand beneath the inhuman skin.

A warm soft hand that squeezed his gently as the thing that he believed to be Caterina Shaw finally spoke.

"Help me."

CHAPTER 5

Even in the murky light, Caterina perceived the battle of emotions on his face: confusion, disbelief, disgust. But she had to try to reach him.

The blood on her palm and fingers had grown tacky as she moved them over the top of his hand and gently squeezed. A shudder shimmied across his body before he pulled his hand away.

He wasn't going to help her, but would he send her back?

She surged to her feet, knowing now she needed to get away from him, but a wave of wooziness weakened her knees, forcing her to lean against the rough brick wall.

"Easy," he said, holding up his left hand the way a cop might while directing traffic as he kept his gun trained on her.

"Can't go back," she warned, but then he urged calm with a slow dip of his hand and said, "I know you can't go back."

Did he know? she wondered, battling for purchase against the wall as her knees wobbled. She dug the tips of her fingers into the soft brick wall and stabilized herself.

His gun snapped up at her action and he muttered, "Holy shit."

He didn't understand.

How could he when she didn't understand?

She had to do something to make things right with him. She had to focus. As she had more than once before that night, she began her mantra, *focus, focus, focus*. She fixed her gaze on the barrel of his gun and experienced relief a moment later when he finally lowered it.

"You're Caterina Shaw," he said.

She raised her gaze to meet his. His earlier emotions lingered there, along with a new one: pity.

Steely determination strengthened her knees. She didn't want him feeling sorry for her. She had never wanted anyone's pity, she remembered, along with another word, "Cat."

He took a step forward as he said, "Your friend Elizabeth calls you Cat."

An image flashed through her brain of bright blond hair, icy blue eyes, and a smile that came quickly and honestly.

"I'm Cat," she repeated, but gasped with fear as he took another step toward her.

He recognized her distress and paused with his approach.

"You're hurt. I want to help you, Cat."

I'm hurt, she repeated in her brain and finally permitted herself to recognize the agony in her shoulder. A deep burn combined with a pulling pain whenever she moved. Wooziness when she tried to walk.

"He shot me," she said, dragging the words from untrustworthy memory.

"Yes, you've been shot, Cat," he said, the tones of his voice surprisingly kindhearted as he took another half-step toward her. "I *will* help you," he added with a conviction that penetrated the last remnants of her fear.

"Okay."

Though Mick heard the word come from Caterina's lips, the only features that seemed arguably human were her intense blue eyes and her hesitant voice. It was as if she was a young child searching for the right words to say, unaware of who she was.

What she was, he thought and heard her whisper, "Focus."

Focus? he wondered, but immediately realized what she was attempting to do and joined in.

"That's it, Cat. Focus," he said, using her nickname to try and build trust.

Her head dipped down in what he suspected to be a nod and then in gradual stages, all the remaining bits of indistinct grey faded and were replaced by the pale tones of human skin.

He controlled his reaction to jump away at the unbelievable change, taking a moment to examine her. He had no doubt she was Caterina Shaw although she was paler and thinner than the photo he had been given. Her hair was the same deep ebony, but tangled, with bits of leaves and dirt caught in the thick curls. A purpling bruise marred one cheekbone, as if she had been recently struck.

Someone had hurt her, but that was not of his concern, he thought, remembering why he was here. He had an assignment to complete. He had to return her to Wardwell's labs.

But then she pulled her fingers out of the brick wall and held out her bloodstained hand to him once again. She repeated her earlier plea. "Help me."

Mick almost wished she had attacked him instead; gone into one of those rages warned about in her medical history. Violence, he could deal with. He considered himself a master in how to respond and protect himself and his men.

Sympathy and compassion? Normally not within his skill set. Yet that's exactly what was needed here.

Fuck.

CHAPTER 6

Mick lifted up his gun hand and Caterina flinched as he did so, obviously assuming he intended to use force.

"Easy, Cat. I'm just putting it away. See." He held the Glock loosely before her and then tucked it into his waistband beside the gun he had taken from Franklin's man.

Slipping off his jacket, he took one more step toward her, closing the distance between them. She leaned precariously against the wall, the effects of her blood loss taking a toll.

"I'm going to put my jacket over your shoulders to keep you warm. Do you understand?"

A bobble-headed nod confirmed it and he moved quickly, helping her slip into his lightweight leather coat to both provide warmth and hide the weird luminescent blood from prying eyes. His car was only blocks away, but he doubted she had the strength to make it that far. Hopefully she could make it out onto the street where they could hail a cab.

Aware that any sudden movement might frighten her, he once again explained his actions.

"I'm going to put my arm around your waist. You can put yours around mine to help you walk out of here."

He didn't wait for her assent, fearful that each passing second created the risk of discovery. Easing his arm around her waist, he sensed the fragility of her body beneath his hand.

Shaw was way too thin, and it made him wonder just how Wells and Edwards had been treating her while she was in their care. She mimicked his actions, wrapping her arm around his waist, her grip surprisingly strong against him.

Turning her away from the stairway leading up to where he had left Franklin's man, he urged her down the hall, keeping his pace measured, since her every woozy step spoke of weakness. Her body trembled beneath his hand and he admired the effort she was making to keep up with him.

At the next set of stairs, he paused, uncertain she could make it up even with his assistance and fearing how slow their progress had been so far.

Meeting her gaze, he noticed that she was struggling to hold on to consciousness. He cupped her jaw with his hand and she jerked back even though his touch had been gentle.

"I'm going to carry you up the stairs and to the exit. You need to stay awake because I'll need your help once we're on the street."

Another wobbly nod of her head confirmed her understanding, but he worried for a moment if he was reading too much into her actions. Even animals seemed to nod on occasion, prompting him to consider that there might not be much left of Caterina's brain. He tamped down the odd sense of loss that thought brought and bent, eased his arm beneath her knees, and swung her up into his arms.

Carrying her, he found his trip up the stairs and to the back door where he had entered was much faster. As he exited into the back alley, he peered into the darkness, but detected no other presence there. Lucky so far, he thought as he eased her upright once again.

He took a step toward the mouth of the alley and she stumbled, but he urged her on. "Come on, Cat. I know you can do this."

She straightened beside him and tightened her hold on him.

"I'm trying," she said in a pained exhale as she took a step and he moved with her.

Together they made it to the curb. Luck seemed to be with him, since an empty cab made the turn off Broad. He picked up his hand and the cab pulled up to them. The cabbie rolled down his window and said, "Lady had too much to drink?"

Perfect, he thought.

"Way too much. We need to go to South and 11th."

"Hop in," the cabbie said and popped the locks on the car.

Mick eased Caterina into the backseat and climbed in beside her. He had barely closed the door behind him when the cabbie peeled away and, with a few sharp turns, they were headed down South Street.

Mick counted the blocks and the minutes, shooting an occasional look back to see if they were being followed.

They weren't.

Caterina's head sagged forward as her body collapsed against him, and his gaze collided with the cabbie's in the rearview mirror.

"She'd better not yak in my cab, mister," he warned.

"She won't." Mick tucked her head close in case she decided to go all camo on him again.

Caterina murmured an indistinct protest and released

a warm sigh that bathed his skin. A human breath with a slight chemical smell, warning that she might be in some stage of ketosis, possibly due to a lack of nourishment.

Anger rose up in him once more as he considered the treatment she might have been receiving in the Wardwell labs. Had such treatment brought about enough rage for her to attack? he considered as he kept a firm but nonthreatening hold on her.

It took only a few more minutes before the cab reached their destination and Mick played up the role of a solicitous date.

"Come on, love. Time to head home," he said as he handed the cabbie a twenty and slid to the door, pulling her along with him.

He opened the door and, with all his strength, extracted her from the car. As her feet hit the ground, she roused. Her body tensed, clearly ready for flight mode until her gaze lifted to his. Then calm settled on her features, unsettling him.

Mick hadn't expected any kind of trust so quickly. He wasn't quite sure he deserved it.

With little wasted motion he had her buckled into his SUV. Once within the car, however, he took a moment to peel away the shoulder of his jacket to examine her wound.

Still bleeding, but substantially less than before. The wound even appeared partially healed. At least enough that he could transport her without worry on that count, although now her condition troubled him for a number of other reasons.

First, the "Is she human?" question.

Second, there was no exit wound, which meant the bullet and any stray bits of cloth were still in her body. Both could cause more serious physical complications if they weren't removed.

A hospital was out of the question.

So were his office/apartment and any of the regular contacts he used for medical emergencies which he wanted to keep private. With Caterina in her current state, there was no guarantee that she wouldn't morph before a stranger. Plus, Franklin was too familiar with all of those places, and if his old friend was that intent on securing the bounty for bringing in Caterina, he would be sure to come after Mick there.

Mick couldn't risk either of those two scenarios, which left only one choice.

With a last quick tug on Caterina's seat belt to ensure she was secure, he retrieved his cell phone from his jacket pocket and hit speed-dial.

His sister immediately picked up. *"Hola, hermano. What can I do for my long-lost brother?"*

It had only been a month since his last attendance at a family gathering, but he knew that for Liliana, a month was thirty days too far removed from family.

"I need a big favor, Lil," he said and shot a look at Caterina as she slumped against the side passenger door.

"You name it," Liliana said easily. Family always came first with his little sister.

"Meet me at the shore house. I'll be there in about an hour and a half. Bring your medical bag."

A heavy sigh came across the line.

"I should have known a call at this ungodly hour wasn't because you missed me."

Damn. His sister had sure learned the guilt trip well from their *mami*.

"You should know by now how much I love you, Lil, but if you don't want to help—"

"You're *mi hermano*. Of course I'll help."

A rare smile broke out across his face. "I knew I could count on you."

"Always, Miguelito," she said, using his boyhood nickname as she usually did when she wanted to annoy him.

Little sisters, he thought, his smile broadening as he turned his full attention back to the road and the drive home.

Home, he thought, and contained the pang of longing.

Home was not the place for a man like him. He didn't deserve that kind of life. Not when he had been responsible for others never making it to their homes.

Hands tightening on the wheel, he shot a quick look at his target. From what he had gathered in his investigations so far, Caterina had known little of a home life.

Mother dead at an early age. A cold and distant father who had not approved of her.

With the exception of Elizabeth, most of the people with whom he had spoken had been more acquaintances and business contacts than real friends.

Could she count on them the way he relied on his family? Did they bring her the same sense of joy and belonging?

He suspected not, and reminded himself of his one objective—return Caterina to Edwards. But as he shot a quick look at his target once again, the niggling voice inside his head warned him that he needed to do more, while the voice of the realist warned, "You can't be everybody's hero."

CHAPTER 7

At that hour of the night, the trip across the Ben Franklin Bridge was quick. The roads through New Jersey and up to Bradley Beach were free of any kind of volume, but not completely deserted. Even in this part of the state there was always a fair amount of activity from cars and trucks, which tonight was both good and bad.

Good because it gave him a way to get lost in case there was a tail.

Bad because it would make any kind of tail harder to notice.

Mick had been vigilant for the first twenty miles or so, always checking the rearview mirror for any telltale signs that he had been made. The roads had been clear of any suspicious vehicles and had remained so for the entire trip.

Occasionally he checked on his passenger, who had barely moved in all that time.

Caterina was battered, hurt, and possibly undernourished. She was also exhausted, judging from the nearly blue-black circles beneath her eyes, which were occasionally illuminated by the bursts of light from a streetlight or passing car.

He let her rest, hoping that with rest would come some greater mental clarity than what she had displayed at the Music Academy. Of course, maybe that was all that was left of her brain after the tumor and treatments.

Once again, he didn't know why that possibility upset him.

Maybe it was because of the impression of the woman he had pieced together through his investigations. The determined, but pleasant and intelligent woman who had not let anything get in her way.

Not even a life-threatening illness.

Not even the good doctors Wells and Edwards.

He wondered what they would make of her condition. Whether they would find it routine or if they would even care. Edwards certainly had seemed more worried about how his partner's murder would hurt the business rather than his violent death.

A death allegedly caused by the woman beside him, he cautioned himself. Emotion could play no role in the job he had been hired to do.

Up ahead on the road was his exit off the parkway. He paid careful attention to the cars around him as he pulled onto a smaller county road. For the few miles on that thoroughfare there were barely any cars, making it extremely easy to see if someone was following.

No one was.

Relief filled him that the existence of this home—a temporary safe house—remained unknown. Neither his old friend Franklin nor any of his current associates knew its whereabouts. The deed was recorded in the name of a business he had set up, lessening any connection to him. That made it a good location for dealing with Caterina for the moment, although he didn't like the idea of bringing work to his home and family.

He had always tried to keep his business life away from his family life. Caterina would be the first business he had ever brought home. For that matter, he had never brought any woman to this house. Caterina was also a first in that category, and under different conditions, he suspected that might have been a good thing, given all that he had learned about her so far.

The turnoff from the county road to the side streets came quickly. Barely a few miles later he was pulling into the driveway of the large old colonial located a little more than a block away from the ocean.

He pushed the button on his visor for the garage and the door rumbled open, the sound low enough that he hoped none of his neighbors would hear it at this fairly late hour. He drove into the garage and shut the door behind him.

With the car in the garage, his neighbors and others would be less likely to notice he was back. For good measure, he flipped the switch he had installed by the door into the house to disable the remote open. Entering his home, he punched in the code to shut off the security system and returned to the Jeep for his captive.

Caterina didn't rouse as he lifted her from the SUV and carried her into the house and up the stairs to the larger of the two guest bedrooms. After laying her on the bed, he rushed back down to close up the Jeep and the house. He was about to enable the security system once more when he caught a glimpse of headlights on the street in front of the house.

A second later his sister pulled up in her dependably boring midsized sedan. An old person's car, but then again, his sister had an old soul. Luckily for him, a reliable old soul.

He walked to the front door and opened it, and as his sister's face brightened with a wide smile when she saw him, he felt a smile erupt on his own face. She hurried up the cement walk, medical bag in hand, and embraced him tightly at the door.

"Missed you, *hermano*," she said as she buried her head into the middle of his chest.

"Missed you, too, *hermanita*," he replied as he hugged her petite body tight to his.

When Liliana stepped away, she inspected him up and down with motherly concern, but there was sisterly sarcasm in her tone. "You're not hurt?"

"I have a ... guest upstairs. She—"

"She?" his sister said, one brow flying upward with interest as she pushed past him, wasting not a second in her quest to discover the identity of his female visitor.

Mick chased after her, wanting to warn her about Caterina's rather unusual abilities, but he was relieved to see that his guest was still conked out in much the same position that he had left her earlier.

Liliana stopped by the side of the bed, perusing Caterina before she turned an accusing eye in his direction.

"Please tell me you're not responsible for the bruises." She flicked her hand at the obvious damage to Caterina's face.

He raised his hands in surrender, although he was slightly annoyed that his sister didn't know better than to ask such a question. "Found her after she'd been hurt. Her name is Cat. She's been shot as well. I'm sure the bullet's still in her shoulder."

He joined Liliana by the edge of the bed, gently removed his jacket from Caterina and tossed it to the side to reveal the bullet wound. Caterina murmured another soft protest as he moved her, but otherwise did not stir.

With the jacket gone, the odd iridescent blood splotch was fully visible as it stained the shirt surrounding the injury to her shoulder.

An injury that seemed even smaller than when he had inspected it in Philly.

Liliana bent to peer at the wound and then reached for the bedside lamp, removed the shade and turned up the bulb as high as it could go.

"What's with the glowing green paint?" Liliana asked as she placed her physician's bag on the nightstand and removed a pair of surgical scissors.

"It's not paint. It's blood."

Liliana shot him a disbelieving stare, but then reached out and touched the splotch on the shirt. When she picked up her fingers to smell the liquid on them, her reaction was much like his had been earlier.

"Definitely blood. How's that possible?"

"Wish I knew, Lil." Mick leaned over his sister's shoulder, watching as she carefully slipped the surgical scissors beneath the sleeve of the T-shirt and began to cut away the fabric.

Caterina immediately roused then, her eyes wide with fear as she noted the scissors and realized what was happening.

"No," she said and jerked away from Liliana. The motion must have caused her pain because she moaned, grimaced, and screwed her eyes shut.

"She's here to help, Cat. Do you understand? *Help*."

Mick repeated the word the way he might speak to a young child.

Caterina shook her head and whispered "no" before passing out once again.

Liliana pressed forward despite Caterina's protest, her movements efficient and so capable that the shirt was cut away from the damaged shoulder without her patient noticing. As she revealed the damage caused by the bullet wound, she muttered a curse. "*Coño*, this is almost closed up, but I can see there are still bits of cloth in there."

"And the bullet. Can you clean it up?"

Liliana nodded as she placed the scissors on the night-stand. "Definitely have to get it clean, otherwise she might go septic. We can admit her—"

"No hospital, Lil, and don't ask me why not."

Liliana turned and planted her hands on her hips, head tilted up defiantly and the lines of her small body vibrating with tension. "You can't expect me to cut her open here."

"I can. It's not life-threatening—"

"It could be if infection sets in. Plus I'm obligated by law to report any gunshot wounds," his sister warned, obviously hoping she could convince him on a different course of action.

Which left only one thing he could do.

"If she's discovered, she could be killed. And how would you explain the lightning bug blood? It's her blood, Lil, and when I found her . . ."

He looked away and dragged a hand through his hair. "It's almost too weird to believe," he admitted.

Sensing the truth and frustration in her brother's words, Liliana reached out and laid a hand on his arm. She had never seen him this upset, not to mention that he had never reached out to her for help on a case before. That he had done so now spoke volumes. And if what he said was true about the young woman's life being in peril, it justified in her mind not reporting the wound.

At least, for the moment.

"If I'm going to deal with the wound, we'll have to sedate her. Then you'll have to monitor her carefully for any signs of infection."

Mick nodded and Liliana reached into her medical bag and removed a vial of sedative that she kept in case of an emergency. It would take very little of the powerful drug to keep Mick's guest knocked out while she cleansed the wound and stitched her up.

She prepped a syringe and then picked up the young woman's arm to administer the medicine. The woman's eyelids fluttered up and down as she responded to the movement, then immediately flew open at the sight of the syringe.

"No," Caterina protested, stronger than before. Suddenly the pale blue of the sheets spread across every visible inch of her body.

Liliana glanced down at where she held the woman's arm, just to make sure she was seeing right. The olive tones of her own skin clashed with the sky-blue hue the woman's skin had taken on. Shock tightened her grasp on the woman, who attempted to break free by wrenching her body away.

"Easy, Cat," Mick said, immediately at her side, grabbing hold of her shoulders in an attempt to pin her down. That only made her react even more forcefully.

She thrashed in earnest, heaving her shoulders up off the bed. Bringing her knees up so she could try to kick at Mick.

Mick climbed up on the bed and wrestled her back down until he was straddling her. He pinned her arms and legs with his body, but she continued to twist and buck upward in an effort to free herself.

"Hurry, Lil. She's damn strong," he said as one powerful surge of Caterina's body nearly upended Mick.

Liliana didn't hesitate. She jabbed the needle into Caterina's bicep and pushed the plunger to administer the sedative.

When Caterina reared up again, nearly snapping off the needle in her arm, Liliana withdrew the syringe. She stepped back and counted down until the medicine took effect, watching as Mick attempted to keep Caterina contained.

He was tempering his force, she could see, while softly murmuring, "We're not going to hurt you, Cat. We're here to help."

Liliana waited anxiously. The sedative was taking much longer to work than she expected. So much longer that it occurred to her she might have to administer another dose, although she feared too much of it might present another round of complications.

Finally Caterina stilled and, as she did so, the blue of the sheets receded from her skin, leaving behind the normal tones of her pale white skin.

Mick slipped off of the bed, pausing by Caterina's side, gazing down at her. The emotions on his face were a mix of confusion and concern.

Liliana stepped close to him. "How does she do that? The skin thing." Her voice was barely a whisper in her brother's ear.

"Don't know. Her medical history mentioned a complication from a full gene expression. Maybe this is part of it. It was some radical kind of treatment."

"Someone's used her for a guinea pig?" Liliana wondered aloud.

"A damn strong guinea pig. I'm going to have to tie her down," he said.

Liliana didn't much care for forceful restraints, and as she considered doing so to this injured young woman, she unconsciously rubbed at her own wrists.

The movement of her hands snared Mick's attention and he finally noticed the bruises on her forearms. Reaching out, he tenderly took hold of her wrist. He raised her arm up higher so that he could inspect it.

"Who did this to you?" he asked, the anger in his voice barely contained.

Liliana shook her head and yanked her arm away. "No one. I hurt myself doing some chores."

A lie and they both knew it. "Did Harrison do that to you?"

Harrison had done that and more, she wanted to say, but worried about how Mick would react. Worried that no one would believe her. After all, Harrison was successful—head of his department at the hospital and well-known in his field.

Who would believe that such a man—her fiancé—was capable of abusing her?

"I got banged up doing some gardening this weekend," she offered up.

Mick wasn't buying it.

"If he's hurting you, we can put a stop to it, *hermanita*."

"I'm okay. Better than you are, obviously," Liliana replied, pointing back to the injured young woman who needed their immediate attention.

A muscle twitched along the hard strong line of Mick's jaw before he reluctantly said, "When this is done, we'll deal with Harrison."

Liliana left it at that, hoping that by the time this problem with Mick was finished, she'd have found her own way to deal with Harrison. For months she had been contemplating leaving him but had demurred, fearful of what he could do to her career at the hospital where they both worked. He was better connected politically and she feared his vindictive nature.

But no career was worth what was happening to her.

For now, however, she had to help her brother.

She handed Mick the scissors. "Cut away the rest of her clothes and get her restrained, but not this shoulder. I'll start—"

She stopped as Mick held up one of Caterina's wrists, drawing attention to the raw spots and ligature marks on her arm. The wrist on the young woman's wounded arm had similar injuries.

"Someone's already restrained her. Repeatedly."

Mick gently laid the young woman's arm back down. With the scissors, he cut away her socks and jeans, revealing additional bruising and ligature marks along her ankles.

"Fuck," he said, his head hanging down as he braced his hands on the bed.

When he raised his gaze to meet hers, Liliana detected anguish in the depths of his dark brown eyes. Laying a hand on the hard muscles of his arm, she said, "Go get a basin with warm water. We'll clean all those areas and get them bandaged."

He immediately did as she asked, and while he was

gone Liliana tackled what remained of the young woman's clothes, cutting them away. With each piece she removed, it became apparent just how badly Mick's guest had been abused.

Her tall body had previously been lean, Liliana suspected, but now was even thinner, the edges of her ribs and hip bones prominent. Assorted bruises marred her body. Fearing her brother's reaction, Liliana worked quickly to remove the clothes and cover Caterina with a light sheet before his return. She would take care of sponge bathing her once she had finished dealing with the wound to her shoulder.

Mick returned a moment later. As he set a plastic bowl filled with water on the opposite nightstand and pulled a washcloth from his back jeans pocket, Liliana reached into her bag and removed a tube of ointment and a roll of gauze.

"Wash her wrists and ankles. Once they're dry, apply this," she said and tossed him the tube and then the gauze.

Mick began to do as he was told while Liliana went to work, carefully cleaning the bullet wound. She picked out pieces of fabric and found that the bullet was not all that far in. If she didn't know better, she would say it was almost like the injured woman's body was expelling it the way it would a splinter.

But a bullet was no splinter and Liliana had never seen this kind of behavior before.

As she worked and more luminescent green blood slowly seeped from the wound, Liliana wondered just what was happening with this woman. Especially since with the bullet and bits of cloth removed, the injury appeared to be healing itself even more quickly.

For a moment she considered that it might not even be

necessary to stitch the wound closed, but decided not to risk it. Working quickly, she made a series of neat tiny stitches to finish, hoping they would not leave much of a scar.

As Liliana straightened, her back protested the hour she had been bent over while she worked. Placing one hand at her waist, she stretched out the kinks and watched as her brother fashioned restraints from what remained of the gauze she had given him earlier.

"Are you sure that will hold her?" she asked, recollecting the force of Caterina's earlier struggles.

Mick examined his handiwork, and tugged on the lengths of gauze he had braided for extra strength and tied to the legs of the bed. Recalling how Caterina had fought him, he had contemplated using handcuffs, but the sight of the ligature marks on her wrists and ankles had guilt-tripped him into finding a kinder way to confine her.

Guilt was not good.

It was affecting his judgment about Caterina, and he couldn't afford that.

He also couldn't afford not knowing what was going on with her, from the weird blood and supernatural healing, to her decidedly diminished mental capacity.

"Do you think you could run some tests for me?" he said, shooting a sideways glance at his sister.

"I'd be remiss if I didn't. Blood test. DNA analysis. Maybe even a full tox screen because something is definitely not right with your friend."

A friend she was not, but his sister didn't need to know that. "I'd appreciate anything you can do only—"

"It needs to be on the down low. I get it, Mick."

He nodded, reached out, and placed his hand on Liliana's shoulder. Gave it a reassuring squeeze. "I need you to be extra careful, Lil. Don't come back to the house without checking in with me first."

Liliana gestured to Caterina. "Are you sure you can handle her?"

Mick didn't respond.

CHAPTER 8

"She'll be fine," Mick finally reassured his sister, but worried whether he could ultimately keep that promise.

This mission was turning out to have too many unexpected variables. Never a good thing when the only contingencies you had anticipated were whether your target would end up dead or alive.

Caterina wouldn't end up dead if he could help it.

The question was, would Mick come to regret keeping her alive?

After Liliana had left to return to the hospital, Mick gave a last tug on the makeshift restraints and, with Caterina sedated, hurried from the guest room to the smallest of the bedrooms at the end of the hall. He had converted that room into an office where he kept a desk loaded with an assortment of computers he used to monitor the perimeter of this house, his office/apartment in Philadelphia, and any location he had decided to bug. On the wall opposite the desk was a large lateral file cabinet holding a varied collection of cameras and microphones he used for surveillance, and first-aid materials.

The closet beside the file cabinet had once been roomy, but now held a built-in vault that housed a cache of guns, weaponry, and ammunition. The vault could only be opened with his fingerprint and a complex security code.

Mick sat down at the desk, powered up the monitors, and checked out the feeds from the various locations. The infrared cameras detected nothing unusual around the perimeter of the house. The remote video from his office/apartment areas showed it was still in one piece, and the control panel on the security system didn't indicate that the area had been breached. The only activity anywhere had been his entry into this safehouse hours earlier.

The last monitor was blank until, with a few quick keystrokes, Caterina's image appeared as she lay on the bed, her arms and legs tied to the bedframe legs and the headboard. A light sheet covered her, hiding the thinness of her bruised body.

His sister had tried to keep the bruises from him, but he had seen them when Liliana had bathed Caterina, much as he had taken note of the purpling marks on his sister's own forearms.

Definitely not bruises from gardening, contrary to her assertions.

He recognized the signs of someone being manhandled. And since as far as he knew Harrison was the only man in Lil's life, he had to assume Harrison had been the one to hurt her.

His stomach tightened with anger at the thought of anyone harming his sister. That it was Harrison doing it only made him angrier.

He had never liked Harrison Edgar Williams. He had always found the supposedly brilliant surgeon to be rather pompous and slow-witted. No match for his smart and effervescent baby sister who deserved much better, as far as Mick was concerned.

Why would Lil put up with such treatment? he thought, gazing at Caterina. Another seemingly smart and capable woman who had been overpowered. Trapped by a system in which she had once had faith.

Did Lil feel the same way? Did she consider herself imprisoned by who she was at the hospital—a newbie resident? One who couldn't challenge an older, better-established surgeon like Harrison?

Mick was going to find out what was happening with Lil and put an end to it, much like he intended to do with Caterina.

No, not Caterina. Shaw. He should start calling her Shaw. He needed to create distance because she was rousing emotions in him that would only complicate the assignment.

Shaw was his target. Just another job.

He couldn't let sympathy for Shaw and admiration for the strength she had shown during her illness get in the way of the mission he had been paid to complete.

How about justice? the voice in his head challenged. Could he let justice get in the way?

He flipped away from Shaw's image to one of the front door. All quiet and dark in the dead of early morning. Dead as he would be if he didn't get some rest, too. He had to stay sharp for what he needed to do tomorrow.

Mick walked out of his office, past Shaw's room, and stopped at the door to his bedroom. The large king-sized bed called to him, but he glanced back at the room holding his captive.

With a muttered curse, he tore off the black knit Henley

he had been wearing, which still bore scattered traces of Shaw's oddball blood. He whipped the two guns from the spot where he had tucked them into the gap at the small of his back and tossed them on his comforter. His jeans soon followed, but fell from the bed and landed in a heap on the floor.

In the master bath, he washed up, removing all traces of Shaw from his hands and arms, then returned to his room to slip into comfortable sweats.

He retrieved the two guns from the surface of the bed, placed them on the nightstand beside him, and lay down on the comforter.

Just a few hours' nap before he got back to work.

Sleep eluded him, however, as images of Shaw's and Lil's bruises juxtaposed themselves in his brain.

Giving up hope of sleep after about an hour, he rose, slipped the two guns beneath the waistband of his sweats, dragged the comforter off his bed and stalked to Shaw's room.

A comfortable overstuffed chair and ottoman were tucked invitingly in a far corner of the bedroom. It was his mother's handiwork when she had helped him decorate this house, hoping that its purchase was a sign that he intended to settle down into a more sedate life. Maybe even take up his cousin Ramon's offer of a spot on the local police force.

His mother had been sadly mistaken, Mick thought as he dropped the comforter at the door and walked to the chair and ottoman. He dragged them to the side of the bed where he could keep an eye on Shaw, as well as on the stairs and bedroom door.

Once the chair was in place, he picked up the comforter,

settled himself into the welcoming cushions, and propped his feet up on the ottoman. For good measure, he removed the guns from his waistband and tucked them into the gap between the cushions and seat of the comfy chair. Within easy reach.

He leaned his head back and closed his eyes to shut out the soft light cast by the table lamp beside the bed. Lil had replaced the linen ivory shade and turned it to a low setting. Listening to the measured cadence of Shaw's breathing, Mick let it lull him into a light sleep.

He walked past the rooms the way a zookeeper might, checking his charges in the early morning hours to make sure they were properly locked away in their cells.

When he reached the last room, he paused and glared at the empty bed through the small glass panel at the door, angry with himself that he had underestimated his patient's abilities and determination.

He wouldn't make that mistake again.

Pivoting on his heel, he stalked back toward the first room and peered within.

Santiago was beginning to stir. His head lolled from side to side as his lips twitched and twisted.

He hit the intercom by the patient's door to listen, but the words, if there were any, were indistinct. The sounds were more like the warning grunts of an animal rather than those of a person. Maybe because in his current state Santiago was more feral than human.

Smiling, he thought about turning Santiago loose on Shaw. He pictured the way the fight between them would ensue, pitting one set of supernatural powers against another.

Santiago had physical strength, but unlike Shaw he was slow both physically and mentally. If it hadn't been for the death sentences imposed by both nature and New Jersey's legal system, he wouldn't have urged Wells to accept the career criminal into the study. But the state had offered to release Santiago into Wardwell's care if he participated in the experiment, and the nature of Santiago's illness—a virulent form of diabetes that modern medicine couldn't control—had sealed the decision.

Finding a gene therapy that would help Santiago might have resulted in a cure.

A very profitable cure for Wardwell.

Unfortunately, the gene strain implanted into Santiago had produced erratic results in controlling his insulin levels. It had, however, yielded a mechanism for burning off all the excess sugar in a way that created immense energy and inhuman strength.

Such possibilities when combined with Santiago's criminal traits and violence...

The smile broadened on his face as he remembered how Santiago had taken care of Wells.

If necessary, he would turn Santiago loose on Shaw to end the threat.

Once that happened it would be back to business as usual and no one would be the wiser about what Wardwell had done.

Caterina woke with a sharp cry that brought Mick to instant alertness.

He whipped his Glock from between the cushions, trained it on the door, but soon realized that there was no one else in the room.

She'd had another nightmare filled with images of blood and death. Fear lingered in her psyche and she tossed fretfully on the bed, yanking and twisting against the restraints. Grimacing as one strong tug brought pain through her injured shoulder, giving her one more reason to wish Mick would relent and set her free.

Instead he tucked the Glock back between the cushions and slipped onto the ottoman. Leaning forward, Mick reached out as if to comfort her, but stopped halfway. Pulling his hand back, he rubbed both hands on his sweats, clearly uncertain.

His hesitation made Caterina pause in her struggles, and with that fragile calm, Mick finally placed his hand at the top of her arm and applied slight pressure.

"Don't hurt me," she said softly.

Mick stroked his hand across her skin tenderly. In patient tones he said, "No one is going to hurt you."

Caterina glanced at his hand and tried to move away, but the bindings made it impossible.

"Let me go," she urged, wanting to be free.

He kept up his slow caress, as if trying to calm her the way one might an injured stray. His cocoa brown eyes filled with a mix of emotions that perplexed her.

She hadn't expected kindness. Couldn't remember the last time anyone had treated her with anything other than contempt or clinical detachment.

"Where would you go?" he asked, shifting even closer to the edge of the ottoman, his presence surprisingly comforting.

"Home. I want to go home."

Guilt flashed across his features, warning her that home wasn't an option he was considering at the moment.

"Maybe later. When it's safe," he urged and shifted his hand up her arm until he was at the binding. "I don't want you to reinjure your arm. I'm going to loosen it a little so you don't hurt yourself."

Caterina warily tracked the movement of Mick's hand as he slackened the ties. Then he surprised her by tucking his hand into hers, his touch compassionate, creating a sudden and silent understanding between them that dissipated the remaining tension in her body.

She finally relaxed down onto the mattress and Mick nodded. "That's it. Rest and get better. Maybe then you can go home, Cat."

Home, Caterina thought, wondering at his actions. Baffled by the kindness he was exhibiting that was so at odds with what she had been experiencing lately. He hadn't really reacted with fear at her strange blood and skin, which even had her scared.

He didn't release her hand as she continued to stare at him. His palm was hard and calloused, but the touch was light. Soothing as he covered her one hand with both of his and once again said, "Rest. I won't let anyone hurt you."

Somehow she knew he was capable of protecting her from others. But as she met his gaze and saw the continued puzzlement there, she sensed that he wasn't sure if he could protect her from himself.

"Will *you* hurt me?" she asked.

His gaze darkened and became shuttered before he pulled his hands away.

"Go to sleep. We'll talk in the morning."

CHAPTER 9

Liliana didn't know who to trust with the blood sample.

Certainly not her fiancé, Harrison. If he thought there was anything of value in the findings, he would be the first to broadcast them to the world in order to benefit himself. He cared nothing for family or friends, just himself, she had come to realize in the last few months when his demeanor had taken a turn for the worst.

It only reinforced her belief that she had to find a way out of their relationship. For months now she had been contemplating it, especially as Harrison's actions in private became more and more violent.

As she entered the hospital lab after grabbing a few hours' sleep in the doctor's lounge, she spotted Dr. Carmen Rojas, a pathologist with whom she had become good friends. The two of them had helped each other through their boards and the mazelike routes of hospital politics.

She hoped Carmen could assist her once again.

Carmen lifted her head from the microscope where she had been examining a slide as Liliana approached. She held her arms out wide in invitation as she said, "Dr. Carrera. What brings you to my dungeon?"

Liliana smiled as she came to stand by Carmen's lab

bench, but her hand tightened on the test tube in the pocket of her white hospital jacket. She looked around the rest of the lab to make sure they were alone before she said, "If I said a science experiment, would you believe me?"

"A science experiment? As in—"

A deep furrow formed between Carmen's manicured brows as Liliana extracted the glowing test tube from her pocket and held it up for Carmen to see. "Somehow a dollar store glow stick isn't my idea of a neat science experiment, Liliana."

"You've got to promise this stays between the two of us."

"Seriously? You want me to keep a glow stick secret?" Carmen questioned even as she held out her hand and wiggled her fingers in a request for the tube.

"It's human blood."

Carmen gingerly took hold of the sample and brought it beneath a table lamp she had at her workstation. She placed the vial beneath the lamp and turned it on. In the beam from the lamp, the blood glowed more brightly than it had with the ambient light.

Carmen punched another button, switching the regular incandescent light in the lamp to blue light. Beneath the blue light, the liquid in the tube phosphoresced into a much more brilliant yellow-green.

"Cool. Is this what Harrison has been up to?"

"This has nothing to do with Harrison. In fact, I'd rather he not know about it. Or anyone else for that matter," Liliana cautioned, needing her friend to understand the importance of secrecy with the sample.

Carmen peered at her askance before extracting a small amount of blood from the tube and placing it on a slide. As she plopped on a slip cover, Carmen said, "No need to worry, *amiga*. I won't spill the beans about this to anyone."

"Gracias, amiga." Liliana watched for a moment, silent as Carmen shifted the slide around and fiddled with some knobs on the microscope. Within just seconds, however, her friend shook her head and shifted away from the eyepiece.

"I've never seen anything like this before. It may take me a day or two to investigate. Find out what could cause this."

"I understand. Could I trouble you for a DNA analysis and full tox screen also?"

Carmen chuckled. "Not asking for too much, are you?"

Liliana jammed her hands into her pockets, slightly uncomfortable with having to ask, but her own expertise lay in bones and not blood. "If it's too much—"

"Just kidding, Liliana. Actually, it'll be an interesting break from the mundane day-to-day, only..."

Her friend paused, then rose from her lab stool and rested her hand on Liliana's forearm. "If you were in trouble, you'd let me know, right?"

While Mick and his friend might be in their share of hot water, Liliana had no such fears about herself. Except maybe for her issues with Harrison. As her gaze connected with Carmen's, she realized that was exactly to whom her friend had been referring.

"Harrison and I—"

Carmen's hand snapped up to stop her. "If you don't want to tell me—"

"It's complicated," she began. "For months now...he's changed and not in a good way."

"Rumor has it he laid into one of the young residents yesterday. Reduced her to tears and then physically pushed her out the door during rounds."

Physically pushed?

At home, what she thought had been a funk had escalated into anger and violence, turning her fiancé into a man Liliana no longer knew. That his behavior was now spilling over into his professional life created even more worry within her. She just shrugged as she wrapped her mind around it, hesitant about providing more fodder for the hospital rumor mill.

"I've been thinking for some time now that it's time to end our relationship," she finally replied.

"Those of us who know you would understand," Carmen said, but Liliana knew there would be those in the hospital who could not imagine why she would break it off with Harrison.

For now, however, she had other worries. She gestured to the tube resting on the lab bench and said, "How long do you think—"

"Couple of hours on the tox screen. DNA analysis will take a few days at least."

"Thanks." With a nod, Liliana turned and walked toward the door of the lab, Carmen in step beside her.

At the door Liliana paused, glancing at her friend, who said, "If you're ever in trouble, with anything, you know I'm here for you."

Liliana had understood that, which was maybe why she had come to Carmen to help her with the various tests. Nevertheless, it was good to hear her friend reinforce that she had made a wise decision.

"I know," she said and hugged the other woman.

When Carmen released her, Liliana hurried up to the surgical wing. As an orthopedic surgery resident, she had to make rounds with the chief surgeon and other residents later that morning. She generally enjoyed rounds, since they provided an opportunity to become involved in a series of different cases, and she liked meeting the diverse group of patients at the hospital.

Unfortunately, the surgical wing was also within Harrison's domain and this morning she dreaded it, last night's fight still fresh in her brain.

The bruises glaringly evident on her body.

She reached the surgical floor and spent an hour preparing for rounds before joining the group of residents already gathering. She braced herself, wondering if any of them would ask about the incident Carmen had mentioned. Liliana walked toward them, aware of how some of their heads were bent together in discussion until they saw her and broke apart.

Clearly they had heard about what had happened.

Straightening her spine, Liliana approached, determined to not let hospital gossip and her association with Harrison weigh her down.

From the stairs, Mick was able to see that Caterina had not yet awakened that morning. Of course it was still early for most. Barely seven.

He had managed to get a few hours of sleep before planting his butt in his office chair to search for additional information on Wardwell and its two founders. Waiting to call his old buddy Franklin.

Franklin Pierce might have been his friend for nearly a

decade, but if Franklin was being paid anything close to what he was for this assignment, that old friendship likely would not count for much. Especially since they hadn't really seen each other very much in the last couple of years.

Taking one of the prepaid cell phones from his file cabinet, Mick dialed the personal cell phone number he had for Franklin. If his ex–Army Ranger buddy answered there, he might be one up on him, assuming Franklin hadn't shut off the GPS tracking on the phone.

Leaning back into his leather office chair, Mick waited while the cell phone rang.

With each ring, he wondered if Franklin had changed much over the years. If his old buddy was still as trustworthy as he had been during their days in the military and after.

His old friend answered with a sleepy, "Hullo?"

In the background a baby cried, possibly awakened by his early morning call. That didn't stop Mick from engaging the GPS tracking service he had hacked from the phone company.

"Don't tell me you're a dad now, Franklin," he said, the tenor of his voice friendly as he waited for the Web site to return a location for Pierce's signal.

"Man, oh man. Is it really you, Carrera?"

A muffled voice said, "Who is it, honey?" as the wailing sounds of the baby grew louder.

A second later, the GPS identified the location of Pierce's cell phone—a building in a residential section of South Philly. Probably Franklin's home, judging from the area and the clear signs of family in the background.

"An old friend," Franklin answered the woman and

then the ambient sounds in the room faded. He was obviously leaving the woman and child behind in the room as he walked away to make their conversation more private.

"Old? Hell, Franklin. I'm not as ancient as you are," he said playfully, prompting his friend to chuckle and reply, "But this old man can still kick your ass."

Mick doubted it, but didn't say. "I know you're on the Shaw job, old man. I need you to back off."

A heavy and tired sigh drifted across the phone line. "Can't do, *mano*. I need the money."

"You need it enough to have your goon kill a helpless woman? She was shot by your em-ploy-ee," he said, injecting each syllable of the last word with sarcasm.

Franklin's words were hushed as he spoke. "My man says she attacked him. That she wasn't human."

Mick forced himself to laugh to attempt to dissuade his friend from such thoughts. "Come on, Franklin. She's just a frickin' musician. Tell your man to stop using the crack. If you give Edwards his money back and quit the job, we'll be square."

"Can't do. Seriously. It's my kid, Mick."

"Is something wrong?" Mick asked, concern for his old friend rising up.

"My daughter's sick and I need the cash," Franklin replied.

Mick sat up in his chair, planting his boots firmly on the ground as he dragged a hand though his short-cropped hair in frustration. "Don't bullshit me."

"No bullshit. Some kind of anemia and the insurance doesn't cover all that much for the treatments. I'm going broke from the medical bills."

In his days as a Ranger, Mick had understood the

meaning of trust. So had Franklin. They had survived more than one hairy mission together based on that trust.

He decided to rely on that trust. Well, trust and a little fear.

"There won't be anywhere for you to hide if you're not being square with me."

"I'm telling you the truth. I'll give you the doc's name if you want."

Mick didn't want it, and it occurred to him in that moment what to do. "Give Edwards his cash back. Tell him you didn't bargain on Shaw being a psycho."

"Is she? A psycho?"

Mick supposed that was as good an explanation as any. "Definitely a major EDP. Anyone who manages to catch up to her needs to watch out."

"But I need the money," Franklin said, the tones of his voice holding a desperation Mick had only heard once before—during their last mission together when everything had gone to hell.

"Just tell me how much you need and I'll wire it to your account. You still have the account, right?" he asked, thinking that Edwards's check in his wallet would go a long way toward helping his friend.

"Still have the account, although it's virtually tapped out," Franklin readily admitted.

Franklin had always been good about keeping that safety account with a nice amount of cash, much like he did. Enough money to last for a couple of years if he needed to disappear. Things had to be pretty bad for his friend to dip into that emergency stash.

"The money will be in your account in the next few days."

"I can't take the money for doing nothing," Franklin replied, pride evident in his tone.

Mick laughed good-naturedly to ease his friend's ego. "Who said you were getting it for nothing? I need you to help me out with some things. Are you game?"

"I'm five-by-five with that. I'd rather work for you than Edwards."

"Good. Do you still have that secure e-mail account?"

When Franklin confirmed that he did, Mick said, "I'll send you some instructions and a cell phone number where you can reach me. Keep your ear to the ground on this case. If you find out anything, send a message to my secure account or call me. Roger that?"

"Roger, Mick. I'll be watching your back."

"I'm counting on it. Don't disappoint me."

CHAPTER 10

Mick hung up and rose from the chair, needing to stretch his legs. He had been at his desk for over two hours since his call to Franklin and he was growing hungry. He hurried to the kitchen to prepare some breakfast and then returned upstairs.

As he reached the door to the bedroom, he paused when he realized Shaw had somehow made a tangle of the sheets which had once covered her body. The shapely length of one leg was now exposed, along with her breasts.

Rather nice, perfectly shaped breasts, he thought, dragging his gaze from them because to continue looking would create too many problems.

Placing the tray on the nightstand, he grabbed the edge of the sheet and carefully raised it back over her upper body.

Not carefully enough.

Caterina snapped her eyes open and, seeing him, strained against her bindings, yanking on them and twisting her body from side to side, the calm of the night before lost.

He held up both hands in a gesture meant to calm her and crooned, "Easy, Cat. Remember. I'm not going to hurt you."

She recalled that voice, offering peace and comfort in the dark of the night. The deep timbre of his voice resonated calm within her and slipped into Caterina's consciousness. It was a pleasing tone, reminding her of something musical.

Focus. *Focus*, she urged herself even as she tugged at the bindings keeping her prisoner. Something else registered as well. The smell of food. Her stomach grumbled loudly and she stopped tugging at the bindings.

She was hungry. Incredibly so.

Caterina dragged the words into her consciousness and said it aloud. "Is that food?"

He chuckled and smiled. "Yes, it's food. If you stop struggling, I'll help you sit up so you can eat."

She did as he asked and he became all action guy, bending to allow her greater slack on the ties on her left arm. When she moved that appendage, the motion brought a painful reminder that she had been shot the night before.

She glanced at her shoulder, noting the clean white gauze bandage taped to her skin.

A second later, the ties loosened on her other arm and she tried to sit up, but the room spun and tilted unsteadily as she did so.

Mick was immediately there, providing a solid place for her to rest her head until the wave of dizziness passed.

He took a moment to drag the sheet upward so she could hold it to her and cover her nakedness before he was in motion once again, returning to the other side of the bed and the chair that sat there.

Who was the real man? Caterina wondered, but that thought was immediately replaced when a fork laden with scrambled eggs came into her line of sight as he began to feed her. He offered bite after bite until she heard the final clink of metal against china. Then came a second desire.

"I'm thirsty," Caterina rasped, suddenly aware of how long it had been since she had drunk or eaten anything substantial.

Mick held up a bright red plastic cup. "Can you handle this on your own?"

The ties were loose enough for Caterina to drink with the cup. She assumed Mick hadn't trusted her with a real glass because it would make an effective weapon if broken, but she was too parched to care. Greedily, she drank the contents of the cup: cold, refreshing milk. "I know you're probably used to champagne," Mick began.

"No, I like milk," she said as a memory popped forth in her mind. Sitting beside her mother as a child and eating wonderfully nutty cookies with ice-cold milk.

She drank down the entire glass and then returned the empty cup to him. He placed it on a small tray sitting on the nightstand, then braced his elbows on his knees and laced his fingers together.

Mick had large hands, she noticed. Nicely shaped with elegant fingers. Along the knuckles of one hand were a series of scars from old nicks and cuts. He wore no rings or other jewelry. Only a large black watch with lots of buttons.

Caterina watched him, uncertain.

And Mick, in turn, watched her, equally puzzled. She had eaten like a bird, literally pecking the food off the fork the action instinctive.

The milk, however, had awakened some kind of thought process within her. A small smile had inched across her lips, and her eyes—those amazing blue eyes—had widened with remembered pleasure.

"Do you know who you are?"

"Cat," she immediately answered but with a hint of question in her voice. It made him worry that the response was merely a repetition of what she had been hearing from him since last night.

"Do you know what you did?"

Her eyes narrowed and she looked away from him, down to where her hands clutched the sheet to her body. After a quick shake of her head, he pressed forward.

"Do you remember Dr. Wells?"

She nodded and began to pluck and wring the sheet with her fingers.

"Do you remember what happened?"

He leaned forward until she couldn't avoid meeting his gaze, confronting her with his presence and the question she needed to answer.

"No," she said and closed her eyes. Mumbled something unintelligible before she started a rhythmic rocking.

Unfortunately, he didn't have time for a Rain Man act this morning.

Grabbing her forearms, Mick lifted her toward him as far as the restraints allowed and brought his face close to hers.

"Open your eyes, damn it."

Caterina did as he commanded but averted her gaze, only glancing at him from the corner of her eye. As she did so, the blue hue of the sheets immediately began to bleed onto her skin.

"What happened that night? Why did you kill Dr. Wells?"

She shook her head and struggled against his grasp, surprisingly stronger than the night before. "What happened that night" was a question Caterina had been asking herself over and over again.

Mick held on tightly, bracing his legs on the ground; maintaining his balance and control of Shaw even as she attempted to break free.

"Please let me go," she finally said. But he held on, needing to break her and get an answer to his questions.

"Who killed Wells?"

"I don't know," she cried and fought him, twisting from side to side as she attempted to break free.

A sharp piercing trill broke into their battle. His cell phone.

He tossed her onto the bed so forcefully that she bounced up for a moment before turning onto her side and curling up as much as the restraints permitted. Small, indistinct noises escaped her lips as she nearly became lost on the sheets, blue on blue, except for the dark wealth of her hair.

He looked at the caller ID and mumbled, "Shit."

Liliana. Hopefully with some news.

CHAPTER 11

"*Hermanita*. Tell me you've got something. Anything."

"DNA analysis will take a day or two, but my friend rushed the tox screens. Cat has been medicated with an assortment of hallucinogenic drugs, including some dissociative ones."

Meaning that maybe she wasn't a raving loon, Mick thought. Maybe something was scrambling the signals to her conscious mind from other parts of her brain, accounting for her erratic behavior.

"I'd ask why, but unfortunately I think I know why— someone wanted to control her," he said.

"As in mind control?" his sister asked.

He shot a quick glance at Shaw. Her knees were drawn upward as far as the restraints would allow. Her earlier cries had subsided, replaced by incoherent mumbling. Some parts of her were beginning to lose their camouflage color, returning to the normal color of human skin.

Interesting. A fight-or-flight response?

He shook his head, wondering, and left the room to keep the discussion with his sister private. Leaning against the wall in the hall, he said, "CIA experimented with LSD and other psychedelic drugs in the fifties and sixties. The MK Ultra Project. Maybe someone took a cue from that."

"If that project involved an assortment of alkaloids, that's a possible scenario. The tests showed small traces of LSD, larger amounts of ketamine and some other spikes of unknown origin, although they contained nitrogen, like most alkaloids."

Mick walked back to the door and examined Shaw as she rested fitfully on the bed. With a heavy sigh, he said, "She could have coded last night when we medicated her. The sedative together with all that crap might have clobbered her heart rate and breathing."

"We can't administer anything else until these other drugs are out of her system," Liliana advised.

Another voice intruded from a distance. "Dr. Carrera. You're needed in the ER."

When his sister spoke, providing a reply to whoever needed her, her words were muffled, as if she had covered the mouthpiece with her hand. Then she came back on the line. "I've got to go."

"Roger, *hermanita*. Call as soon as you've got anything else," he said and hung up.

He stalked back to the side of the bed and glanced down at Shaw. She had quieted somewhat, but he didn't trust that she wouldn't become agitated again, especially considering the mix of drugs someone had pumped into her.

The LSD alone could have residual effects that might linger for some time, depending on how much of it she had received and for how long. He'd even heard of cases where people tripped years after receiving the drug. Since Liliana had mentioned that the traces of LSD had been small, he hoped the effects might be gone within a few days.

With the drugs out of her body, Shaw might become more coherent and cooperative, although doubts lingered about her condition. And about the weird traits she was exhibiting—the extra-human strength, skin that went all camo when she lost control. That was something she had done a few times, but was it only due to the drugs?

Could she have committed Wells's murder during one of those incoherent and possibly violent times?

Mick had to figure out what was going on, and he had to figure out what had actually happened with Wells before he turned Shaw over to Edwards.

Shaw might be a drug-crazed lunatic, possibly even a murderer, but she was still higher on his list than the urbane Dr. Edwards. Even if the physician hadn't actively participated in what had been done to her, he'd had a hand in it as the owner of the company.

He didn't much care for people who took advantage of those who were weaker.

Mick tossed down his pen, frustrated by his enforced confinement.

Although he had taken care of more than one wounded comrade and enjoyed his time as an EMT, being a nursemaid was an entirely different thing. Especially when combined with his patient's continued outbursts.

He'd been listening to them for the better part of the late morning as he attempted to obtain more information on Wardwell. He surged from his office chair, determined to put an end to the noise, when he spotted his iPod sitting beside the computer.

They say music quiets the savage beast. Maybe it could

quiet Shaw. If she connected with the music, she might also make some kind of association with who and what she had been. That in turn might trigger more recollections about the night of the murder.

He snagged the iPod and bounded down the hall to the guest bedroom.

As she had before, Shaw immediately reacted to his presence, her skin transforming before his eyes. He tempered his actions, measuring his pace as he neared the bed. Keeping his movements nonthreatening and his voice even.

"I won't hurt you, Cat."

He slipped the iPod into the unit on the nightstand. With the push of a button, Shaw's music spilled from the speakers.

Dvorak's *Cello Concerto in B minor*. She had played the piece at the Kimmel Center last year.

"That's you, Cat. You playing the cello," he said in soft tones, crouching down so that he would be eye level with her.

"Do you remember? Do you remember what you were? Who you are?"

"I'm Cat," she said brightly, but her answer seemed to displease him.

"My name is Cat," she repeated more forcefully and tapped a spot close to her heart with her fingers.

He reached out and took hold of her hand. His was hard, the pads of his fingers calloused, but as he had been the night before, his touch was surprisingly gentle.

"I wish I could believe that you weren't just repeating what you've heard."

Suddenly Mick shot upright, his manner hard once

more. "You've been drugged, Cat. It may take some time for the drugs to wear off."

"My name *is* Cat," she insisted, but the music coming from the machine by the bed called to her. It was so beautiful. The tones rich and melodious. Soothing. A smile came to Caterina's face as the music wrapped itself around her. Tangled with her thoughts to drive away some of her fear.

Mick grudgingly smiled as well.

"Glad to see that you like it," he said and then walked out of the room.

She did like it. She closed her eyes and fragments of images spilled from her brain, filling up her limited consciousness. The black and white of notes on paper. Honey-gold wood, cold and smooth against her skin. Coarse hair, sticky with rosin.

His words repeated in her brain.

That's you, Cat. You playing the cello.

Like two pieces of a puzzle coming together, the pictures in her mind joined with the words.

A cello. She used to play the cello and it had brought her joy. It had to have made her immensely happy before because it was bringing her a great deal of peace now.

She shifted her position, turning on the bed. Yanking on the restraints to get closer to the music.

With the notes embracing her, she released herself to the melody washing over her.

"You left the condo very early this morning, or maybe it's more accurate to say late last night," Harrison said. From the corner of his eye, he shot a look around to see who might be in the hall in the surgical wing before he laid his hand on Liliana's sleeve.

Easing his index finger beneath the edge of her jacket, he inched it up to reveal the first hint of a bruise. "Was it because of our fight? I didn't mean to hurt you," he said, leaning toward her and speaking in hushed tones, the gesture seemingly nonthreatening.

Unfortunately, Liliana knew what would usually follow. He used his size, coupled with his proximity, to intimidate. When that failed, his fists reinforced who was lord and master in his domain. In their relationship.

It hadn't always been that way. At first he had been a caring and solicitous fiancé. Then a few months ago he had withdrawn, seemingly worried about something. But he had not revealed the source of his concern to her, no matter how hard she had tried to reach him.

The depression had cemented itself in him. He became more possessive and increasingly angry and prone to violence.

Needing distance from him, she took a step back and inched her head up to meet his gaze, refusing to be cowed. His light blue eyes chilled at her actions and the muscles of his jaw clenched tight. She knew she needed to avoid confrontation at all costs, especially now when Mick and his guest needed her help. But she would not let Harrison control her with fear any longer.

"I wanted to check up on one of my patients before rounds," she finally answered.

"Is that right?" He took a small step toward her, the tightness of his body causing an instinctive response in her to avoid the threatening gesture. Unfortunately, the wall was at her back and he had effectively cut off any forward retreat.

Stiffening her spine and pulling back her shoulders, she tilted her head and defended herself in the only way she could at that moment. Calmly she said, "Do you really want to do this here and give the hospital even more to gossip about?"

He narrowed his eyes, considering her.

"What do you mean? Gossip?"

The squeak of a rubber-soled shoe on the gleaming tile floor intruded.

Harrison's head snapped around as the nurse turned the corner and came into view. He took a step away from Liliana and, with that step, his entire persona morphed.

"See you at home later, honey," he said, the tones of his voice light and cheerful. A movie star smile brightened his face.

She barely controlled the flinch when he dropped a quick kiss on her forehead and sauntered away with that phony grin.

"Morning, Nurse Edmonds," he said, his tones almost too friendly.

The nurse gave a curt nod and chill look to Harrison. As Liliana stopped at the nurse's station to slip a patient's chart into the chart rack, the nurse offered her a warmer greeting. "Good morning, Dr. Carrera."

When the nurse's gaze met hers for one brief second, understanding blossomed there.

"Good morning, Sara. How is Mrs. Rodriguez this afternoon?"

"Better than you are, I suspect," she said beneath her

breath as she removed the Rodriguez chart from the rack and handed it to Liliana.

Liliana buried her head in the papers, reviewing the patient's vitals and progress. "Looks good. I'm going to pop in and check on our patient."

"By the way, Dr. Rojas was looking for you. She came up to the floor about half an hour ago."

With a quick nod, Liliana walked away, chart in hand to see to her patient, but all the time she was wondering what Carmen could want, since her friend hadn't been expecting the results of any of the other tests so soon.

At the patient's door, Liliana stopped to see if Mrs. Rodriguez was awake. The hip replacement surgery had gone well, but had taxed the older woman.

When Mrs. Rodriguez noticed her waiting by the door, she grinned happily and waved her in. "Come in, *niña*."

The welcome on the older woman's face filled her with satisfaction and confirmed yet again the reason why she had gone into medicine.

Something that whoever had worked on Mick's friend seemed to have forgotten.

CHAPTER 12

Mick's investigation was being seriously hampered by his having to babysit the unpredictable Ms. Shaw. Luckily his sister's schedule had some freedom for the next few days. Until then, Mick had figured out what to do to keep Shaw contained, which was why he was waiting for his cousin Ramon. Sheriff Ramon Gonzalez, now that he was all grown up. Head of one of the local police departments.

Ramon had agreed to meet Mick at the Dunkin' Donuts in Belmar, which was buzzing with an assortment of the resident clamdiggers and the Bennies who rented shore homes in town during the summer months, inflating the town's population and filling many of the local shops along Ocean Avenue. The place was crowded, but far enough away from his usual haunts that it was safe to meet Ramon there.

At Mick's request, Ramon was dressed in civvies to avoid attracting attention. His cousin slipped onto the cement bench opposite him at the outdoor table where Mick had settled down to wait for him. On top of the table were Ramon's favorites: black coffee with a chocolate frosted donut.

As his cousin noted the treat, his eyes lit up with joy, reminding Mick of the Ramon from their childhood.

"Thanks, *mano*." He picked up the paper cup and took a sip, wincing at the heat of the coffee. His hand was headed for the donut when Mick stopped him.

"Did you bring what I asked?"

Ramon rolled his eyes. "When you called me, I thought, Miguelito is finally going to do the right thing and join the force."

Mick shook his head. "You know that I can't consider joining the force—"

"On account of your parents? Because of the money they need?" Ramon immediately challenged. He braced his hands on the edge of the thick cement tabletop and leaned forward. "They're almost finished paying off that bank loan. You don't need to keep on sacrificing what you want—"

"No sacrifice, Ramon. It's what I like to do," he replied and picked up his own cup of coffee to take a sip.

"Bullshit, *mano*. You were always a White Hat. You can't have changed that much over the years."

A White Hat, he thought, clenching his jaw to contain a retort. If he was, that hat was a mite muddied and grey in spots these days. Life had taught Mick that nothing was ever black or white.

"Did you bring what I asked?" Mick repeated.

Ramon looked from side to side, clearly cautious. Then he plopped a plastic bag from a local grocery store on top of the table. "Everything you need is in the bag, but if you get caught—"

"I'll explain how I stole it from your police station. Does Mabel still leave the women's bathroom window open so she can sneak a smoke?"

Ramon shook his head and in a chiding tone said,

"Mabel retired last year. You might have known that if you came to visit more than once a month."

Mick knew that Ramon wasn't just talking about visiting the people he had befriended while working as an EMT for the town. Ramon was trying to make him feel guilty about visiting his family.

Mick raised his hands and held them out in a now-you-see-me gesture. "I'm here."

Ramon rolled his eyes again, picked up the donut and took a big bite. Gesturing to Mick with the half-eaten confection, he said, "You're here out of the blue and I bet you haven't called your *mami*. You know that the last thing you want is to have her show up at your door uninvited."

Mick could well imagine it. His loving but demanding mother descending on his home in the midst of this mess with Shaw. He could just picture her going all camo in front of his mother. Hell, he wished he could hide out when his *mami* was on one of her missions.

Snagging the plastic bag from the middle of the table, Mick opened it and peeked within. Inside was the electronic monitoring device he had requested, as well as a small piece of paper. He didn't need to look at the paper to know it held information on how to access the system to activate and track the ankle bracelet.

"Thanks, *mano*. Now what do you know about McMahon and Hernandez?"

Ramon took another sip of his coffee. "The two detectives manning the Wells murder?"

Mick nodded and Ramon continued. "Met them years ago at a police conference. I thought they were straight-up guys. I hear they're stuck waiting for the state lab guys to process the evidence."

"So they can't release the crime scene yet?" Mick said with a smile.

"Don't know, but I can find out. What's your interest in the case?" Ramon asked.

Not that Mick intended to answer. Instead he stood, grabbed the bag and jiggled it as he said, "Thanks again. Could I ask you to do me one more favor?"

Ramon grew serious and once more perused the area around them before responding, "You name it."

Mick nodded, leaned forward, and whispered, "Keep *mami* away for the next few days."

Mick hadn't been gone for long. Not more than an hour. The *beep beep beep* of the alarm system announced his return.

Caterina wondered where he had been while she lay tied to the bed, the soft strains of Vivaldi's *Four Seasons* playing in the background. Her one hand moving against imaginary strings, recalling how to play the piece.

"Summer" was playing. Somehow appropriate. She couldn't remember how long she had been in the Wardwell facilities, but recalling the heat and humidity after she had escaped, she definitely knew it was summer now.

Noise came from downstairs. Mick's voice, muted from the distance between her room and wherever he was on the lower floor.

Then silence.

A few seconds later she heard his tread on the stairs. It was surprisingly light. She caught a glimpse of him through the open doorway as he climbed up the stairs, and then he was at the entrance to the room.

He said nothing as he entered, walked to the chair and sat, a plastic bag in his hand. Opening the bag, he slipped a small piece of paper into the pocket of the button-down shirt he wore and then removed a small black box connected to a black plastic band of some kind.

He rose, stepped to the foot of the bed and grabbed hold of her heel. He held it steady as he slipped the band around her ankle, joined the two ends and then snapped them into place to secure it to her leg.

"What is that?" she asked.

"An electronic monitoring device. If you attempt to leave the area, it'll warn me. If you continue beyond the perimeter of the house, I'll still be able to track you down. And I will."

Caterina stared at him hard, anger vibrating through her body at his threat.

Mick wasn't sure why, but he suddenly felt like he needed to defend himself. "I'm not a monster," he said, as if reading her thoughts.

"Prove it," Caterina challenged. "Let me go."

CHAPTER 13

Surprise, and even a pleased smile, flickered across the harshly chiseled lines of Mick's face before he reined himself in. "No can do."

He returned to the chair, staring intently at Caterina as he said, "I have to go, but I won't be gone long. Don't think of running away."

Without a second glance, Mick left again.

Over an hour later, he parked the Jeep in the visitor section, taking a moment to survey the three different wings of the Wardwell facilities.

The center wing held all the corporate staff and security. He had met with Edwards there the other day.

Based on the research he had done, he knew the wing to the left housed the sterile lab areas responsible for creating the cloning products and tests Wardwell manufactured, while the wing to the right held the medical complex where Caterina and the other patients were housed.

He entered the center wing, where he stopped for a moment to check out the guards at the security desk. As he had hoped, a different set of guards was on duty than had been present when he had visited the other morning.

He sauntered up to the desk and waited for the guard to acknowledge him.

The ill-fitting suit he'd chosen to wear was tight across Mick's shoulders and the starch in the collar of the shirt had chafed a spot on his throat raw, but the outfit certainly screamed underpaid cop.

When the guard finally looked up from his papers, Mick reached into the suit jacket pocket and flashed a fake local police department badge. Fake, but good enough to pass.

"Detective Ramirez," Mick said, tucking the badge back into his jacket pocket.

"I thought you guys were done already," the guard asked as he pushed forward the log book for Mick to sign.

Mick scrawled a name in the book and answered, "State lab boys needed another sample. Asked me to come down and get it so they can finish up their investigation and release the crime scene." He held up a briefcase as if to confirm that he intended to put the evidence within it.

The security guard nodded and handed over a visitor's badge. "Third door on the right. Then go through the breezeway into the next wing and follow the hall to the very end. You'll need the badge to open all the doors."

Mick shot him a quick salute and did as the man said, swiping the badge at the door to access the breezeway before he walked down to the end of the hall. Even if there hadn't been crime scene tape everywhere, a quick peek through the glass panel in the door would have confirmed that something major had gone on in the room.

Blood spatter marred the walls and a larger splotch stained a spot in the center of the floor. Pieces of lab fur-

niture, shattered beakers, microscopes, and other equipment littered the room. Across the room, large pieces of
plywood closed off what had once been a large plate glass
window.

Mick slipped beneath the crime scene tape, swiped the
card to open the door, and entered the laboratory, where
he took photos with a camera and made mental notes of
everything in the room, including the destruction in various areas. Then he strode to the lateral file cabinets along
the far wall. The doors of the cabinets were dented and
blood-splattered.

He cracked open the first drawer. Lots of files, but with
very few papers. The second drawer held more of the
same.

The next lateral file was locked.

He removed a locksmith's pick from his suit jacket pocket
and slipped it into the opening. A few pokes and twists and
the lock on the cabinet popped out with a *ka-thunk*.

Patient files filled the top drawer. Files with red labels
that read TERMINATED took up the bulk of the space. The
name on the last file in the cabinet was Jenkins.

He closed the drawer and opened up the second one.

Bingo. Shaw's file was smack in the middle. He
removed it and for good measure grabbed two of the
nearby files labeled with the troublesome TERMINATED
stickers.

He tucked the files into the briefcase and locked the
cabinet, returning it to its original state. He hurried back
out into the hallway and as he did so, a woman in scrubs
turned the corner and headed toward him.

When she realized he was by the door to the lab, she
paused, clearly uncertain.

"Detective Ramirez," he said, as he reached into his jacket and extracted the badge.

She nodded and he said, "Do you work here? In the lab?"

"I did until Dr. Wells was murdered. They've closed up the facility for now," the woman said, fingering the hem of her shirt nervously. She motioned to another door farther up the hall. "I was just going to pick up some samples in there."

"Where are the patients?" he asked.

The woman shrugged. "Gone. Dr. Edwards thought it would be better to move them away from the violence."

And away from anyone who could question them about what really went on the night Wells was murdered, Mick thought. Edwards was certainly trying to cover up the incident. He wondered why his client hadn't already called him about the progress he was making on the case.

"Thank you for your time," Mick said, and with a polite nod of his head he exited the Wardwell facilities.

Outside the building, he hurried around the exterior of the structure to the spot where Shaw had supposedly made her escape by tossing a heavy piece of lab equipment through the glass. Several large pieces of plywood sealed off the damage.

He bent down and examined the base of the makeshift plywood barrier and bits of broken window glass glinted in the sunlight.

Very little glass.

Someone might have cleaned up, but if the glass had shattered as badly as indicated in the police reports, he would have expected a fairly large area where bits of the window glass would have been broadcast by the force of the blow.

He stood and surveyed the area in a six-foot-or-so radius from the window.

Nothing, which didn't seem possible to him even if someone had cleaned up. Human nature being what it was, they would have focused on the area close to the window and likely missed the pieces scattered farthest by the impact.

The lack of glass raised another possibility in his mind—that the window had been broken from the outside, spewing bits of window glass inward.

He made a note to review the police reports again when he returned home.

The files in the briefcase were heavy, dragging at his arm as he rushed back to his car. Dragging on his conscience as he recalled how many red TERMINATED labels there had been in the two drawers.

If either he or Franklin had completed their mission, would Shaw have been the next patient with the Terminated designation?

He intended to find out just what that status meant and who was responsible for the deaths of so many.

Later, Mick paced the length of the living room in his home, his booted feet sounding loudly on the polished wood floors, making him wish for once that he had put carpet down. The carpet would have muffled his sounds, but then again, it would also provide stealth to an intruder.

Not that he had ever meant for his chosen profession

to intrude in this place, even though he had secured this home as thoroughly as he had his apartment/office.

A car door slammed outside and he went to the door and peered out the spyglass.

Liliana was hurrying up the walk, medical bag in one hand and a white paper bag with the familiar logo of his family's Mexican restaurant in the other. His stomach growled in anticipation of what was in the bag.

At the door he disarmed the security system and admitted his sister. Re-armed the system once she was safely inside.

"You've got news—"

"And nachos in addition to some other goodies," Liliana said, holding up the bag. Inclining her head in the direction of the stairs, she said, "How's the patient?"

Mick shook his head. "Determined to get free, and luckily more coherent than yesterday."

"Considering the dissociative properties of some of the drugs she's received, that's surprising."

Liliana walked down the hall toward the kitchen and Mick followed. She placed her medical bag on a kitchen chair and went to the oven. After she turned it on, she placed the contents of the bag inside.

It occurred to Mick as he watched her that his baby sister had the mom act down pat.

"We can eat and talk about the test results after I check out . . . You said her name was Cat? Any last name?"

He hesitated, unsure of just how deeply to involve his sister.

"Let's leave it at just Cat."

"Justcat? An unusual surname, wouldn't you say, *hermano*? But it seems appropriate for such an unusual woman." She grabbed her doctor's bag and brushed past

Mick on her way to the guest room, stopping short at the foot of the stairs.

"Has she had a chance to relieve herself? Or to move about to avoid the risk of DVT?"

"About an hour ago, she relieved herself and took a shower, although she was none too pleased with my company in the john. Also gave her some of my sweats to wear."

Seemingly satisfied, his sister went to check on her patient.

At the door to the room, Liliana stopped, surprised by the sight of the cello in the corner and the sound of the softly playing music. "Is that—"

"Tony's old cello," Mick called as he climbed the stairs to follow his sister. "I snuck by the house and borrowed it. Left him a note that I needed it for a friend."

"I can't remember the last time our baby brother played it," Liliana said.

"That's why I figured it wouldn't bother him. Thought it was worth getting the cello, since Cat responded favorably to the music."

Liliana nodded, proud of her brother for making such a kind, albeit surprising, gesture. She went in and walked to the bed. As she had the night before, Caterina grew fretful at the sight of her.

Placing her medical bag on the ottoman by the chair where Mick had slept the night before, Liliana sat down and laid her hand on Caterina's pale blue forearm. In her best bedside manner, her voice soothing, she said, "How are you feeling today, Cat? How is your arm?"

Caterina eyed Liliana up and down before her movements quieted and, as they did, the camouflage staining her skin receded like the wash of a wave along the shore.

"Please let me go," she said.

Mick muttered a curse under his breath.

His sister glared at him. "Why don't you go get some dinner for Cat?"

Caterina looked from the young woman sitting beside her to Mick. Her captor, since she recognized now that she had escaped one prison merely to end up in another.

Mick shot an annoyed look at them, but did as his sister asked.

Liliana scooted to the edge of the chair and patted Caterina's arm reassuringly. "Don't mind my brother. He means well."

Caterina examined the doctor more carefully. She and the man shared the same dark brown hair and eyes, but Mick's skin was a darker color, like the burnished wood of her cello.

Yes, her cello. She had remembered that during the many hours that she had lain in the bed, listening to the music that continued to play softly. Recalling how her fingers would shift along the strings while her bow worked against them to bring forth the strains of a symphony.

When Mick had brought in the beat-up old instrument, she had known it wasn't hers, but despite that had twisted on the bed until she could touch the wood, feel the cool of the varnish beneath her fingers, pluck a string or two only to wince at its out-of-tune sounds.

"My name is…" she started to say, but then her mind processed another thought that yanked a wide grin to her face. "Caterina. Caterina Shaw."

CHAPTER 14

"Caterina Shaw, the cellist?" Liliana was taken aback by the revelation.

Caterina nodded. "I play the cello. I'm a musician."

"Dios mio," Liliana whispered before recovering her poise. "I'm Liliana. Mick's sister and a doctor. May I look at your arm?"

Caterina moved her wounded arm and experienced a slight pull, but little pain. Feeling an unexpected sense of security with the other woman, she nodded and permitted her to check the wound.

"It's knitted closed and almost completely healed," Liliana said with some surprise in her voice. "I'm going to take the stitches out, so it may feel a little weird."

As Liliana cut the stitches and pulled them out, Caterina felt like someone was tracking a thin string over her flesh, but there was no pain. When she finished, Liliana placed a fresh bandage on Cat's arm and returned to her seat.

"Are you feeling better? You seem more alert."

Amazingly Caterina was feeling almost...human. The long periods of rest had allowed her to focus, and with that focus had come more and more memories. Despite that, there were still some ideas that failed her, and she was frustrated that communicating her thoughts remained difficult.

"I feel . . . well, but . . . confused at times."

Liliana nodded and grasped her hand, the gesture comforting. "Someone has drugged—"

"You did. And Dr. Wells. Edwards," Cat offered, remembering that they, too, had regularly injected her during her stay in their lab.

"Did Dr. Wells and Edwards hurt you?" Liliana asked even as her brother walked back into the room with a tray.

"Dr. Wells was my . . . friend."

"We're your friends also, Caterina," Liliana said.

"Caterina?" Mick immediately chimed in.

Liliana shot him a sisterly look filled with condemnation. "Caterina Shaw. The world-famous cellist. She seems to finally have remembered who she is."

As Caterina glanced at Mick, she caught part of a look between the two siblings, but like so many things, she had trouble understanding the meaning of it.

Mick stood by his sister, holding the tray of food, but he shifted his attention to her. "If I undo the ties so you can eat, do you promise not to put up a fight?"

The idea of being free, if only for a short moment, firmly pushed away any ideas she might have been having about how to get away from this place.

"Promise," she said and held up her bound wrists.

With an annoyed exhalation, he handed his sister the tray. "Hold this."

He went to the legs of the bed and one ankle at a time, untied the restraints. Then he shifted to her arms, removing those ties as well.

"Thank you," she said, relieved at even the smallest liberties he had provided.

A second later, he placed the tray over her lap and the aromatic smells teased her nostrils, creating a deep loud rumble in her stomach.

The scents kindled memories from the deepest recesses of her brain. Suddenly she was a child again, her mother beside her.

Mick sat on the edge of the bed, examining her as she contemplated the food. "You remember something."

"Mami," she said, straining for more, and he helped her along.

"Your *mami* was Mexican. Did she cook food like this for you?"

She had, Caterina realized, only it had been a long time since she had eaten such food. Since she had seen her mother. With that realization, a wellspring of sorrow rose up, bringing tears to her eyes.

"My *mami*'s dead."

Liliana squeezed her hand. "I'm so sorry."

With the barest hint of sympathy Mick advised, "It happened a long time ago. When Cat was six."

"If anything, that makes it harder," his sister scolded.

Her dad was dead as well, she remembered, but that knowledge brought only a scintilla of the pain of her earlier enlightenment.

Mick motioned to the food on the plate. "Eat up. You need to build your strength."

She dug into the meal with the plastic fork he had provided.

An enchilada, she recalled. The corn tortilla was filled with flavorful cheese and covered with a delicious chili pepper sauce. Beside the enchilada rested refried pinto beans and yellow rice with vegetables.

With each forkful she ate, her hunger grew until the plate was clean.

"Still hungry?" Mick asked, arching a brow as she contemplated the empty plate.

"Sorry, but it was good. Can't remember eating anything so good. Long time ago."

Once again, Liliana reached out and offered a reassuring pat on her arm. "Don't be sorry. My *mami* will be happy that you enjoyed the food."

"Drink," Mick commanded. She did, gulping down the sweet grape juice in the plastic cup he handed her.

When she was done, he tied her back up. She wanted to protest, but at her first chirp, Mick silenced her with a threatening glare.

"We'll be back later," Liliana said and grabbed hold of her brother's arm, dragging him out of the room.

Caterina lay back against the sheets, the music from the iPod relaxing her once again. The fullness of her stomach was satisfying, until the tastes that lingered on her tongue elicited more memories of her mother.

She did something she knew she had not been able to do before.

She cried for her mother's loss until the pain emptied from her body, leaving behind only the memories of precious times shared.

Then she waited for her captor to return.

CHAPTER 15

In the kitchen, Mick placed the dirty dishes in the sink while asking his sister, "Can you fill me in while we eat?"

"Trying to get rid of me so quickly?" Liliana challenged. She set the table while Mick removed the aluminum take-out plates from the oven.

He paused, faced her, and leaned his hands on the edge of the counter. "Actually I was hoping you could stay the night in case I need help."

His sister hesitated, then surprised him by saying, "To be honest, I was hoping you'd let me crash here for a little bit. Just until I can find somewhere else to live."

He walked to her side and cupped her cheek, applying gentle pressure to raise her gaze upward.

"You're doing the right thing. If you want me to take care of him—"

"I appreciate the offer, big bro, but I need to handle this on my own."

He nodded. "Use my bedroom. It's more comfortable and I need to keep a close eye on Cat anyway."

"Caterina Shaw." Liliana shook her head in disbelief.

"The famous cellist, and according to the local newscasts, a murderess."

He remained silent, which prompted his sister to ask, "You're not denying the latter?"

"Don't have enough information to either deny or confirm." Mick returned to the counter where the take-out containers rested.

"Lose the military speak," Liliana chided.

"Yes, sir," he teased as he placed the aluminum containers on the trivets his sister had laid out on the large oak kitchen table.

Liliana chuckled, sat down and quickly served them a sampling of the food their *mami* had prepared. It steamed on their plates and the aroma enticed. The first few minutes at the table were quiet as they took the edge off their hunger, but then Mick broke the silence. "When you called, you said you had more news."

Liliana nodded and blew on a bite of tamale on her fork. "Surprising news. My friend wasn't expecting any results for a day or so, but she was able to get an analysis earlier than she thought."

"Some new test procedure?"

"Exceptionally fast DNA replication. So fast that she ran the analysis a second time to make sure it was right," Liliana replied. She rose from her seat and pulled some papers from her medical bag, laying one on the table beside Mick.

He recognized it immediately as an electrophoresis gel result from a DNA test. A series of parallel columns contained a number of differing bands in each column. Someone had circled several of the bands on the paper.

Liliana ran her index finger along the test results.

"These bands here and here are what you would expect to see in a human DNA test."

She jabbed at the circled sections. "But not these."

She slipped another piece of paper, showing what looked like a graph, before him. "So my friend did an electropherogram using an automated sequencer for determining the DNA series. Same weird results."

"'Weird results.' So you're telling me we still don't know what's going on with her?" he said with frustration.

Liliana whipped out one last piece of paper: a page printed from a Web site showing a photo of a Petri dish with a number of phosphorescent colors in the shape of a palm tree and ocean.

"Look familiar?" she said and walked back to her chair, sat down and resumed eating.

Mick picked up the paper and read aloud the caption beneath the photo. "This scene shows the plethora of colors available in various mutations of fluorescent protein-producing bacteria."

"The GFPs—the green fluorescent proteins—in the bacteria physically show how genes express themselves," Liliana explained.

"So she's contaminated by some kind of fluorescent bacteria?" he asked, putting down his fork. But then the answer came to him before Liliana could reply. "They used the fluorescent proteins, these GFPs, as trackers for the genes they implanted during her cancer therapy. That could explain what happened to her blood."

Liliana nodded. "Some scientists have even produced transgenic rabbits and pigs that glow in the dark because of these proteins."

A glow-in-the-dark animal, only the woman upstairs

wasn't an animal. Although he still wasn't quite sure what she was right now.

Or what she was going to become.

"I've got her supposed medical history up in my office, but I also managed to steal her real file today."

Liliana placed her fork on her nearly empty plate. Only a bit of beans and rice remained. "You think the scientists at Wardwell doctored the one they had given you?"

"Possibly. I'm going to review the files tonight. Compare them and see what I can discover." Mick rose from the table. He was heading out of the kitchen when his sister stopped him. "Not so fast, *hermano*. I brought the food, so you're going to clean up before you go to work."

"You're a hard taskmaster, Lil," he said, but returned to the table, wrapped her in a bear hug and dropped a kiss on the top of her head.

She returned his embrace, burying her head in his chest. "Tell me this will all work out, Miguelito."

"It'll work out, Liliana. I promise."

Softly murmured words, spoken in Spanish, awakened old comforting memories.

Caterina fought the urge to rouse, wanting to bask in the newly recovered recollections of her mother. The gentle touch of her mother's hand as she brushed her unruly locks at night, rousing the scent of the orange blossom bathwater she had dribbled onto her freshly washed hair; the passion in that same touch as her mother's hands alternately caressed and struck the keys of the upright piano they had owned, playing a difficult symphony or concerto. Playful as she morphed the song into some ragtime or a variation on a mariachi tune.

Her father had said that she had inherited her mother's ear, but hidden behind the compliment had been censure. Caterina had realized that even as a child.

He might have loved her mother at one time, but he had grown to disapprove of her, and the love, if there ever had been any, had died beneath his controlling ways.

When her father had gazed at her, she saw the reflection of her mother in his eyes. A passionate and carefree woman who had made the mistake of marrying a formidably powerful and unyielding man. One who had chipped away at her mother's spirit with his demands.

As Caterina half-opened her eyes, wanting to return to the good memories in her head, she saw them—brother and sister—heads bent close together as they spoke softly in Spanish. Was it to avoid her understanding them? Her Spanish was rusty from years of disuse. Maybe they were assuming that, or maybe she was just being paranoid.

Liliana was crouching down, eye level with her brother, who sat in the chair beside the bed. He had been in that same spot for the last few hours, as far as Caterina could tell. She had awakened a couple of times from a fitful rest to find him there. Mick had urged her back to sleep with a consoling touch and a comfortably issued command to rest.

Now his sister was back, and seeing that Caterina had roused, she reached out and gently touched her arm. The gesture was familiar—like a mother's touch.

Liliana even looked like Caterina's mother. Petite. Slender. Olive-skinned with cocoa brown hair and dark eyes, only now as she met Liliana's gaze, she realized the other woman's eyes were a deep green, almost emerald.

"You're awake?" Liliana asked as she leaned forward.

Mick rose from the chair. Dressed in black from head to toe, he possessed a dangerous aura that awoke conflicting emotions within Caterina.

Fear.

Attraction.

Caterina suspected it would be hard for any female not to respond to his blatant masculinity. And as she came to that realization, another tagged along with it.

Her brain actually seemed to be working with more clarity than it had in a long time.

"I'm awake," she confirmed and for good measure added, "And I'm remembering things. My mother and father."

"The drugs must be wearing off," he said, the tone of his voice flat. Offering no comfort, but no condemnation, either.

Caterina had expected the latter, although her mind wasn't processing thoughts clearly enough yet to comprehend the *why* of that expectation.

"I don't understand what's happened to me," she said.

Mick blew out a rough sigh and jammed his hands into the pockets of his jeans. He rocked back on his heels. "That makes three of us."

With a reassuring pat of her hand as she sat down on the chair, Liliana began to fill Caterina in on what she and Mick had been doing. "Mick's managed to get your real medical file. We've been going through it tonight to find out what's been done to you."

What's been done to me? Caterina thought and closed her eyes, attempting to drag forth some kind of recollection of what had happened to her. She was sorry that she did so when the memories came, lashing out at her with their violence.

The scent of blood, earthy and metallic, filled her nose and mouth. Wet and sticky, it covered her hands and arms.

A face emerged from all the blood.

"Dr. Wells is dead," she said aloud. "Someone killed him."

"*You* killed him," Mick replied callously.

Caterina shook her head emphatically. "No. He was my friend. I wouldn't hurt him."

Mick seemed inclined to argue with her, but Liliana reached out to stop him.

"*I* know you wouldn't hurt him, or anyone else."

Liliana's message was clear, but Caterina didn't have any way of convincing the taciturn Mick, who reminded her a little too much of what she had remembered about her father.

For that matter, she might not even be able to prove to herself that she'd had nothing to do with Dr. Wells's death.

She was tired, more tired than she had ever been at any time in her life. Not even the days she had undergone chemo could compare to how she now felt.

This kind of tired was soul deep.

Whispering, she said, "I want to rest."

Mick controlled the urge to shake her as Shaw closed her eyes and sank back onto the pillows. As he glanced at his sister, she inclined her head in the direction of the hall and he walked out. Liliana followed.

"You've got to be patient," she counseled.

He couldn't argue, although he was finding it difficult

to contain his frustration. Ducking his head down, he said, "You're right, only ..."

Liliana eased right before him, making it impossible for him to avoid her. "Only what, Mick? I mean, you got her to safety. She's starting to remember. That's all good, right?"

It was all good for Shaw, but she wasn't his client.

"I was hired to bring her in, Lil. I'm surprised my client hasn't already called to find out what I'm doing to earn my money. It's been several days already."

"Does it matter? Caterina's safe. Isn't that what—"

"I don't think my client cared whether Shaw came back dead or alive."

Confusion slipped across Liliana's features. "What do you mean?"

"I mean that since he sent someone else after her as well, my client is probably hoping someone might be bringing her in dead."

"He hired you to kill her?" she hissed and shot an anxious look toward the doorway of the guest room.

Mick shrugged and eased the tips of his fingers into his jeans pockets. "No, but with the kind of money he was paying—"

"You understood that having to kill Caterina might be a possibility." Accusation was thick in her voice. With an abrupt shake of her head, she whirled on her heel and took a few jerky strides away, before she whirled back and faced him. "You used to be my hero. Not anymore."

Her words cut him deeply, but she was right. Hell, he had never wanted the responsibility that being a hero brought.

But the nagging voice that remained buried deep within him answered back.

"I don't eliminate people for money. *Coño*, I wasn't even going to turn her over without finding out what really happened in that lab."

Liliana came to stand before him again. "What did happen in that lab, Mick?"

He focused on a spot in the distance, his mind's eye recalling the pictures Edwards had provided. Recalling what he had seen today—the blood all over the lab and the damage in the room.

"Something awful," he said before finally facing his sister. "If Shaw did it..." He exhaled roughly. "I need you to be careful until we can figure out what's going on with her. And Edwards did hire someone else for this job besides me, but that's been taken care of."

"Should I reconsider my request to stay here?" Liliana asked, but her tone was teasing, an attempt to lighten the earlier tension between them.

Mick thought about how it might look to the neighbors that Liliana was coming and going. If anything, it might make it appear that nothing was happening in the house except a visit from his sister.

"If you decide to stay, you need to be extra careful."

"Promise."

Knowing Liliana, he was sure that promise would be kept. But he also needed something else from her.

"Do you think you could help me review her medical history again? Just in case I missed something?"

Liliana nodded, but inclined her head down the hall to his bedroom. "I just need a few minutes to call Harrison. Let him know I won't be home tonight, or for that matter, anytime soon."

"What about your stuff?" he asked.

"I'll swing by during the day while he's at the hospital and get my things."

Mick reached out and dragged her into his arms. "Like I said before, if you need me—"

"I know and I appreciate the offer, but this is something I have to take care of myself."

The call came well beyond midnight.

Mick and Liliana had been discussing and researching various experiments and treatments based on Shaw's file for a couple of hours.

"Tell me this isn't a BFD," he said to Franklin as he answered.

"Sorry, *amigo*, but the camel's on fire."

Shit, he thought, but forced a smile on his face for his sister. He motioned with his head that he wanted her to leave the room, needing privacy for the upcoming discussion.

"I'll go check on Caterina," she said, rising from the chair and hurrying out.

Mick closed the door behind her and leaned against it. "What's the SNAFU?"

"Edwards was way too calm when I told him I was off the assignment."

Mick processed that comment, but it didn't take much to realize why.

"We weren't the only two he hired."

"Sorry, man. When I was going through security at the end of the day, I noticed some guest names on their list. Mad Dog paid Wardwell a visit also. I tried to get more info only—"

"Fuck," Mick muttered and raked his fingers through his hair.

Matthew Donnelly, aka Mad Dog, was nothing but trouble.

"But you're not sure that Edwards hired him?" he pressed.

"This is the kind of job Mad Dog would do for free," Franklin retorted with a rough laugh.

Beautiful woman.

Big challenge.

Possible death.

Definitely the kind of assignment Mad Dog would relish.

"Do you know what Mad Dog's been up to lately?"

"Private security black ops. Heard he was doing some time in the Middle East, but got booted. Then he headed down to South America on another assignment. Never really wanted to stay in touch with him, if you know what I mean," Franklin replied.

Mick knew exactly. Mad Dog was a sick miserable fuck. Most people wanted to keep off his radar.

"Thanks, Franklin. Keep me posted on anything else you hear."

Mick snapped the cell phone shut and took a deep breath as he considered Franklin's news.

Mad Dog had probably been spreading mayhem wherever he went, Mick thought, recalling his last mission with the other mercenary. Two innocent civilians had become collateral damage, not that Mad Dog had cared.

Mad Dog had been fired by the large private security firm after that incident and had seemingly disappeared. Mick had left the firm of his own volition and set up his private agency to deal with different kinds of problems. Not that those problems hadn't occasionally involved the possibility of death.

But not cold-blooded murder.

And a man like Mad Dog would help himself to Shaw in other ways as well. In her almost-returning-to-normal state, it was hard to ignore how attractive she was in person.

The professional photographs hadn't done her justice.

But as he had thought in Edwards's office days earlier, he reminded himself that beauty didn't preclude violence.

Not to mention that violence had its own beauty.

Mick was an artist of that kind of beauty.

Raising his hands, Mick examined them, almost as if they belonged to someone else. They were hands capable of brutality, but not cruelty. Hands that could bestow tenderness, not that he'd had much opportunity for that lately. Hands capable of passion, which he could easily get and give.

Women seemed to be drawn to him, or maybe it was better to say they were drawn to the aura of danger around him. Enticed by the prospect of a risky tryst with a handsome man who knew how to satisfy.

That kind of attraction didn't really make for anything but a passable fuck.

And a sad existence.

Jerking away from the door, he opened it and returned to the guest room where Liliana sat in the comfy chair, laptop on her legs, reading something online.

"You may want to reconsider staying here after all," he said, leaning against the door frame.

She looked up, her dark eyes filled with puzzlement. "You want me to go back to Harrison?"

Mick strode over to her, kneeled before her, and tenderly took hold of her hands. Strong, capable, loving hands. Hands that could never be violent.

"Someone else has been sent after Shaw. Someone nasty."

"So? More reason for me to stay and help out," she said and twined her fingers with his.

"You don't understand, *hermanita*," he said, shaking his head.

"I get it. He's the Big Bad, but you're here. You'll watch out for us."

Her trust in him warmed a long-lost piece of his soul and yet...

"You didn't think that before. When you said—"

"That you weren't my hero. I was angry. I wanted to lash out because..."

She looked away from him, but it wasn't enough to hide the tears shimmering in her eyes.

"Because why, Lil?"

She sucked in a shaky breath and bit her bottom lip. "Because for months now I've been losing control of my life. I was angry about that."

He cupped her chin and urged her to face him. With a proud smile, he said, "You are a beautiful and amazing woman. One who can take care of what she needs to do."

One lone tear spilled down her cheek. She braved a watery smile and said, "Then trust that I can handle myself now. That I can help you with this assignment."

She was his blood and they had overcome a great deal of adversity together. The early days when they had first arrived from Mexico and everything had been scarce. As children they had faced the challenges of being different in a predominantly white community. Survived the near ruin of their family's business several years earlier.

He wouldn't dismiss her abilities when he needed them the most.

Recognizing that she needed to be here and involved to regain what she thought she had lost, he said, "Watch your back when you're coming and going. If you see anything that seems suspicious, you call me and head to the nearest police station."

"Copy that," she said and shot him a playful salute.

Gesturing to the laptop, he said, "Get anything else out of there?"

Liliana's smiled firmed and broadened.

"You bet I did."

CHAPTER 16

Mick nudged the door open and walked in, looking fresh and well-rested, but Caterina knew he had spent the night in the chair by the bed again.

Whenever she woke from a sleep packed with fitful images, he had been there, alert as well. Offering comfort. His dark eyes seeming to register every little facet of what was happening, as if to catalogue the events for further analysis.

He had even released her once during the course of that uneven night, escorting her to the bathroom so she could relieve herself. This time he had waited outside the door, sparing her the ignominy that he had visited upon her the day before.

Back in the room, he had tied her up again, but not as tightly.

Has he come to believe I'm not a threat? Caterina thought.

As Mick approached the bed, Caterina wondered how he could have reached such a decision when she herself still doubted.

The images that had come to her during the night had been violent. Horribly so. A slideshow of blood, destruction, and death. Vividly real in her mind, but with enough gaps that it made her memory inconsistent.

Through every nightmare he had been by her side, providing stability and comfort.

"Good morning," he said, walking to the foot of the bed. He released the bindings, but didn't retie the restraints.

At the headboard, he did the same, freeing her from her bondage.

She rubbed at her wrists, not that they were sore. She had stopped fighting against the restraints last night after supper, realizing that this man and the young woman didn't intend her harm.

Not like she had struggled at Wardwell.

Wardwell.

She remembered now the names of her captors. Remembered that Dr. Wells hadn't necessarily been all goodness and light, although he had befriended her.

"They used to tie me down," she suddenly told Mick.

A flicker of emotion darkened his almost impenetrable gaze as his eyes met hers.

"Edwards?" he asked, seeking confirmation.

She nodded. "Wells, too. And Dr. Morales."

He plopped down into the chair, but leaned forward, his elbows resting on broad powerful thighs. His fingers loosely laced together.

"Morales is their assistant." His tone seemed to seek confirmation of that statement.

Caterina searched her brain, trying to remember more about Morales. The name had popped into her recollection last night as she forced herself to try and recall what had happened to her.

Nothing came to her about Morales. She shook her head. "I can't remember."

He thought about what he had learned from the files he had taken. "Dr. Morales isn't a physician. He's a geneticist, from what we could gather from your files."

Caterina again tried to place the name. In a burst of intense, powerful images that blinded her, the doctor's image flashed into her mind.

A dark-eyed little man.

A thin smile as sharp as the instruments in his hand.

Burning pain in her veins from his needle.

The images came over and over, interspersed with agony so real, she needed to escape it. She shifted forward, but encountered a hard chest. Buried her head there as he wrapped his strong arms around her.

"Easy, Cat. They're just memories," Mick said softly.

She grabbed hold of his T-shirt, her hands fisted tightly into the fabric as she keened like a child. Only the press of her body against his was very womanly.

Too much so, Mick realized, fighting his visceral reaction to her proximity.

"Why is this happening?" she murmured against his chest, rubbing her head there, as if by doing so she could erase the images.

He cradled the back of her head with immense restraint and tenderness, sifting his fingers through the thick curls. "They gave you small doses of LSD in addition to a bunch of other hallucinogenic drugs. It may take a little while for all that medication to work out of your system."

"What's a 'little while'?" she asked, wagging her head more forcefully, as if trying to dislodge the visions. As he glanced down, he realized she had gone all camo on him again.

Her hands were the color of his dark blue polo shirt and the rest of her was beginning to blend into the rust brown of the oversized T-shirt he had offered her to wear.

"A few days or even weeks. It's hard to tell with LSD. But try to focus," he urged, recalling the mantra she had used the day before to regain control.

She heeded his command. Repeated the word over and over, and as the tightness left her body, so did the color, but not before she caught a glimpse of herself in her altered state.

She released him and held up her hands. Held them before her and examined them while her skin slowly faded back to normal.

"What am I?" she asked, puzzlement in the stormy ocean blue of her eyes when her gaze skipped to his.

He could have lied. Tempered his words with tenderness, but he had a limited quantity of that and holding her had expended most of it.

"A science experiment," he said, then released her and returned to his spot in the chair.

Her eyes narrowed as she considered his statement. The soft curls of her hair bobbed back and forth with the motion of her head as she said, "They were supposed to help me."

"You're not blind anymore," he reminded her, although he wasn't sure she would consider that a worthwhile trade-off to becoming someone's lab rat.

He wouldn't.

She leaned back against the headboard, raised slender elegant fingers to her temples, and rubbed tiny circles there. "Toward the end, when I was sick, I couldn't see. But it was the pain..."

Meeting his gaze directly, she said, "It was the pain that stole the music." Tapping a spot above her heart with one hand, she added, "*My* music."

The passion in her words was unmistakable.

He understood it. Admired it.

But he couldn't allow those sentiments to change what he had to do. "Someone killed Wells. Do you know who?"

"If I did, don't you think I'd tell you so you'd let me go?" Shaw shot back.

"Not if you were the one who did it," Mick replied calmly, barely controlling his smile at her show of spunk. He liked feisty Cat much more than the mewling weak Cat the drugs had created.

Damn it, not Cat. *Shaw.* He had to think of her as Shaw to maintain distance, but it was becoming increasingly difficult to do so.

She dug her hands into her hair, pulling it back off her face. Releasing the long locks to fall back onto her shoulders as she said, "Why don't you turn me over to the police? Let them decide."

He shrugged and intentionally kept his tone neutral. "Because I've been paid to return you to Edwards."

Her skin paled for a moment before a bit of the T-shirt's rust color leaked onto her body.

Fight or flight, he thought again.

"You're afraid of Edwards. He hurt you?"

"Morales. Edwards," she admitted, looking downward at the sheet covering her body. Plucking at the folds of it nervously before she asked, "Are you going to—"

"Give you to Edwards? Do you think that's what I'm going to do?" he said, perversely intrigued to hear her initial thoughts about him.

She slowly picked up her head, tilted it at a slight angle. Intently she examined him, but the look wasn't one like he generally received from most women. This one reminded him of the look from one of his elementary school teachers.

Exasperated described it best. That brought a disappointment he didn't understand, so he arched a brow and said, "Well?"

She raised her chin a defiant inch. "I think that if you were going to do that, you would have done it already."

Her slightly rebellious response roused his smile once again. "So what do you propose I do?"

Her chin shot up another tiny bit, but there was nothing tiny about the determination in her voice.

"Help me find out who killed Dr. Wells."

CHAPTER 17

Mick considered Shaw's request and the challenge she had presented since the moment he'd seen her photo.

"I'll think about it," he said, unwilling to admit that her request had him intrigued. And then, "It's still early. Why don't you try to get back to sleep." Dark circles lingered under her eyes.

"I can't sleep anymore. Besides, when I sleep…" She hesitated, afraid to reveal more. But there was apparently little she could hide from him.

"You see too much," Mick said softly, completing her thought.

When Shaw nodded, he continued. "I know what it's like when there are only nightmares, but…if you let them come, eventually they won't be as scary."

She couldn't imagine the visions that visited her in the night not being frightening unless you had somehow shut off your soul. Or worse: lost it.

As Caterina lifted her face, Mick's deep brown gaze locked on hers. He seemed so steady and controlled on the surface, but in the depths of those eyes, she imagined she saw his demons. Realized they weren't as frightening because he had mastered them. She supposed he had controlled his fears much the way he had dominated her over the last few days.

Much like her father had mastered her mother until nothing remained of her spirit and passion.

Her father had tried to do the same to her over the years, but somehow she had survived it. Could she survive this man's controlling ways until she was free again?

"You think I'm guilty, don't you? You think I—"

Mick surged toward her on the bed and covered her mouth with his hand. His palm was rough against her lips. His grip hard, but not so hard as to hurt.

"What I know is that someone violated your trust. Violated you. If I had been in the same position, I might have done the same thing, so I don't care right now whether you did it or not."

Before she could respond, or even fully process his statement, he was in motion.

He stepped away from the bed, back to the door. With a desultory flick of his hand he said, "We're having breakfast before Liliana goes back to the hospital. After that, you and I are going to go over your medical files. Understood?"

"Understood," she replied and resisted the urge to snap off a salute.

Definitely ex-military, it occurred to Caterina now. His tone, posture, regimented attire, and haircut screamed it out loud at full volume.

She rose from the bed and stretched, working out the kinks from being bound for so long. When she was done, she took a moment to walk around the room, examining it more fully.

The furniture was simple. Heavy rustic oak pieces.

Simple fabrics that would wear well. Above the dresser was a mirror and as she caught a glimpse of herself she was once again shocked by her appearance.

She leaned on the surface of the dresser and peered at her image. So much thinner. Paler. Her face almost swallowed up by the long rebellious locks of her dark hair. But it was still a human face, the strange skin color that came and went notwithstanding. She even tried to call forth the camouflage, focusing on her hand as it rested on the wooden surface, but it wouldn't come.

She ambled to the old cello leaning against another chair close to the bed and touched it lovingly, the rough feel of the strings and slick varnish ingrained in her memory. She itched to sit down and play, but Mick probably expected her to join them downstairs for the meal. She was surprised he had released her, but then again, she still wore the bracelet that would allow him to track her. Like a prisoner.

A prisoner who had been treated relatively well, she had to admit. Liliana had taken care of her injuries, which they had discovered were completely healed when she had taken a shower the night before. They had fed her. Provided some clothing, she thought, readjusting the overly large shirt that kept on slipping down one shoulder.

Mick's shirt, judging from the size and the smell of it. If she inhaled, she detected remnants of his scent on the fabric.

The sweatpants he had provided were also large at the hips, but close to the right length. She had tightly knotted the ties to keep the pants from falling off her hips, which had been made almost boyish by her weight loss.

Walking down the hallway, she stepped into the room

at the head of the stairs. Clearly Mick's bedroom. She paused at the door. A large king-sized bed occupied most of the space. The dresser surface held a few pictures, but not much else. Everything was militarily neat.

Caterina went to the dresser and examined the pictures. The people in them had such strong physical similarities that she didn't doubt they were related. Which meant that besides Liliana there were two other siblings, as well as a mother and father.

No girlfriend, she thought as she picked up and looked at the remaining photos in the frames.

She laid the frame back down, making sure she returned it to exactly where it had been. Her father had always insisted that there was a place for everything and everything should go back in its place.

Exiting the room, she paused at the top of the stairs, uncertain of just how much freedom Mick intended to give her. She should just go downstairs, she told herself. A cold tremor snaked through her gut as she recalled what would happen to her at Wardwell when she disobeyed.

The sensation was so strong that something shimmered along the edges of her vision, creating a weird halo effect over all that she saw. She remembered seeing something similar before. Maybe when she had first escaped into the forest.

She gripped the banister more tightly, disoriented as she discerned the shapes of the real images sporting unusual and colorful auras.

Her hand on the railing. The steps leading downward.

The images were all there, oddly limned, but there.

She took a first tentative step down the stairs, her knees wobbly from the shock of the change in her vision. Then she straightened her spine, closed her eyes for a moment, and inhaled deeply. Held her breath as she took one step and then another until she was finally at the bottom of the stairs.

She landed on the polished wood floor in the living room immediately off the stairs. Heard voices to the right of her, down a small hall that ran beside a comfortably sized dining room.

Mick's voice. Liliana's voice. Vibrating loudly in her brain. More loudly than was normal. Talking about her.

"You can't turn her over to Edwards. You read the file. You know what they did to her."

A tired sigh followed, filled with more regret than Caterina had expected. "If she killed Wells, I have to turn her over to somebody."

Somebody.

The police, Caterina hoped, until it occurred to her that in her current state, the police would not know what to do with her. Or worse, that . . .

"How long before they turn her back into a science experiment?" Liliana said, stealing the thought from Caterina's mind.

Caterina turned to go to the kitchen, but then realized she could see them. Or rather, she could see weird-colored outlines of their bodies through the walls ahead, like some kind of radar sense.

The irrational images dizzied her as she tried to put things to right. As the room began a slow lazy spin, she fumbled for purchase against a large oak sideboard nearby.

A terra-cotta pitcher on the surface flew off and crashed to the floor as she misjudged the edge of the furniture.

Once she latched onto the edge of the heavy sideboard, the wood gave slightly beneath her fingers as she stabilized herself.

The noise of the pitcher smashing against the floor brought the two siblings running, but Liliana paused halfway down the hall, a shocked expression on her face. She raised her hand to her mouth, disbelief on her expressive features.

Mick had no such hesitation.

He plowed forward toward her, his mouth a tight line across his face. His dark brown eyes blazed with anger.

She flinched as he neared, but his touch was gentle as he wrapped one arm around her shoulders, offering support.

"You can let go. I've got you," Mick said in soft measured tones.

She sagged against him and her fingers popped free from where they had dug into the hardwood of the sideboard.

"That's it. Easy," he said, worried that if the medical file was accurate, rage might follow Shaw's current state.

Her skin had taken on the colors of the room around her—a deep coral color but with a slight shimmer like diamonds in spots. As he locked his gaze on hers, he detected bits of glowing green in the normally deep blue of her eyes. The GFPs tracking the expression of the genes Wardwell had implanted, he guessed.

"What's happening?" Shaw whispered, giving him some measure of relief that she remained aware that something unusual was going on. Unfortunately, he didn't have an answer.

"I don't know, Cat. I'm going to pick you up and take

you over to the couch," he said. At her nod, he did just that, slipping his arms beneath her knees and carrying her.

She eased her arms around his neck and laid her head against his shoulder, the action so trusting that his heart skipped a beat from the emotion of it.

Somehow, Shaw trusted him. Possibly believed in him.

It had been a long time since that had occurred with anyone outside of his family. Not since his days in the Army or maybe the year or so after, when he had been an EMT.

Certainly never with a woman.

And despite the camo and the glow, Caterina was all woman and he could never think of her as just Shaw ever again.

Her femininity was there in the press of her breasts against his chest as he eased her onto the sofa and held her. In the softness of her hair which tangled with his fingers as he pushed it back from her forehead, offering comfort.

"It'll be okay, Cat," he said and she sighed softly, her warm breath against the side of his neck.

Liliana gingerly entered the room, concern etched onto her features. When she saw Mick had the situation under control, she sat down in the chair across from them, vigilant.

Mick continued with his soft caress and leaned his head against the top of Caterina's as it rested on his shoulder.

He looked across to Liliana and she bopped her head in Caterina's direction. He knew what she wanted to do.

"Will you let Liliana examine you so we know what's happening?"

Caterina shivered in his grasp, but nodded.

Liliana popped up from the chair, rushed from the room, and then came back with her medical bag. She laid her hand on Caterina's forearm and stroked it gently. "Let me see your eyes, *amiga*."

Caterina turned her head toward Liliana, but her gaze remained downcast. Fearful.

Liliana tucked her forefinger under Caterina's chin and urged her head up slightly. With her penlight, she illuminated Caterina's irises, activating the phosphorescent trackers which shot off a bright blue-green glow.

Releasing her chin, Liliana swept the penlight across her skin. Reflected light, as if Caterina had dusted her skin with body glitter, twinkled in reaction.

"I don't recall seeing this behavior before. How about you?" Liliana asked Mick.

He thought back to the night he had captured Caterina. There had been the weird fluorescent blood and skin camo, but nothing like this unusual glow.

"Definitely a no. I'm gathering that's not good news."

Liliana shook her head. "Carmen said the cells were replicating at amazing rates. Maybe so much so that they're overwhelming the true cells in her body."

Caterina uttered a shocked, "I want to stay human. I want to stop this."

"Focus for me, Cat," Mick murmured.

Caterina gripped his shoulder roughly, experienced the jerk of his body as she did so, and tempered her hold. She concentrated on the gentle tug of his hand against her hair, on the constant heartbeat beside hers.

Before their eyes, the deep coral color and glowing bits on her skin and in her eyes faded, while the outlines disappeared and Caterina's normal sight returned.

When Caterina dared to look up at Mick, she tried to explain what she had experienced.

"I wasn't sure I was supposed to come down. When I got downstairs, I heard you, but all I could see were weird auras around everything and strange colors," she said and shot an anxious look from Mick to Liliana and then back. "I don't want to be someone's lab experiment. I want to be normal again."

A muscle twitched along the line of Mick's jaw and his eyes became flat as he looked at her. "I have no control over that."

She doubted his words. He seemed to have control over so much, but she wouldn't push the issue right now. Not when she was relying on the two of them for her safety.

Since Mick's face had become hard and unyielding, she grabbed hold of Liliana's hand. "You'll help me, right?"

Liliana squeezed Caterina's hand, trying to keep her calm and avoid another transformation. "I'll do what I can."

Facing Mick again, Caterina spoke in a tired, but determined voice. "Isn't there anything in my medical file that can help?"

Mick closed his eyes, as if mentally scanning the file again. "Plasmapheresis was one of the treatments mentioned."

Liliana let out a low whistle. "Plasmapheresis will be tough. It's not like I can whip up a cell separator to bring here. The machine is too big. Plus it'll require us getting information on what needs to be filtered out of Cat's blood for the plasmapheresis to be effective."

Caterina glanced back at Mick. "Was there any other treatment in the file?"

Liliana answered this time. "It mentioned an inhibitor drug, but didn't state its composition."

"Inhibitor?" Caterina asked.

"I'm assuming from the file that it's some kind of chemical concoction they worked up that slows down the gene replication going on in your body," Mick advised.

"But if you don't know what's in it—" Caterina began, but Mick cut her off.

"We would need to get the medication from Wardwell."

"You can't risk going back there," Caterina said.

Mick exhaled roughly and slipped her off his lap and onto the sofa. Jamming his hands on his hips, he considered her, rattled that she seemed more concerned for him than for herself. He wasn't used to people other than his family caring for him. And he didn't like that he was starting to care for her in ways that had nothing to do with the job.

He needed distance from Caterina, physically and, more importantly, emotionally. "What made you think I was volunteering for the job?"

CHAPTER 18

Mick had been expecting the call from Edwards for days. It finally came while he was on his way down to the Wardwell facilities. He held the phone in his hand, tempted to answer and rattle Edwards's cage, but he held back.

He needed to save any shock-and-awe tactics with Edwards for when they would be most effective. Luckily the call reminded him of one thing—to silence his phone.

Half an hour later he had reached his destination.

Caterina had traveled for miles after escaping the Wardwell labs and finding refuge at the Music Academy. He estimated it was only about a mile from the roadside rest area where he had stopped to the woods nestled against the Wardwell complex. The woods were one of the farthest western edges of the Pinelands. Because of the complex's location close to the National Park and on top of the state's largest natural aquifer, the Wardwell facilities had generated controversy amongst local environmentalists during construction.

The protests had resulted in quite a number of public meetings, which in turn had created lots of news about Wardwell, including various published versions of the physical layout of the facilities in relation to the nearby Pine Barrens. This made it easy for Mick to find a back way toward the labs through the woods.

The very muddy woods.

Mud was not good. It would provide too much evidence that someone had been there. Someone who shouldn't be.

Mick was about two hundred feet away from the first Wardwell building when he noticed tracks in the soil. Booted footprints from one person.

Someone other than Mick had been reconnoitering the area. Maybe mud wasn't so bad after all.

Given Franklin's warning, Mick had an idea about who it was. Mad Dog might be keeping an eye on those places connected to Caterina until he had a lead on where she might have gone. He may even have been aware that Mick was working for Edwards and might also need information from the lab to locate Caterina. Mad Dog was mean, but he wasn't stupid.

Easing on his night vision goggles, Mick perused the perimeter of the buildings. Aside from the faint signature of a night watchman in the guard booth at the gate to the complex, nothing registered.

Turning his attention to the woods, Mick caught a sign of motion close to the edge of the broad manicured lawn that formed a barrier between the trees and the building housing the medical complex where Caterina and the other patients had been kept.

He hunkered down, training his attention on the area. Another short rush of movement came, confirming that someone else was out there in the woods.

A glint of moonlight against glass—likely binoculars—

became clear in the dark of night. They were pointed in his direction.

Shit, Mick thought as he hit the ground to avoid detection. He pulled his Glock from the holster tucked into the small of his back.

Someone was clearly waiting for him. Maybe had even known about Mick's previous visit, since the person had positioned himself close to the area Mick had canvassed the afternoon before.

Mick crawled hand-over-hand, cautiously propelling himself forward. The soil was wet and cool against his body. The soft ping of a gunshot traveled across the night, but the harder thunk against wood that followed sounded far from his current position.

Whoever it was had lost track of him, but that wouldn't last for long.

Mick pushed ahead more quickly, his attention focused on the blob before him, a person kneeling in a sniper's practiced stance. When he was about ten yards away, it was time to act.

Reaching into his satchel, Mick pulled out a flash grenade, pulled the pin, and immediately tossed it forward and away from him.

As the grenade exploded, the shooter rose, turning toward the light for a moment, his back to Mick.

Mick charged, plowing forward like a fullback, body low. He connected with the shooter mid-spine at full force and the man flew face forward hard, losing his grip on the rifle. The weapon skittered off into the underbrush.

Mick jerked his gun toward the man, but his opponent half-rolled to his side and snapped off a quick chop to Mick's wrist that deadened his hand.

Exerting force, he once again got the man lying flat beneath him, but the man followed up with a sharp jab toward his face.

Mick avoided it by rolling off and coming to his feet, training his gun on the weaponless sniper, who rose slowly from the ground, hands outstretched in a sign of surrender.

"Should've known you wouldn't be an easy kill, Carrera," Mad Dog said and took a step toward him.

Mick jerked the nose of the weapon upward in warning, and then steadied it with the hand that still had feeling.

"No need for bloodshed, Mad Dog. I just have to get something from the lab."

"Guess you found Shaw, then. She must be really good in the sack if you're willing to sacrifice the bonus to bag her."

Bonus? The original check had possessed enough zeroes to tempt a saint and now there was a bonus?

"Haven't found her yet, but thanks for the heads-up about the bonus," Mick lied, but Mad Dog clearly wasn't buying it.

"Let's make this interesting. You want something from the lab?" Mad Dog said, slowly, carefully reaching down into his pocket. Just as judiciously, he pulled out some kind of card. As the moonlight illuminated the plastic, Mick realized it was a key card like the one he had used the day before to enter the facilities.

"What do *you* want, Mad Dog?"

A cold smile crept across his face. "What I've always wanted, Mick—a piece of you."

"A piece of me in exchange for the key?" It almost wasn't fair. He would gladly have a go at Mad Dog with no prize on the line. Getting the key out of the deal was gravy.

Mick took a step toward a fallen log and put down his gun, wanting it to be a fair fight.

"I'm all yours, Mad Dog. *Mano-a-mano* because I want to feel you break beneath my hands," he said and urged the other man onward with a wiggle of his fingers.

"You always were too honorable," Mad Dog replied. With a quick snap of his wrist, he suddenly held a small knife in his hand.

Before Mick could go back for his gun, Mad Dog had cut him off, the knife held out in front of him. With the repetitiveness of a pendulum swing, Mad Dog slashed back and forth, but Mick avoided the razor-fine point of the knife, his steps quick-footed and sure. Dodging each feint of the knife as he sought an opening to reach Mad Dog.

Finally Mad Dog pushed him back toward the edge of the lawn with a swift lunge. Mick stumbled on a tangle of roots, but quickly got his feet back under him.

Mad Dog immediately seized on that minute slip, swinging his hand in a wide arc that caught Mick on the forearm with the knife.

Heat erupted where the blade skimmed across his skin, but he didn't let that deter him.

As Mad Dog's arm swept by and he reversed the blade for another swipe, Mick moved in and grabbed hold of his opponent's wrist. He jerked it against his knee and the blow loosened Mad Dog's grip.

Mad Dog slapped out with his free hand, trying to get a hold on Mick's head, but he yanked away. Slipping beneath Mad Dog's arm, Mick delivered a punishing blow to the other man's ribs.

His ex-colleague grunted and doubled over.

Mick drove up with his knee, connecting with Mad Dog's face. Immense satisfaction came with the crunch of bone that followed.

The satisfaction was short-lived.

Mad Dog retaliated with an elbow that caught Mick close to his liver, driving his breath from him. He stepped back to avoid the blow he knew would come next.

He wasn't fast enough.

A hard jab connected with the side of his face and Mad Dog followed with an uppercut that had Mick staggering backward.

"Slowing down in your old age," Mad Dog taunted. He was clearly ready for action despite the blows Mick had landed.

But Mick was ready as well.

The night became peppered with their grunts as fists or legs connected. With the slap of a deflected blow and the scuffling sounds of their boots along the underbrush and fallen leaves in the woods and along the edge of the lawn.

Mick bided his time, waiting for the perfect opportunity. He would have to win the battle to get the key. He knew Mad Dog would only consider it a win if Mick ended up dead.

The moment came sooner than Mick expected.

CHAPTER 19

Mad Dog lashed out with a high roundhouse kick, but missed badly and lost his balance on some slick leaves.

Mick took advantage, driving an elbow sharply into Mad Dog's kidney.

Mad Dog groaned and dropped to the ground, grabbing at his side. Mick seized his arm and twisted it upward, and Mad Dog sagged even farther. With that opportunity, he drove his knee into the middle of his opponent's back and flattened him against the ground.

"Ready to say uncle, Mad Dog?" he asked, leaning close to the other man.

Mad Dog glanced up at him sideways, one part of his face plastered against the wet leaves and mud. "You know me better than that, Carrera."

Sadly Mick did know him that well. Someday he would have to kill Mad Dog if he was ever going to have any peace of mind.

But not tonight.

With two quick punishing blows to the side of Mad Dog's head, he knocked him out, then trussed him up with the cable ties in his jacket pocket. Whipping the key card out of Mad Dog's front pocket, he retrieved his gun and headed for the Wardwell facility.

With Caterina's permission, Liliana had taken a second sample of blood for a twofold purpose.

The first was to find out if the abnormally speedy gene replication was ongoing.

The second was to determine if they could somehow re-create the parameters that her medical file indicated for the plasmapheresis. With that information, they could prepare the cell separator so that they could filter Caterina's blood.

As Liliana hurried down to the pathology lab during her break, she hoped the latter could be delayed until they had the time to prepare it properly. That Mick would come through as he always did by retrieving the inhibitor drug.

At the door to the pathology lab, she paused, peering through the glass in the door to see who was within.

Only Carmen once again, pulling another late shift, head bent over the microscope at the back of the lab.

She walked in and her friend's head popped up. A welcoming smile blossomed on her face as she approached.

"*Amiga*! Are you going to make my day again?" she asked excitedly.

Liliana shot her a puzzled look. "What did I do?"

"That last blood specimen—major-league interesting. High-tech stuff. Those GFPs, or should I say, YFPs and other amazing science."

Liliana sat on the lab stool next to her friend, peered back around the lab to make sure they were alone, and whispered, "You didn't say anything to anyone, did you?"

Carmen emphatically shook her head. "You asked me not to, but I couldn't resist doing further analysis based on the results from the electropherogram."

She tucked her hand into her lab jacket pocket and fingered the test tube there, worried that she possibly had made a wrong choice by involving Carmen. "You didn't tell anyone else—"

"I didn't," her friend reiterated. "But I will tell *you* that what I found was a mix of human gene fragments spliced together with those from squamates and amphibians."

"Squamates and amphibians? As in—"

"Lizards. Frogs," Carmen quickly supplied and then added, "Probably because some amphibians have the ability to regenerate the tissues in their bodies in a way that's identical to the original tissue."

"So if someone had harm to a particular kind of tissue—"

"You join a little piece of the tissue before it was damaged with the right kind of amphibious genes and you could conceivably regenerate mounds of new injury-free tissue," Carmen advised.

Which might explain why Caterina was now able to see. If the cancer had left behind even a small part of her optic nerve, it could have been regenerated to restore her eyesight. But that didn't explain the skin thing or the weird auras that Caterina claimed to have experienced.

"*Hola*, Earth to Liliana," Carmen said and snapped her fingers in front of her face.

"Sorry. I was just thinking about the possibilities."

"Revolutionary," Carmen said in awed tones.

She tightened her hand on the test tube, but then relented and pulled it out of her pocket. As she held it out to her friend, Liliana wondered if it was glowing a little more than it had the last time.

"May I?" Carmen asked as her hand hovered over the sample.

"Would you check this out? See if the replication is still as fast as you thought?"

"That's easy. Ask me to do something hard," Carmen quipped, clearly unaware of the importance of what was happening, much less of the real reason behind the request.

Something hard?

"Can you find out exactly what kind of lizard or frog? Let me know what might happen if those non-human genes keep on replicating."

For the first time, Carmen grew serious. "This is more than some science experiment for you, isn't it?"

Liliana narrowed her eyes and examined her friend, trying to decide just how much Carmen needed to know. After a hesitation, she finally said, "It's much more than that. Life and death more than that."

Carmen leaned against the edge of the lab bench and cautiously placed the test tube on its surface. Leaning forward, she took hold of Liliana's hands. Carmen's were smooth and slightly cold from the temperature in the lab, which explained why Carmen always wore a sweater— usually a funky one—beneath her white jacket.

"I'm sorry, Liliana. I didn't realize it was something personal. Of course I can try to find out, although it may be a little beyond my expertise," her friend said.

"I'd appreciate it, *amiga*."

Liliana hugged Carmen, hard and quick, and then made a hurried escape from the lab. As she walked out she plowed right into Harrison.

His presence surprised her, since he normally had little to do with the pathology department. He snared her upper arms in a cruel grasp and jerked her to the side.

"Is that why you haven't been around? Playing both sides of the field now?" he whispered through clenched teeth and shook her hard, rattling her teeth.

"Stop it, Harrison." She pushed against his chest, trying to break free.

Her actions didn't deter him. He shook her roughly again. Moved forward until her back was against the wall and he had boxed her in, preventing her escape.

"But that's where you've been. With Carmen."

She forced her forearms up between them and shoved him hard, regaining her space. Recapturing a piece of herself.

It surprised him that she was fighting back. He stepped away and stared at her as if seeing her for the first time. Strange considering they had been involved for two years. Engaged for the last six months.

Engaged until right now.

She pulled the ring off her finger and held it out to him. "This is over, Harrison. I won't be your punching bag anymore."

He stared at the ring in her hand, then returned his gaze to her face. He placed his hand over the ring, but grasped both the ring and her hand in his much larger one and squeezed painfully. The pressure forced the ring against her palm and as the strength of his grip increased, the sharp prongs of the elaborate diamond cut into her flesh.

She tugged to escape, but he only held on tighter.

With another sharp tug, she finally broke free and the

ring dropped to the floor, pinging against the tiles until it came to rest.

Harrison only shot it a sideways glance as he drove her up against the wall once again. Bending down from his greater height, he warned, "I will not let you do this to me, Liliana."

He stepped away from her, gracefully swooping down to recover the ring from the ground, and then headed toward the elevator bank. As the door opened and one of the other doctors stepped out, he offered them an engaging smile and warm greeting.

He received a genial response, which grew confused when the doctor noticed Liliana standing down the hall.

She forced her own smile at the female physician as Harrison swept by her and into the elevator.

After a steadying breath, she took her first hesitant step to return to her rounds.

Her second step was more certain. Stronger.

CHAPTER 20

Now that she had the freedom to move around, Caterina could see that the home was one of welcome, filled with warm vibrant colors that reminded her of Mexico and of her own happy times with her mother.

Caterina ran her hand over the rough-hewn oak sideboard, regretting the roundish dents left behind by her fingers. She traced the rough edges of the crudely elegant cast-iron candelabras resting on the wooden surface. They were beautiful despite the lack of gloss or adornment. Simplistically functional, like the man who owned them.

Leaning toward the fat pillar candle on one of them, she inhaled deeply, but only a hint of the fragrance remained. She suspected Mick didn't spend enough time in this place to use them or keep them fresh.

If the house was well-maintained, it was likely by someone else's hand.

The rumble of the garage door alerted Caterina that Mick was back.

She walked to the kitchen and stood just a few feet away from the side door that opened into the garage. He came through a moment later and the alarm began its warning chirp. He quickly shut it down and as he turned, she realized he was hurt. A blood-soaked bandage was stark against his black shirt. His face bore a multitude of scrapes and bruises, as did his hands.

It would have been stupid to point out the obvious. Instead Caterina grabbed the top rung of a kitchen chair and swung it around. Motioned to it and said, "Sit. I'll go get something to patch you up."

His eyes narrowed as he said, "Since I'm the one who knows where everything is—"

"I'm sure I can find the supplies." She jabbed her index finger at the chair again. "Sit before you bleed all over the kitchen."

Mick stalked toward the oven, snagged one of the kitchen towels hanging from the door handle, and wrapped it around the wound on his forearm, since blood was beginning to escape the gauze he had wrapped around the wound earlier. When he took two big strides toward Caterina, she controlled the urge to flinch. Miraculously, he obeyed her and plopped down onto the kitchen chair.

"There's a small linen closet in the master bathroom. Medical kit is in there," Mick said, cradling his injured arm to his midsection.

Caterina rushed upstairs and found the kit right where he'd said. Grabbing the plastic olive-green box with the red and white cross, she hurried back downstairs, but stopped short as she entered the kitchen.

He had pulled off his black sweater and the blood-soaked gauze. The naked expanse of his shoulders was leanly muscled. On one shoulder he bore a bruise in the shape of a hand—her hand.

Caterina bit her lip and walked around him to the table

where she set down the medical kit. While she opened the gear, she glanced at him sideways, slowly inventorying the damage to his body.

On his left shoulder, the vivid imprint of her hand. Farther down, a series of reddish blotches sure to turn into more bruises.

She skipped over the sight of his lean sculpted abs, her hands shaky as she took out some gauze and butterfly bandages from the medical supplies. As she removed pre-packaged alcohol swabs, she said, "Let me see your arm."

He shifted the chair to better face her and it squeaked against the tile floor. Laying his hand flat on the table, he removed the towel and splayed his fingers against the thick wooden surface to allow her to examine the wound.

She winced as she noted the length and depth of the knife cut.

"That looks like it'll need stitches."

Mick grunted in agreement. "Lil can close it later if we clean it up."

Caterina nodded and ripped open a few alcohol pads. Wadding them together, she faced him to start the clean-up, but as she did so she again noticed the cuts, scrapes, and bruises on his face. Once again she winced, earning an amused chuckle from him.

"Don't worry. The other guy looks worse."

His comment, undeniably macho as it was, dragged a chuckle from her before she dabbed at the areas around the wound. Gently she wiped away the dried blood and smudges of dirt. Tossed aside the dirty pads and opened up new ones.

As she finally cleaned the slice in his arm, he sucked

in a breath. His fingers turned white as he pressed down on the table from the sting of the alcohol against the open wound.

"I'm sorry," she said, and guilt rose up even more sharply as she took note of her handprint against his collarbone and shoulder.

Mick tracked her gaze, but shrugged off her apology. "You didn't mean to do that."

"Doesn't make it right, or any less painful, I suspect," she said and brushed the tips of her fingers across the bruise.

That touch—innocent and honest—ripped through his body, tightening his gut and creating an unexpected and unwanted reaction.

From the tremble of her fingers a millisecond before she yanked her hand away, she clearly had experienced something intense as well.

When he lifted his head and examined her features, he couldn't fail to notice how her irises had widened and a blush—a very human blush—had blossomed across her cheeks.

Needing to return their interaction to a more neutral plane, he said, "Can you put some butterfly bandages on it for now? Cover it up for me."

She shifted away from him and her fingers pecked at the contents of the kit. She carefully applied the butterfly strips and then covered the area with gauze.

"Thank you," Mick said, relishing the softness of her fingers on his skin.

"Raise your head." He did as she asked, amused by the command in her voice, at odds with the tenderness of her touch.

Carefully Caterina tended to the cuts and scrapes on Mick's face, her expression intense as she worked. Concerned and guilt-ridden.

Mick tried to reassure her. "Like I said, the other guy looks worse. Besides, the fight had little to do with you."

"I don't understand." She leaned one hip against the edge of the table as she worked.

"The guy I fought has a problem with me. We used to work together."

"In the Army?" She started to pick up the dirty swabs and remnants of gauze and tape, shooting him a half-glance as she waited for his answer.

"They'd never take a psycho like him into the Army."

Mick rose from the chair and stood close to Caterina. Too close. Her shoulder brushed against the wall of his chest, creating that skitter of reaction once more.

Cautiously she tilted her head up toward Mick. Her eyes were an intense ocean blue, the pupils wide. The blush was even stronger across the high slashes of her cheekbones. She licked her lips in a nervous gesture.

Very luscious womanly lips.

Mick dipped his head down, hesitating when he was about an inch away. Warning himself that if he took a taste...

CHAPTER 21

Mick barely brushed his lips against hers, but he still felt the hitch in her breath that spoke of surprise before turning into acceptance.

Caterina joined her lips to his, the need for human contact overwhelming any caution about the logic of what she was doing. His lips were warm and soft above hers. Mobile as they gently explored. She laid her hand against his rock-hard chest to steady herself. Warm beneath her hand. The skin smooth as she skimmed her fingers down the length of his body.

Then suddenly Mick ripped away, toppling the kitchen chair behind him.

He raised his hand in front of himself like a shield. "That should not have happened. I'm sorry."

Caterina hated that he was right. It shouldn't have happened. "I'm sorry as well, it was just..."

"The satisfaction of surviving. I've been through it before. It's a natural reaction after a battle," Mick said as he ran his hand over his face.

She understood. The conquering hero coming home to whatever woman awaited him in that place. Celebrating the victory over an opponent. Thumbing his nose at

Death. Her father had been a warrior in a suit, vanquishing opponents in the marketplace. He would come home, drunk with victory and liquor. Beating his chest and belittling her mother's accomplishments and joys. Diminishing them to aggrandize himself until her mother had stopped believing in herself.

Until her mother had ceased to exist.

"I get it," she said. Not that she approved. She wanted to seem unfazed, but she couldn't stop herself from running her fingers across her lips to savor the lingering feel of him.

Mick's eyes tracked that motion for a second before he quickly shuttered his gaze. His face turned stony and his lips thinned into a tight line as he reined himself in.

"I'm going to go get changed," he said and left the room.

Caterina watched his retreating back, wondering about the kind of man he really was. Was there anything in him beyond the warrior? Was his only interest the success of his mission and accompanying monetary gain?

The gain that had to be substantial, she assumed, thinking that Edwards would be willing to pay a great deal to get her back. Would Mick tire of the challenge she seemed to be presenting and turn her over for that bounty?

Or was he a man of honor beneath the dangerous and hard persona he displayed?

As Caterina stood there, she realized either scenario was risky for her. And she realized that just like she had refused to let her father determine where her life would go, she couldn't rely on Mick to get her life back for her.

She had to find a way to take care of it herself.

*   *   *

The scientist stared at the bloodied and dirtied face of Matthew "Mad Dog" Donnelly. At the leaves and bits of twig glued to him by the drying mud.

"You assured me you could deal with Carrera," he said, gesturing to the cabinet on the wall. One shelf was completely empty. The shelf had held half a dozen vials of the inhibitor medication necessary for controlling the gene replication in their patients. It would take only a day to make more of the compound, but with the vials taken, Shaw could easily last another six months. Maybe more.

"I *can* take care of Carrera," Mad Dog reassured, rubbing at his wrists, which still bore the markings from the cable ties with which Mick had secured him.

The man examined the paid mercenary, circling around him the way a guard might a prisoner, hands held behind his back. Assessing the dirt all along his body and the bruises and scrapes on his face.

"Carrera has Shaw," he said.

Mad Dog denied it with a quick shake of his head. "Carrera said—"

"He has Shaw," the scientist nearly shouted and jabbed his hand toward the telltale empty row in the cabinet. "He took medicine to treat her."

Mad Dog's gaze flickered to the vacant space before he pulled his shoulders back and a steely glint came into his glacial ice-blue eyes. "If he has her, I'll deal with both of them."

"I won't pay extra for Carrera."

A twisted gleam took hold in the mercenary's eerie crystal cold eyes.

"When the time is right, Carrera is a dead man," Mad Dog responded, his voice bone-chillingly cold.

The scientist walked up to the hired man and peered at Mad Dog. "Do you know what Machiavelli said about enemies?"

At the mercenary's hesitation, he continued. "'The injury that is to be done to a man ought to be of such a kind that one does not stand in fear of revenge.'"

Poking a finger into the hard wall of Mad Dog's chest, he warned, "Don't play with Carrera. Eliminate him."

CHAPTER 22

Mick controlled his grimace as Liliana finished tying off the last stitch in his arm. Barely a flicker of discomfort crossed his face thanks to his restraint.

Too bad he hadn't used such restraint earlier with Caterina.

"You'll need to keep this dry for twenty-four hours."

"*Coño*. There goes that bubble bath I planned on taking," he teased, but it failed to bring a smile to his sister's face.

"You okay?" he asked, worried at the troubled look in her eyes. Sorry that he might have placed it there.

"Okay? You want to know if I'm okay."

With jerky motions Liliana cleaned up the materials she had used for the sutures and stalked across the kitchen to toss them away. Rounding on him, she jammed her hands on her hips. "You're hurt. Someone named Mad Dog is after you and Caterina. And speaking of Caterina—"

"I got the inhibitor. Several vials of the medication are in my satchel." He jerked his hand in the direction of the worn black satchel resting on one of the kitchen chairs.

Liliana walked to the chair, picked up the bag, and removed a handful of the vials. Weighing them carefully in her hand, she said, "Based on the dosages indicated in her medical file, these should last for some time. Certainly long enough for you to figure out why someone wants her dead."

The relief on his sister's face was incomplete. Mick pressed on. "Something else is bothering you."

Liliana placed the vials on the table, and then removed the rest from the satchel. As she did so, he noticed the bare spot on her ring finger.

"You broke it off with Harrison."

Nodding, she replied, "He didn't take it well."

Mick rose from the chair, flinching at the ache in his ribs as he stood. Mad Dog hadn't broken them, but they still hurt like hell.

He took a step to close the distance to his sister and laid his hands on her shoulders. "I'll make sure he doesn't hurt you."

Liliana shrugged his hands off. "You'll protect me. Caterina." She whirled on him, laid a hand on the middle of his chest. "*Mami* and *Papi*. Tony. You'll take care of all of us."

She shoved his chest hard enough to make him recoil, tender as the area was thanks to the blows from Mad Dog.

"Who will take care of you, *hermano*?"

Apparently recognizing that her question had no answer, she grabbed one of the vials and her medical bag and stormed out of the kitchen. Mick could hear the heavy thump of her footsteps on the stairs, a testament to her anger.

He could have followed, tried to reassure her he had things under control, but opted instead to give her time to cool down. Since Liliana had once again brought home food from the family restaurant, he placed the take-out dishes in the oven. While he welcomed the food, he worried it came with a very large price tag—a visit from his *mami*. She was bound to be wondering about what was happening with him and why Liliana was involved.

When the food was in the oven and the kitchen table was set, Mick took a steadying breath and headed upstairs.

Caterina was sitting on the edge of the bed with Liliana perched across from her in the recliner. In her hand his sister had a syringe which she had plunged into the vial he had taken from Wardwell's lab. As he walked in Liliana said, "I'm using the dosage indicated in the file."

Liliana pulled the syringe from the vial and in a fluid move, swapped the vial for the rubber hose sitting on the nightstand. She wrapped the hose around Caterina's bicep, tapped her arm for a vein, and then injected her with the medication.

Caterina jerked as she did so. "I didn't mean to hurt you. Sorry," Liliana apologized.

Caterina shook her head. "It's not you. It's burning."

"That happens with some medications," Mick explained as he walked into the room.

Caterina looked up at him and offered a brave smile. "Thank you for getting the medicine."

"Hopefully it'll keep things under control until we can find out what really happened to Wells."

Liliana withdrew the syringe, placed an adhesive bandage over the injection site, and urged Caterina to bend her arm to apply pressure.

Caterina did as instructed and turned her attention back to Mick. "I can help you with the investigation now."

Mick shook his head. "Maybe if the meds work, but first... It would help if you could try to remember more about what happened that night."

Caterina nodded. "I'll try. Only every time I do..." She shrugged and wrapped her free arm around her waist. "There's always blood. Lots of it. All over Dr. Wells and me."

Mick nodded and sat down on the edge of the bed beside her. She averted her gaze, but he tucked his thumb and forefinger beneath her chin and urged her face back toward his.

"You need to get past that to try and remember what happened before. To how Wells was killed."

Caterina nodded. "I'll try."

He brushed away some stray unruly locks from her face. "You can try later. Liliana was kind enough to bring dinner again and I suspect you're hungry."

Caterina smiled. It caused a funny hitch in the middle of Mick's chest. "I thought I smelled something tasty."

"Let's go get some eats then," Liliana said and rose from the chair. Watching the gentle way her gruff brother touched Caterina, Liliana couldn't help but suspect his feelings for the sick woman were no longer strictly professional. But she said nothing, only led the way down to the kitchen, smiling to herself as she went.

With dinner over and the two women sharing an easy conversation as they cleaned up, Mick had felt driven from the kitchen, unable to stand the way they chatted about everyday things seemingly without a care to the danger which existed. He had not wanted to burst their fragile bubble with the reality that so far he had nothing to prove that Caterina wasn't a murderess. He also couldn't abide the sense of homecoming he felt sitting at the table with them.

Locking himself away in his office, he spent the night perusing the Internet for additional information on Edwards and Wardwell Biotech, and discovered more than he had expected.

News from various science sites confirmed that Wardwell was a leader in developing a number of different fluorescent proteins for use in various applications, as well as an innovator in the field of gene therapies. Much had been made of one of their early experiments, using genes spliced from a urodele amphibian to successfully regenerate nerve tissue.

That would explain Liliana's comments at dinner about the test results reported by her pathologist friend.

As he sat back, Mick realized that advances from such a success might account for the restoration of Caterina's sight, but confusion remained about the strange halo sight and skin camo she displayed when stressed.

Why implant even more genes to create a human chimera? Especially one half out of her mind from a powerful combination of dissociative drugs, unless...

MK Ultra, he thought once again, thoughts returning to the CIA experiments with mind control. If Edwards thought he could create and control chimeras with useful traits, those genetically modified humans could be quite useful and profitable.

Only nothing in any of the online articles supported such a crazy hypothesis. He leaned over the keyboard and continued searching. By the end of the night, Liliana had been called back to the hospital for an emergency and he had unearthed a small article from a financial news site.

Edwards had recently met with the head of Gates Genengineering, a larger biotech company whose new drug application had suffered a rejection from the FDA. The NDA was for a therapy similar to the Wardwell process Mick thought had been used on Caterina. The article mentioned possible discussions of a merger. Given the size of the other company, a merger might be worth millions to the owners of Wardwell.

Of course if anyone got wind of what Edwards and his researchers had done to people like Caterina and those unfortunates with the TERMINATED stickers, no legitimate company would touch Wardwell. In fact, Edwards and his cohorts would be lucky not to end up in jail for the rest of their lives.

If Wells had somehow developed a conscience and had been about to blow the whistle on the entire experiment, it made perfect sense as to why Edwards might want his partner dead.

With a merger imminent, it also made sense why Edwards would hire not one but three hunters to go after Caterina. He couldn't take the risk that she could expose what had happened and ruin the multi-million-dollar deal.

To prove motive, however, Mick had to confirm that the merger was actually proceeding. Opening his e-mail program, he right-clicked on one of the e-mails from Edwards and checked the message header. Buried in the header was the IP address for Wardwell's system. Launching a hacking program a friend had provided years ago, the system started searching for open ports and found several of them in the firewall.

He used one of the open ports and accessed the Wardwell system, hoping that someone in IT had been lazy and left at least one of the servers with its default settings. Sure enough, one server still had the "no password" default. Shortly after this discovery, Mick entered the Wardwell system. He didn't want to linger long, afraid that someone might eventually catch on to his break-in.

He started a search for "Gates" and within just a few short minutes had located a Word document on the server. Better yet, it was in a directory that appeared to belong to Edwards. He quickly downloaded the document and exited.

When he opened the document, it confirmed the merger had progressed substantially.

Gates Genengineering had made an offer of 100 million dollars to acquire Wardwell. With that much money at stake, he now had possible motives for Wells's murder, whether to silence a whistle-blower or get a bigger share of the money from the deal.

He had to warn Franklin.

He dialed his friend, who immediately answered.

"I've got some information and you're not going to like it," he said and explained about the merger.

"I'm liking this less and less every day, Mick. I've got a family now," Franklin said. For the first time ever, Mick heard something in his friend's tone that he had never expected to hear.

Real fear. The kind that grabbed hold of your gut and made you doubt. Even a scintilla of doubt on a mission was not good.

"I understand, Franklin. So here's what I want you to do."

CHAPTER 23

Mick provided Franklin with the basic information about the deal and asked him to try and track down more information as to when it might be finalized. Then he gave him the names and addresses of the two terminated patients whose files he had stolen. He needed to know more about what their families had been told regarding their progress and deaths.

"What about Donnelly?" Franklin asked, concern in his voice.

What about Mad Dog? Mick thought, recalling his earlier encounter with the man. "Whatever happens with Mad Dog won't involve you. I promise you that. It'll be between him and me."

Because they had a score to settle.

"Thanks, Mick. I've got too much to lose," his friend said and hung up.

Mick snapped the phone shut, Franklin's last words digging into his brain.

I've got too much to lose. Mick had little if anything to lose.

He rose, intent on checking on Caterina, when he heard the insistent *beep-beep-beep* of the alarm system signaling that someone had opened a point of entry into the house.

He rushed to the guest room hoping it hadn't been Caterina, but she was gone.

Cursing, he grabbed the stair railing, vaulted down to the middle of the stairs, then up and over the handrail to the next level. He landed on the wooden floor with enough force to rattle the nearby furniture.

Ahead of him the kitchen door leading to the backyard was wide open.

He ran toward the door and the cell phone at his hip began to buzz. A message flashed, alerting him to the fact that Caterina had breached the designated perimeter for the ankle bracelet she was wearing.

He rushed outside, believing he would have to give chase as she ran off the property, but instead he watched as she executed a graceful dive into the built-in pool in the backyard.

Shocked, he was about to go after her when the house alarm increased in pitch, alerting him to the fact that it would soon trip and dispatch instructions to the central station.

Since Caterina didn't seem to be going anywhere and he didn't need the police coming to check out the call from the central station, he returned inside and shut off the alarm. He answered his phone when it rang a second later.

"I got a warning here at the station about the ankle bracelet. Do I need to send in the troops?" Ramon asked.

Mick walked toward the edge of the pool where Caterina was treading water in the center, her arms wrapped tight around herself, shivering. The violent chattering of her teeth visible even with the long distance.

Something was wrong, but it was nothing that needed to involve Ramon.

"No, *amigo*. Everything is under control here," he said, but as Caterina's skin faded away to the bright blue of the pool lining, nothing could have been further from the truth.

Mick walked to the edge of the pool and crouched down, meeting her gaze, made an almost iridescent aqua from the reflection from the pool water and the increasingly intense hue of her skin.

"What are you doing?" he said.

"Hot...burning up," she replied, and slowly sank beneath the surface of the water.

Shit, he thought. Liliana would be pissed as all hell if he let Caterina drown on his watch.

He quickly yanked off his shirt, pants, and shoes, placed his cell phone within easy reach on the pool deck, and dove in.

With one powerful stroke he reached her.

Wrapping his arms around her body, he dragged her to the surface, where they both gulped in a big breath of air.

To his surprise, she laid her head on his shoulder and once again said, "I'm burning up."

She was. Even with the cool water surrounding them, heat poured off her skin. Her body shivered against his with brutal force, her teeth rattling together until, with each second that passed, the chill of the waters penetrated her body and brought some relief.

Relief from the fever racking her body didn't bring an end to the transformation of her skin. Luckily the high fence surrounding the property offered some privacy for the moment, but not much.

Anyone with a second story facing their way could get a good look once they left the water, since the back porch light illuminated a wide swath of the yard and pool area. He had to get her to restore more of her human state before they could return to the house.

He raised one hand and ran it across the slick strands of her hair in a soothing gesture. Bringing his lips close to the shell of her ear, he whispered, "Are you feeling better?"

She nodded and finally relaxed a bit, releasing the tight hold she'd had on her own body to wrap her arms around him.

So not good, he thought at the soft press of her body against his.

Think baseball, he said to himself as he cupped her cheek and urged her to lift her head. When she did so, he said, "I need you to lose the camo, Cat."

Realization sank in as she examined her arms.

She screwed her eyes shut and beneath her breath began her mantra. Her lips barely moved as she said, "Focus. Focus. Focus."

He braced one hand in the middle of her back and joined in the mantra. Only it distracted him from safe thoughts of baseball.

Caterina clearly noticed the natural reaction his body was having to her being so close.

"Focus," she said more loudly, and opened her eyes.

They were back to normal, not that he could ever call eyes that blue and beautiful normal.

She bit her bottom lip, worrying it with her teeth as she raised one hand to steady herself against his shoulder.

The movement only pressed them closer together and

revealed another truth—he was not the only one who was possibly aroused.

Her pupils were wide and a bright stain of pink colored her cheeks. A flush of passion and not fever. The pebbly hard tips of her nipples rubbed across his chest and he would have had to be a saint not to touch.

He was no saint, but somehow he restrained himself.

He cupped her cheek, leaned his head close and asked, "Do you feel well enough to go back into the house?"

Caterina focused on his warm breath and the hard palm of his hand against her skin. Closed her eyes and imagined it was a lover's touch. A touch that begged for sweet compensation in return.

Opening her eyes, she inched toward him until her lips almost brushed his and whispered, "Yes."

His breath hitched in his chest and against her body; his erection jumped in response. He applied gentle pressure and urged her face upward as she acquiesced to that demand.

Human demand.

The call of male to female somehow reaffirming that she was still a woman. Still so much more than someone's lab experiment.

When she brought up her head, he was bending toward her. He paused as his lips brushed hers, the warm spill of his breath enticing her to savor his mouth.

She touched her lips to his, telling herself to focus on them. On him. On the pleasure his touch brought her.

Mick groaned at her consent, certain that this was insanity and yet he couldn't stop kissing her.

She brought both hands to his shoulders. They were still hot against his skin, but not as hot as before.

But way more hot than was right, and he knew that as good as this felt and as much as he wanted to part her thighs and drive himself into her, honor demanded that he stop.

Easing himself away but keeping a steadying grasp on her, he said, "We need to get you back inside. Make sure you're okay."

Puzzlement traveled across her features, followed by confusion and possibly disappointment. "You don't want—"

"I do want, but not like this," he explained.

He'd had one too many cases of want with little else attached to it.

She was a case of too much want with too much luggage, none of it good.

Until it could be more and be something less dangerous, she was off limits, he told himself.

"Let's go in," he said, noting that her body had returned to normal during their interlude.

She confirmed his instruction with a nod of her head. With a kick and one strong swipe of his arm he propelled them from the deeper end of the pool to where they could stand.

Side by side they walked to the stairs and stepped out onto the pool deck, the summer night air balmy against their skin. The wet oversized T-shirt clung to her body, shaping every curve. Exposing her long legs and the graceful sweep of her neck and one shoulder as the shirt slipped downward from the pull of the sodden fabric.

His own state was too obvious through the boxers he wore.

A bright flush stained her cheeks as she noticed. With

a quick pivot on one heel, she raced back into the house, leaving him to mutter a curse and hurriedly scoop up his clothing and cell phone.

Inside the house, he re-armed the alarm system before snagging a beach towel from the mudroom off the kitchen. He wrapped it around his body, grabbed another towel, and followed the trail of wet footprints up the stairs.

The door to the bathroom was closed and he knocked on it. Caterina only partially opened the door, but it was enough for him to see that she was now totally naked. He thrust the towel through the opening in the door and stalked to his room, where he changed into dry sweats.

With Caterina's fever, she needed something more lightweight to wear. He located an old cotton robe that would do.

He exited his room and found she was already back in the guest room, sitting on the bed, her knees tucked up to her chest and the beach towel encircling her body. Arms wrapped around herself in a defensive gesture.

She had brushed her hair and it was slicked back from her face, bringing to stark notice her wide eyes and classically perfect features.

Mick stalked to the recliner, held out the robe, and sat down.

She took the robe from him, eased it on, and tied it closed. She then proceeded to do that shimmy thing that all women seemed to learn as some part of the growing-up ritual, shifting a bit here and there to slip the towel off without dislodging the protection of the robe.

"What were you thinking?" he said.

She looked away toward the window at the far side

of the room and shrugged. "I felt so hot and all that cool water was out there. . . ."

Her voice trailed off and she faced him once again. "I won't do it again."

It was difficult to be angry when she was so damned agreeable and innocent-looking, sitting there with her arms wrapped around her bent knees. Head leaning on those knees as those damned blue eyes locked on him. The black of the waterproof ankle bracelet glaring against her creamy skin.

"When you trip the alarms, remember that it may not all be White Hats that answer," he said, forcing a roughness to his voice to reinforce his concern.

"Are you a White Hat?" she asked, but beneath the innocent tones of her voice lay challenge. She suspected that on occasion he walked the line between black and white.

"It depends," he said, confirming her suspicion. And because he was becoming too interested in her as something more than his target, he inched to the edge of the recliner and placed his hand on the crook of her neck. One hand was all it took to almost encircle that fragile column as he slid his thumb over her larynx.

He tightened his grip just a bit, enough for her to realize his intent. Her eyes widened with apprehension and she grabbed hold of his wrist with both hands.

"You won't hurt me."

CHAPTER 24

"I won't?" Mick replied, increasing the pressure on her throat even though doing so made him cringe inside. Still, he achieved the result he'd wanted.

Caterina's fight-or-flight response kicked in. Her skin erupted with the deep maroon color of his cotton robe and her hands tightened on his wrist, almost painfully so.

He could handle her like this, he thought. He could handle her when she wasn't all soft enticing female.

"You want me to believe you're a killer, but you're not," Caterina said, her grip as firm as his.

Reason told Mick to increase the pressure at her throat, to disprove her belief. But he couldn't, because she was right.

Caterina met his gaze as her heart thumped in quick allegro beats. She held fast to his wrist and as she did so, the weird halo sight she had battled earlier returned, outlining his body in a bright blue, while his center appeared as a combination of other colors, communicating to her brain the heat of his body.

Like one of those cheap gum machine love-test strips, she saw the cooler outside edges of his limbs and the increasing warmth toward his core. In the middle of his chest, the brightest of all the colors. The most intense spot of heat.

Caterina shifted one hand from his wrist to that spot. Absorbed the thump-thump of his heart against the sensitized pads of her fingers. Thump-thump. Thump-thump. A steady reliable beat like that of a conductor's baton.

Splaying her hand against that beat, she closed her eyes and concentrated on it. As she did so, the pressure at her throat eased until Mick finally moved his hand completely away.

But she didn't remove hers.

Opening her eyes, she met his gaze. The color of his dark brown eyes had deepened to almost black. Beneath her hand, the thump-thump remained steady, but tension had crept into his body.

Finally she pulled her hand away and wrapped her arms around her knees once again.

"You know what I think?" she said, alternately confused and accepting of what was happening between them.

"I don't care what you think," Mick replied, still obviously struggling to convince her that he was dangerous.

"I think you're a White Hat, only you're afraid to admit it because you won't be able to control people if they think you might actually have a heart."

She'd learned about fear and control from her father. She understood it well.

Amazingly he saw past her words to the emotion that drove her. "Not all control is bad, Cat. And you will do what I tell you."

On some level, she knew he only meant well. That he wanted to protect her and his sister and anyone else who came under his charge. But she had struggled to be free for too long. She had lost that precious freedom at Wardwell and she'd be damned if that happened again.

"We'll see," she said.

Dog tired, Liliana plodded up the three steps, stumbling on the last one despite the post lantern lighting up the walk in the late dawn hours. She caught herself before she fell and continued up the walk.

At the door, she fumbled to find the keys in the bottom of her purse.

A big mistake.

Someone covered her mouth with a large masculine hand and wrapped an arm around her midsection, trapping her arms against her sides. Her purse and medical bag fell to the ground with a noisy clatter. She prayed someone inside would hear the ruckus.

With little effort, her assailant picked her up off the ground and moved toward the side of the wraparound porch. She tried to scream but she could barely breathe, much less muster any kind of noise. Mick's words reverberated in her brain about being careful. About the danger they all might be in. She'd let fatigue make her careless, but knew she had to act now.

Twisting and turning her body, she managed to free one arm. Curling her hand into a claw, she reached behind her, raked her assailant's face, and heard his surprised yell. His grip on her mouth loosened with her attack and she followed up with a sharp backward elbow to his midsection.

He grunted and released her, freeing her to swing around with her other elbow. The blow connected with his nose, the sound a sickening crunch.

Her attacker released a groan and fell away from her.

Liliana didn't wait to see who it was.

She raced to the door just as Mick flung it open and stepped out onto the porch, barefoot and bare-chested, Glock in his hand. If the weapon wasn't scary enough, the bruises and scars on his body screamed, *Don't mess with me.*

Mick immediately pulled her behind him, using his body as a shield. Then she heard his amused chuckle.

"Always thought you were no match for my lil' sis."

At that comment, she poked her head around Mick's broad back in time to see her fiancé...no, make that *ex*-fiancé rising from the floor of the porch.

Three angry scratches ran down the left side of his handsome face. Bright red blood streamed from his nose and down onto the expensive Brooks Brothers suit and shirt he wore.

"I just came to talk to her," he said, whipping out a handkerchief from his pocket and gingerly placing it against his abused nose to stem the flow of blood.

"I should press charges," Harrison added, glaring at her as she finally took a step to stand beside her brother.

Mick tucked his gun into the waistband of his jeans and crossed his arms against his chest.

"*Por favor*, press charges. I'd love to explain to the police how you assaulted me," Liliana shot back.

Harrison took a menacing step toward them, and then, glancing at Mick, seemed to reconsider. "You think they'll believe you?" he said, his face contorted into a sneer.

Mick chuckled, surprising her by the mirth until he pointed to a spot just above and to the right of the door frame, where a small camera was trained on the front door and porch.

"It's all recorded, Harrison. I'd consider seeing a lawyer if I were you."

Harrison's face first paled and then erupted in a flare of angry red. Liliana worried he might stroke out, there was so much tension visible in his body, but instead he merely turned and rushed down the walk. After he crossed the street, she noticed his car parked there for the first time.

Had he followed her home or had he been there all along? she thought, the terror of the attack finally setting in. She was shaking as she retrieved her purse and bag from the ground.

"You're lucky it was just Harrison," Mick admonished.

"*Yo sé.* I won't let it happen again," she replied, her hands trembling while she put to right the contents of her purse.

Mick nodded, seemed about to chastise her again, but then enveloped her in a big bear hug. "You did fine, *hermanita.*"

Liliana let herself linger for a moment in his protective embrace before shaking off the nervous energy pumping through her body and walking into the house. She glanced up to the second-floor landing, wondering about Caterina.

"She was running a high fever. Had to cool her down," Mick explained, as if reading his sister's thoughts.

Liliana tossed her things onto a chair by the front door and faced him, her arms encircling her waist as she willed away the last remnants of fear from the attack.

"Is the fever gone?"

Mick shook his head. "Still low grade. Her sleep is really erratic. She's having nightmares."

"Or post-traumatic stress disorder. Maybe what she's seeing is a replay of what happened in the lab that night or whatever else was done to her."

Feeling more in control of herself, Liliana placed a hand at her side and stretched to work out a kink in the small of her back from the many hours she had been on her feet during her shift.

"Let's hope she can replay that night. I've got nothing to say she did it, but nothing to say that she didn't," Mick said.

Liliana thought about the condition Caterina had been in when Mick had first brought her home. Barely aware of who or what she was. Lacking control and understanding.

Liliana *tsk*ed. "Even if she did kill Wells, she probably lacked the mental capacity to understand what she was doing. You know how she was when you found her."

Mick knew. He also knew how she was now.

The latter was more dangerous to him than the former.

"What do we do if the fever continues?" he asked.

Liliana shrugged. "Her file mentioned the plasmapheresis was undertaken after a couple of doses of the inhibitor. Maybe the treatment isn't to deal with the gene replication. Maybe it's to clear her blood of whatever is left after the inhibitor drug takes effect."

Mick shot a quick glance up the stairs and dragged a hand through his hair. "Do you think it's possible that what's left behind is what's causing the fever?"

Something strong enough to stop or maybe undo the wild gene replication could possibly leave behind remnants that could contaminate her blood and cause a reaction, Mick thought.

"The fever could be from her body fighting off some byproduct of the inhibitor drug. With each treatment, more byproduct remains behind until the patient's blood needs to be cleansed."

Mick recalled the size of the cell separator necessary for the plasmapheresis, not to mention Liliana's earlier comments about the need to know just what to pull out of Caterina's blood. Neither could be done here, but he couldn't risk Caterina going out in public.

"I don't have much time left to figure this all out, do I?"

Liliana walked over and gently placed her hand on his shoulder. With a reassuring squeeze, she said, "No, you don't. But I have total faith in you, *Miguelito*."

He had been on many a tough mission in the past, but this one was proving far more difficult than he had anticipated. Still, he forced a smile and said, "I'll try not to disappoint."

Caterina didn't feel well. A warming heat had remained although the dip in the pool had driven away the worst of the fever. It felt like the start of the flu. She felt assorted aches in her joints and head, but suspected the ache in her head might also be from the lack of any restful sleep.

Mick had been by her side again all through the night. Vigilant but distant after the incident in the pool.

He'd seen her toss and turn, but had elected to allow her the privacy of her demons rather than comforting her as he had before. Maybe a good thing, since after he had left the room for a moment, she had finally remembered more about that night.

She hadn't killed Wells.

She hadn't heard Mick return to the recliner because with that revelation, sleep had finally come. But not enough, she thought as the full daylight streaming through the back window warned it was time to rise.

Stretching, her muscles and joints protesting the movement, her head pounding from either the lack of rest or fever, she alerted Mick as she stirred. He instantly sat up and shifted to the edge of the chair.

Mick was barefoot and bare-chested, wearing only a pair of well-worn jeans. The top snap was undone, revealing an intriguing vee of skin leading...

"Done looking?" he chided.

She snapped her gaze up as heat blossomed across her face. There was one way to avoid answering his question.

"I remembered."

Mick sat up higher at the edge of the chair. "You remember what happened to Wells?"

Caterina nodded, but then gave an uneasy shrug. "Bits and pieces of it," she confessed.

"More than just the bits and pieces of Wells, I hope."

Macabre humor, but she supposed that it was required in order to stay sane while he worked on this case.

"There were two other patients in the medical facility that sometimes became violent. I remember them being restrained and taken away. Sometimes it took three or four men to hold them down."

Mick held up two fingers to confirm. "Two patients?"

Caterina nodded and continued. "One looked familiar. Like I should know who he was, but the other... Rough-looking with all kinds of dark blue tattoos on his body. Not pretty ones."

"Prison tats, maybe."

Screwing up her eyes, she forced a picture of the large man into her memory. Had he looked tough enough to have served time?

"Maybe," she said with a sigh.

"Is that all you remember?" he pressed, clearly wishing she would move on with her story.

Typical man, Caterina thought, but revealed what else she had finally recalled during her restless night.

"I remember lots of loud yelling. Then a number of crashes and glass breaking. I was in my room and went to the door, but it suddenly flew open. One of the patients—the familiar one—flew past me and landed on the floor of the room. He was covered in blood."

"Was he dead?" Mick asked.

She struggled for more detail from the fragments of memory, but couldn't recover them. "I don't remember."

"What happened next?"

"I went out into the lab. Things were tossed around. There was broken glass everywhere and one of the windows had been smashed."

"Do you remember seeing anyone else in the lab?"

Caterina closed her eyes, replaying the scene in her head like she might a movie. The images stark. Dangerous.

"The guy with the tats...He had pieces of a chair in his hands and he was standing there, beating his chest like a gorilla in a zoo and howling. This weird unnatural howl..."

She sucked in a rough breath, continuing to recall the images. Piecing them together like a puzzle so she could complete the picture in her mind.

"I moved away from him. Scared. Then I fell over something and landed on the wet floor."

Mick had no doubt about what she had tripped on as her eyes filled with tears and spilled down her pale, stricken face.

"It was Dr. Wells," he said softly, evenly.

She nodded, her mouth open as she pulled in a rough inhalation. She pressed on with her story.

"He was staring at me. His head was at a weird angle. I thought his mouth moved...."

A shudder shimmied across her body and she grabbed hold of her biceps with her hands. "I picked him up, but he was all warm and wet. His body was in pieces and there was something sticking out of the back of his skull."

"A piece of a chair leg. Someone drove it into him," Mick advised.

"I didn't do it," she reasserted.

"I know." No sense denying that he believed her. The more Mick had found out about Edwards, the more sure he was that the man was behind whatever had happened. And if he had been Edwards, he wouldn't have picked Caterina as the one to do the killing. Especially not if he'd had not one but two men, both bigger and stronger than the fragile musician, capable of such violence.

"You don't know the names of the men?"

Caterina shook her head emphatically, sending the loose curls of her hair shifting with the movement. "The patients used to spend time together at first. But then people started not coming back from their treatments. Dr. Wells said that it would be better if we didn't get too attached to each other."

Or it would be better that the patients didn't figure out that some of them were being disposed of when they had ceased to be useful to Wardwell, Mick thought.

"Wells, Edwards, and Morales. All of them were aware of what was happening with the patients?"

Caterina nodded.

"Anyone else? Nurses? Other staff or family—"

"A limited number of people had access to us. Even visits from friends and family were restricted. Dr. Wells told me it was because we were immunologically compromised." A harsh laugh escaped her and she wagged her head in chastisement. "I was such a fool."

Mick didn't want to feel sympathy. But he did.

"You made a difficult choice. Don't second-guess it."

She snared his gaze with hers. "Would you have made that choice?"

He recalled the decision he would have made—to put a gun in his mouth and blow out what was left of his brains.

She exhaled sharply once more and said, "I didn't think so."

Raking her fingers into her curls, she pulled her hair off her face and then let it tumble down again. "What do we do now?"

We?

"*We* don't do anything. *I* am going to up security around here and try and get more information on the two men you thought were patients. Find out what the dead patients' families were told."

He rose from the recliner, but she surprised him by laying a hand against his waist. A tender touch. One that stirred emotions best left buried.

"You don't have to always go it alone."

"Wrong. Alone is all I know. Don't forget that," he said and hurried from the room. As he had indicated, *he* had things to do.

Alone.

CHAPTER 25

After Harrison's attack on Liliana, Mick activated the perimeter warning systems running all along the edges of the property. He didn't normally keep them live, since they were too easily tripped by a stray dog, cat, or errant beachgoer, but it worried him that it could just have easily been Mad Dog grabbing Liliana instead of her ex.

That he had made a good choice was reaffirmed when just before lunch the system was tripped, alerting him to a security breach.

A major one, he thought as he watched his mother stride up the walk, a minor hitch in her gait thanks to the knee she refused to get replaced. In one hand she held a large bag emblazoned with the restaurant's logo, while in the other she carried what looked like a delivery receipt.

As she paused by the steps to the front door, perusing the slip as if to confirm the address, it occurred to him that his *mami* had become quite an actress in her old age.

When someone opened the door—Liliana, he hoped—his mother played it up, although anyone who knew them would be confused as to why she would be lost at her own son's home.

Anyone else, however, might think it a routine take-out delivery and discontinue their surveillance.

He pushed away from the desk, and walked into the hall where he heard his sister say, "Come in, *mami*."

"Sshh, *niña*. Someone might hear you," his *mami* whispered.

As the door closed, that hushed entreaty was immediately followed by, "*Dios mio*. You're the lady from the news."

Coño, Mick cursed silently and hurried down the stairs just in time to catch his sister introducing the two.

"*Mami*, meet Caterina Shaw. She's Mick's...houseguest. Caterina, this is our mother, Mariel."

So much for keeping things secret, he thought.

As he arrived where the three women stood staring at one another with some trepidation, he enveloped his mother in a bear hug and said, "It's good to see you, *mami*. I missed you."

With a sharp elbow to his abused ribs that shoved him away and forced him to contain a groan, his mother said, "You missed me so much that I had to guess from Liliana's take-out orders that you were home."

"I didn't spill the *frijoles*," Liliana confirmed to him, miming that she was zipping her lips.

"I'm on a job, *mami*—"

"And you involve your sister!" she chided, rising up on tiptoe and wagging a finger in his face.

He snagged that digit before it took out an eye. As he did so, he noticed Caterina's amused face. Before he could do anything else, Liliana jumped back into the fray.

"I asked Mick if I could stay here. I broke off my engagement with Harrison."

His mother immediately launched into action. She pressed the bag of food into Caterina's hands and embraced Liliana.

"*Ay, niña. La virgencita* has answered my prayers," she said. Then she released his sister and wrapped her arms around him, pressing her head against the middle of his chest, which was the only spot her petite stature permitted her to reach.

"*Mi'jito.* Why didn't you say you were helping your sister?" The grip of her arms was tight, but there was a doughy softness to them and her bosom, which reminded him of his youth and the comfort of that embrace.

He hugged her back hard, bent, and dropped a kiss against the side of her face. "I'm glad you're here. I was hungry."

In answer to the enticing smells from the bag that had wafted into his vicinity, his stomach growled loudly.

The three women all laughed in unison, although their laughs couldn't have been more different. His mother's loud and slightly hoarse. Liliana's like a short burst of gunfire.

Cat's almost melodic, with a freedom he suspected she hadn't experienced in quite a long time. The smile on her face confirmed that impression, as did the deep blue of her eyes.

When he took the bag from her hands, their fingers brushed, kindling the need he had tempered last night. Bringing a spark of awareness in her as well, he realized.

Caterina quickly withdrew her hands from the bag, ignoring the sensation jumping alive within her at the simple and innocent touch of their fingers.

Mick rushed away with the bag, leaving her to follow

Liliana and Mariel as the two women walked arm in arm toward the kitchen.

The resemblance between the pair was strong, much like that between Mick and Liliana, only Mariel's eyes were neither green nor brown, but a light-colored hazel.

Their mother was petite like Liliana, but with a stout figure which said she clearly enjoyed a lot of her own cooking.

The sight of them—mother and daughter, clearly friends—roused memories of Caterina's own childhood. Of strolling beside her mother in the park or sitting beside her on the piano bench as she played, the notes from the piano resonating through the space of their small apartment.

An apartment similar to this home with its rich colors, artisanal furniture and collectibles that spoke of a love for culture and tradition.

Interesting for a man who Cat might have guessed spent little time in one place. Someone had definitely used some loving care in building this home, although there were things which also hinted that he neglected it.

In the kitchen they gathered at the table. Mick was quick to empty the bag of the aluminum pans filled with an assortment of foods while Liliana retrieved beverages for everyone. Anyone looking in on the tableau would say it was just another family gathering.

Only Caterina wasn't part of this family, or any other. She swiped at her eye, brushing away a tear. Mariel immediately noted her disappointment.

Patting Caterina's hand as it rested on the tabletop, Mariel said, "Do not worry, *niña*. If Miguelito is helping you, all will turn out well."

Caterina met Mick's gaze from across the width of the table, almost daring him to admit that when it came to her, there would be no happy ending, but he remained silent.

When Liliana placed a plate laden with a sampling of Mexican foods before her, Caterina thought she had little appetite, upset as she was by the current state of her life. But it was difficult to ignore the enticing and earthy smells of the food which resuscitated happy memories in her brain and had her mouth watering as if she were one of Pavlov's dogs.

"I remember some chef saying that as long as you kept your food, your culture would stay with you," she said, carefully forking up pieces of a tomato-laced meat that had been stewed until tender.

"Did your *mami* cook Mexican food for you?" Liliana asked.

"Your *mami* was Mexican? *Que bueno.*" Mariel clapped her hands together and riveted her gaze on Mick. "She's a *Mexicana, mi'jito.* Isn't that wonderful?"

"Her father was an *Americano, mami.* Irish, right?"

"Of Irish descent," she replied after swallowing the delicious meat.

"Irish and Mexican. Two cultures rich in the arts. That must explain your love of music," his mother said before daintily digging into her own plate of food.

"*Mami* was a pianist. A very good one, but . . . My father didn't approve of her performing. He wanted her home and taking care of him while he built his business." Mention of her father diminished her hunger, so she pushed around a bit of enchilada on her plate.

"He didn't approve of your choice of career, either, did

he?" Mick asked, a tenderness in his voice that made her jerk her head up in surprise and meet his gaze.

"No, he didn't approve."

"His loss, Cat. You're an amazing musician and your mother must have been as well to instill such passion in you," he said.

All three women turned to peer at him: Caterina in surprise, Liliana with a knowing grin, and his mother with pride and hopefulness.

"Thank you," Caterina replied, pleased by support she had not expected. In the little time they had spent together, Mick had been controlling and determined. She had even come to accept what he was—a man who would take on a dangerous and possibly illegal job for money.

But this was just another of those fragile moments where he also showed her he was capable of tenderness and caring, confusing her.

Caterina couldn't wrap her head around what the real Mick was like.

"Nice to know you're finally liberated, *hermano*," Liliana teased, dispelling the growing seriousness of the discussion.

Mick chuckled at her comment and resumed eating, and so did Caterina. The food had been prepared with care and loving, adding a special essence to it that filled more than just their bellies.

By the time they had finished eating and sharing a few stories about Liliana, Mick, and their other two siblings, she felt relaxed, but also tired and achy. There was a growing heat in her body and pain in her joints. Caterina understood it to be a reaction to the replication inhibitor Liliana had injected her with the night before. She wondered when she would be due for another shot and whether her body could handle it.

As Mick was ushering his mother out the door, insisting that Caterina had to rest and he had work to do, Mariel trailed her motherly eye over the sweats swimming on her body.

"Surely you have something else for Caterina to wear, Miguel?"

Mick released an exasperated sigh and said, "There hasn't been time—"

Mariel slashed her hand through the air and eyeballed him before facing Liliana. "Caterina seems close to Roberta's size, don't you think?"

Liliana examined her, appearing like a younger version of Mariel before she confirmed the assessment with a determined tilt of her head. "About the same as Bobbie. She left some clothes at home, didn't she?"

"*Sí*, just like Roberta. She won't be home on leave for a couple of months, so she won't miss them. Liliana can come get them later."

Before Mick could argue, Mariel was bustling out the door, leaving the three of them standing there in her wake.

Mick was quick to say, "I'm sorry, Cat. I know she can be a handful."

Caterina thought about Mariel's food, concern, and high-handedness. She could find nothing for which Mick should apologize.

With a smile, she said, "She reminds me of my *mami*. I like her."

Caterina expected both the siblings to argue with her, as siblings were wont to do when it came to their parents, but they didn't. Instead, Mick said, "You're looking a little pale."

"Tired. A little sore," she confessed and rubbed the top of her bowing arm, which was always the one to give her the most trouble. She'd battled with some bursitis there for years.

Liliana frowned. "You're not due for another shot until tomorrow, but if the aches and fever haven't subsided by then—"

"I'm with you, Liliana. I don't like feeling like this," she said.

Mick jammed his hands into his pockets and inclined his head in the direction of the stairs. "Why don't you go get some rest?"

Caterina thought about the rest. Thought about an old saying she'd heard from her father more than once.

"I'd rather find a way to help the two of you. There'll be time enough to rest when I'm dead," she said.

Somehow his immediate nod of agreement brought little comfort.

CHAPTER 26

The three of them sat around the table for the bulk of the afternoon until both Caterina and Liliana were close to dropping off from lack of sleep.

Mick, damn him, was like an automaton, able to function on little rest. Caterina assumed that during his time in the Army he had likely gone days without anything more than short naps.

When he urged both her and Liliana to go get some rest, Liliana demurred, determined to walk the few blocks to their parents' home in order to get clothes for Caterina. Since she wasn't due back at the hospital until the next day, she assured both of them that she would be able to get all the rest she needed after that short errand.

Mick indicated that he would accompany her, clearly fearful that Liliana would encounter Harrison once again.

As much as she wanted not to display her weakness, Caterina's eyes were heavy-lidded. All she could think about was sinking into the comfort of the bed.

She started up the stairs but tripped on a step.

Mick was immediately there to help her, sliding an arm around her waist and walking beside her to the guest room. She eased beneath the covers and he tucked her in, pulling a sleepy smile to her face.

"You're not such a hard nut after all," Caterina whispered before closing her eyes.

Not such a hard nut, Mick thought, a wistful smile on his face as he considered a sleeping Caterina.

She was on her side, her face resting against the pillow. One hand tucked beneath her cheek. There was a rosy hue to her skin, but it wasn't a healthy blush.

He placed the back of his hand on her forehead and measured the heat there. Still lower than it had been the night before, but based on the papers in the medical file they had reviewed yet again that afternoon, each dose of the inhibitor might bring ever higher temperatures as the drug attacked the replication going on in her body. That attack unfortunately produced an immune response in the patient, leading to the fever and sometimes muscular and skeletal pain.

The only treatment—the plasmapheresis to remove the antibodies and debris left behind by the inhibitor. If a patient's blood wasn't cleansed in time . . .

There was no time to rest if they would keep death at bay, he thought.

Which meant that it was time to pay Edwards a visit. Rattle the cage and see how he reacted when pressed.

Gently passing a hand across her hair, he vowed to make sure that whoever had done this to Caterina would get their just rewards.

For now, he would take a short break by walking Liliana home. Then he had to figure out the best plan of attack against Edwards.

*   *   *

It had been a toss-up between confronting Edwards at his offices at Wardwell or his home in nearby Marlton.

The home won out.

Edwards likely had less security there than he had at the Wardwell facility, thinking that his castle was a safe place.

Mick had dressed for the mission, black on black on black. In his satchel he had the equipment he would need to break into the home. He was well-armed, his Glock in a holster secured at the small of his back, and a smaller pistol tucked into an ankle holster beneath the hem of his black jeans. For good measure, he had a knife in a sheath strapped to his left arm for easy access.

He would not let Mad Dog get the upper hand tonight, should he be there.

When he walked from his office to the guest room to check on Caterina before leaving, he found her awake and easing a black sweater over her head. The action provided him a quick glimpse of the slender lines of her body, which were already looking fuller than they had a few days ago. Her skin was creamy against the ebony of the shirt and the black jeans she wore.

Black on black on black. Not a good omen.

Mick leaned a hand against the frame of the door and coughed to let her know he was there.

She whirled to face him and finished pulling down the sweater. As she did so, the midnight-colored curls of her hair spilled down over her shoulders.

"What do you think you're doing?" he asked.

"I'm going with you." She dug her fingers into her hair,

pulling it back and securing it with a band. It exposed the fine lines of her pale face, made more severe by all the darkness surrounding her.

At his perusal, a slight blush came to her cheeks.

"You're staying here. Where you'll be safe."

Hands outstretched, Caterina stated her case. "I need answers. I *need* to face that son of a bitch and know why he did this to me."

Mick understood what she needed. He just wasn't sure that it was wise for her to be with him when he confronted Edwards. He shook his head. "It's too risky with the way you are."

"The way I am?" she asked and took a step toward him. "You mean like this?"

Before his eyes, her skin darkened in color, becoming almost as black as her clothing. The only remaining sign of color was the compelling blue of her irises and whites of her eyes.

"You've been practicing?" he said and quirked an eyebrow to emphasize his point.

"Not really," she said with a shrug. "It just kind of happens."

Before his eyes, she returned to normal. "I need to go head to head with him."

Mick thought about what he had to do that night. Considered what role, if any, she might play in the mission.

A risky business, taking her along, and yet...

He understood she needed to control her own fate. He also realized that giving Edwards a show of what he had created might help them get more information.

He stalked to her and kneeled before her. "Bring your leg here," he said and tapped his left thigh.

Caterina did as he asked, stepping onto his thigh.

He pulled down the sock she wore and deftly removed the electronic monitoring device. Tossing it on the bed, he said, "I hope I don't live to regret this."

"You won't," she urged and removed her foot so that he might rise.

"We'll see," he said.

Google Street View had accurately depicted Edwards's home and the surrounding residences.

He wouldn't be able to park the Jeep on the street without attracting attention, Mick thought as he drove to the end of the court before circling around and back off the block.

Thanks to suburban sprawl, however, the next block down to the enclave of McMansions was an everyday middle-class street of medium-sized lots and single-car driveways. A number of vehicles were parked along the street, including another black Jeep Liberty much like his, even down to the American flag cover on the spare wheel.

He pulled into an empty driveway and did a K-turn. Returned to an open space at the mouth of the street and abutting a wooded corner lot that belonged to one of the McMansions. He parked the car and cut the ignition.

Removing the keys and tucking them into his jeans pocket, Mick stared past Caterina as she sat beside him. She had been dozing off and on during the nearly hour-long drive to the area, her strength clearly still not back to normal. As she roused and glanced in his direction, the slight flush of her fever was visible even in the dark.

He was concerned about her role tonight, but he couldn't have left her home after her plea.

He motioned to the lot as she gazed at the wooded area.

"We'll cut through that stand of trees until we reach the back of Edwards's home. Then we'll move toward the front door and catch Edwards off guard when he answers. Is that understood?"

A curt nod of her head acknowledged his instructions.

He handed her a spare set of keys and said, "If anything goes wrong, you drive home using the GPS. Wait for Liliana and ask her to call Ramon."

She took the keys from his hand and said, "Will do."

"Good. Let's get going."

He popped open his door, but the car's interior lights did not come on, keeping their exit secret from any eyes on the street.

Caterina immediately ducked into the woods and he followed, but as they left sight of the street, she paused and waited for him to take the lead.

He did so, but kept his pace moderate, aware of Caterina's condition. If he was going to push her, it would be when they had to make their escape. He slipped an occasional glance her way, making sure she was with him. Cautious not to make too much sound as they traversed the land behind two of the homes, undetected.

Ahead lay Edwards's home and Mick slowed his pace, vigilant for any security systems. As at Wardwell, there were no perimeter alarms. Together they skirted the woods until they were directly behind their intended target.

There were no lights on, from what was visible of the house or along the back of the building.

"Do you think anyone is home?" Caterina asked in a low whisper as she leaned toward him.

Mick brought his index finger to her lips to urge her to remain silent. Her lips were soft and warm. Maybe too warm, but he battled back his apprehension.

They were committed to the mission now and there was no turning back.

He eased his hand into the satchel and withdrew his night vision goggles. Slipping them on, he searched for signs of any lights or motion sensors.

There were lights at the two farthest corners of the large home, but they had no sensors attached to them. They might be time-activated, although if they were, Mick would have set them to come on well before now.

The area beside the garage was lined with a straight row of fast-growing arborvitae and would provide little coverage. The woods in which they were hiding, however, continued as an arm's-length-wide strip of trees and underbrush at the opposite side of the home.

Sufficient cover in which they could hide.

Bending close to Caterina, Mick whispered, "Follow me."

Crouching low, he advanced through the woods and up that strip, Caterina close behind him. Their footfalls were soft against the leaves and underbrush until she stepped on a twig that snapped loudly, like a gunshot in the night. He paused then, as she did, waiting to see if anyone from either home might notice.

No one did, blissfully convinced of the safety of their suburban environs.

Their gazes connected and as they did so, Mick realized Caterina had gone camo. A useful trait for tonight's mission, he thought. Inclining his head toward the home, he indicated they would proceed.

More carefully, he worked his way through the remaining underbrush and trees until they were beside Edwards's home. Only a narrow strip of grass and some landscaping around the edge of the edifice separated them from their goal.

He perused the area with the goggles, but she whispered, "Edwards is home alone."

Exactly what the goggles had confirmed. "How did you know?"

She shook her head and as he met her gaze, he noted the glitter of the inhuman there. She held up her hand before her and glanced in the direction of the nearby house. "I can see multiple shadows there." Then she pointed to Edwards's home. "But not in there. There's only one shadow."

Her halo sight, he realized, must be capable of sensing heat.

Caterina waited for his reaction. Tried to curb the fear running rampant through her body that had released her camouflage powers. Powers which she didn't yet understand.

Mick cupped her cheek and ran his thumb across the side of her face as if to remind himself of what she was beneath the odd-colored skin.

"Good job," he said, the tone of his voice low.

"Are you ready?" He faced her and for good measure, reached beneath the hem of her black sweater to tug into position the Kevlar vest he had insisted she add for protection. Mick didn't trust that Edwards wouldn't be armed.

Caterina met his gaze square on and nodded. "Ready."

He glanced back toward the house and noticed a light going on in one of the rooms.

Taking hold of Caterina's hand, he said, "Let's go."

In a low crouch, they circled around the side of the home, cut across the landscaping close to Edwards's house. They had to duck low to avoid being seen through the two big picture windows in the front. Pausing at the edge of the front-door landing, Mick reached up with a gloved hand and unscrewed one lightbulb, providing Caterina some cover.

As they had planned during their trip to Edwards's home, she took a spot in the shadows right by that darkened side of the door. She laid her hands on the red brick and closed her eyes. A furrow appeared in the middle of her forehead as she concentrated. Little by little the transformation took place.

By the time Mick rang the doorbell, every inch of her visible skin was the rusty red color of the brick along the wall. The black of the vest and sweater blended into the shadows, making her nearly invisible.

Footsteps sounded from within and Mick took two steps back from the door, wanting to draw Edwards out onto the landing and away from Caterina.

The muffled *beep-beep* of someone disarming an alarm system came seconds before the door opened.

Edwards stood there. Annoyance sprinted across his features before a smug look took control.

"Mr. Carrera. A personal visit wasn't necessary. It would have been sufficient for you to answer all the calls you've been ignoring."

"And here I thought that you would be happy to

hear that I've brought you something. Or should I say someone?"

Interest flared in Edwards's features and he took that first expected step over the threshold and looked behind Mick.

"You have her here?" he asked.

Mick chuckled and shook his head, chastising the other man. "You paid me to find her, didn't you?"

Edwards squinted, peering at him intently and then craning his neck toward the driveway and woods. He took another step forward, as if to improve his line of sight, which was exactly what Mick wanted.

"Don't see anything? Look behind you, Dr. Edwards."

The other man half-turned and looked straight back toward his doorway. Straight at Caterina, but he apparently didn't see her.

Tracking Edwards's gaze, he knew why. The black of Cat's clothing and hair appeared to be nothing more than shadows. Her eyes were closed, giving away nothing of her presence thanks to the redbrick color of her skin. But then she opened her eyes—those amazing sapphire blue eyes—and they were like a beacon in the night.

Edwards gasped and that stunned second was all it took.

Mick grabbed Edwards from behind, encircling his neck with one arm while jabbing his gun into the scientist's ribs.

"We need to talk," Mick said.

CHAPTER 27

Mick forced Edwards forward across the threshold and into the house. Caterina followed, closing and locking the door behind them.

He marched the doctor through the house until they reached the kitchen. Tossing Edwards into a chair, Mick ripped some cable ties from his pocket and bound the scientist to the arms and legs of the chair, not that Edwards had put up much of a fight.

Maybe because his stunned gaze had been focused on Caterina the whole time.

As Mick finished securing him, he turned to find Caterina losing the brick camo and going back to her normal skin color.

"Long time no see, Dr. Edwards," she said, the tones of her voice controlled although her body was taut with anger.

"You've got some nerve bringing her here," Edwards said, glaring at Mick as he stood beside him. "She's dangerous. She killed Wells."

Mick *tsk*ed and shook his head. "There are lots of reasons why I think Caterina didn't do the skewering. Let's start with reason number one—Gates Genengineering."

Edwards paled. "How do you know about—"

"I hacked your servers," he said.

"You found the Gates documents?" Edwards sputtered.

Mick nodded and walked around the edge of the chair to crouch right before the doctor, not wanting to miss a second of his response.

"What happened? Did Wells find out about the experiments you did on Caterina and the others?"

Confusion clouded the other man's eyes as he shot a look back at Caterina before returning his gaze to him. "What are you talking about?"

"This is what *you* did to me," Caterina said and approached. To leave no doubt about what she was referring to, she laid her hand on the maple surface of the table. Her anger made the transformation quick as her hand almost disappeared onto the surface of the table.

"I didn't know that's what Wells did. I just knew something wasn't right," Edwards replied, his eyes wide with fear.

"Wells was trying to help me when you had him killed," she nearly screamed and advanced on him.

Mick jumped in her way, and as had happened before, her extra strength surprised and nearly toppled him. "Calm down, Cat."

"See how violent she is," Edwards asserted, and the chair bucked as he tried to escape his restraints to get away from Caterina.

Caterina did as Mick requested, backing away and tucking her arms tight to her sides to assert control. "I'm sorry. It won't happen again."

Mick stood before Edwards once more, arms across his

chest. His stance loose, but ready for action. "If I thought Caterina would do it, I'd gladly let her at you. Someone has to pay for what's been done to her."

"I told you. I had nothing to do with that," Edwards hissed, the skin taut across the almost ferretlike lines of his ascetic face.

"Nothing to do with it, but you found out about it, didn't you?"

Hot color erupted on Edwards's cheeks. "Wells came to me right after I told him about the merger."

"He wanted to tell Gates about the experiments," Mick prompted.

Reluctantly, Edwards admitted it, which was not what Mick had been expecting. "He wanted to come clean, but that would have jeopardized everything."

"So you killed him," Caterina said and came to stand beside Mick, the intensity of her fury apparent but under control.

"As far as I know, you're responsible for Wells's death," he said, jerking his head in Caterina's direction.

"You know this based on what? Video feed? Eyewitness testimony?" Mick asked.

Edwards shrugged. "I can't say."

Caterina leaned down until she was almost face to face with Edwards. "You mean you can, but you won't."

As she rose upright and stood beside him again, Mick laid a calming hand on her shoulder as he looked straight at Edwards and said, "Call off Mad Dog."

Edwards raked his gaze over him intently before saying, "Who is Mad Dog?"

"Matthew Donnelly. Mad Dog. Soldier of fortune. Psycho security expert. Call him off," Mick repeated.

Edwards shrugged and shook his head. "I don't know any Mad Dog."

He was either a damned fine actor or he was telling the truth, but just in case...Mick pulled out an old photo of him with Mad Dog and shoved it in Edwards's face.

"You've never seen this man before?"

"Never," Edwards immediately asserted.

Mick actually believed him, but he also suspected the good doctor might have an idea as to who had called in Mad Dog. "Who do you know who might have hired him?"

"Don't know." Clearly lying this time, Mick thought.

"Mad Dog's name was on your security department logs," he said and crouched down once more until he was eye to eye with Edwards. He wanted his message to be clear.

"You've got until noon tomorrow to check the logs and call me with the name of the person Mad Dog visited."

A shrewd look crept onto Edwards's features. "What if I don't?"

Mick smiled and glanced at Caterina before he rose and joined ranks with her. She slipped her hand into his as he said, "I can show you a world of hurt you can't even begin to imagine. Physical and financial hurt. Understood?"

Edwards's gaze narrowed at their show of unity and then he nodded.

"Understood, Mr. Carrera."

Despite the other man's words, Mick didn't trust him. There was too much at stake financially for Edwards. If he had hired Mad Dog, Mick suspected the scientist would not call the mercenary off so quickly.

But Mick hoped the warning would spur Edwards into

action that would help him confirm the doctor's involvement in what had happened to Wells. He would be tracking Edwards's every move so he could better understand the kind of battle he faced to safeguard Caterina's life.

The ride back to Mick's home in Bradley Beach was quiet.

Mick was lost in his thoughts, probably considering what they had learned from Edwards.

Edwards, Caterina thought with disgust, had been so smug and too calm. Clearly unremorseful of all the pain, suffering, and death that had come about because of the contract with Gates Genengineering, which Mick had told her about before their arrival at Edwards's home.

One hundred million dollars for the loss of how many lives? Caterina wondered as another shiver racked across her body.

At the movement, Mick quickly looked in her direction before returning his attention to the road. "Are you okay?"

The low-level heat she had been tolerating all day had been steadily growing until her head had begun to pound. Now the chills had started.

"I'm hot," she admitted and tucked her arms tight around herself to contain the involuntary spasms of her body.

Mick's hands tightened and relaxed on the steering wheel. "It's about ten more minutes to the house. Can you hold on that long?"

Caterina's head hurt so much that even the off–on of the passing streetlights was creating agony in her skull. Only ten minutes, she told herself.

"Only ten," he repeated and she realized she had vocalized her last thoughts.

Another rough shudder slashed through her body, but she lied past her chattering teeth and said, "I can do it."

She repeated those words silently to herself, trying to ignore the pain and the nearly uncontrollable tremors of her body.

Mick increased his speed, mindful of Caterina's deteriorating condition, but drove within reasonable limits so as to avoid being pulled over. Finally he parked the Jeep in the garage and turned in the seat. "Cat, we're home."

She nodded, or at least he thought she did. She was shaking so violently that it made it impossible to know whether or not the motion had been in response to his question.

Mick sprang into action, exiting the Jeep and swinging around to her door. Opening it and reaching in to carry her from the car and into the kitchen where Liliana was making herself a cup of tea. At her questioning glance, he said, "Cat's burning up again. I'm taking her to the pool."

After closing the door to the garage and disarming the alarm before it could trip, Liliana followed Mick to the edge of the pool where she hovered nearby anxiously. He toed off his boots, ripped his cell phone from his belt, slipped his gun holster from the small of his back, and removed his ankle holster.

"Get some towels," he instructed and walked with Caterina in his arms to the stairs at the far end of the pool. He carefully moved down the steps, the chill of the water seeping through his jeans as he descended into the pool.

Caterina was mumbling incoherently, something over and over again, when he finally entered the water with her.

An immense tremor racked her body at the contact with the cold water and her eyes flew open, bright orbs of blue made brighter by the reflection from the moonlit pool water. She grabbed hold of Mick's shoulders and buried her face against his chest.

He tucked her close, laying his face next to hers. He could feel the heat burning up her body.

"How is she?" Liliana called out as she tossed some towels by the lip of the pool and crouched down to get a better look at them.

"It'll take a little time to cool her down. I'm worried that the fever returned without another injection of the inhibitor drug."

As Mick examined Liliana's face, her similar concern was plainly evident.

"I'll go get her room ready." She rushed off, leaving him alone with Caterina.

Mick bent his knees, dipping down so that they were covered in the cool water up to their necks.

Caterina's face bore a ruddy blush from the fever, but as he cradled her, the heat from her body slowly receded, as did the rosy flush. He brought his lips to her forehead, pleased that her body temperature was substantially lower.

"How are you feeling?" he murmured.

"Better," she replied.

"Let's get you dry and back to bed to rest. You probably overdid it tonight by coming with me." Or at least, he hoped that was the reason for the return of the fever and not something else going on in her body.

At her nod, he carried her out of the water to the pool deck, released her legs so she could stand on her own.

She was wobbly, so he kept one arm around her. Together they bent and retrieved the towels, drying off their hair and faces. He wrapped a towel around her body to collect some of the water dripping off her clothes. Scooped up his cell phone and weapons, and then picked her back up and took her upstairs to the guest room.

Liliana waited there with yet more towels. On the nightstand by the bed she had set up a small bowl and washcloths. The bowl was filled with water and ice in the event the fever returned.

Mick walked to the edge of the bed and let Caterina slip to her feet again.

"I'll help you get out of those wet things," his sister said. He took that as a cue to leave and also as an opportunity to change into something dry himself.

In his room, he ripped off the sodden clothes, tossing them into the bathtub. Briskly rubbing a towel across himself to counteract the cold pool water, he dried off and eased into a T-shirt and sweats. Brushing his hair back with his fingers, he returned to the room where Liliana had managed to get Caterina out of her clothes and into bed.

Liliana was drawing another sample of blood, and when he walked in she explained, "I want to make sure there's nothing new causing this fever."

After the vacutainer was filled with phosphorescent green blood, Liliana efficiently removed the needle from Caterina's arm and bandaged it. As she finished, Caterina reached out and grasped her hand.

"Thank you, Lil," she said. Liliana returned the gesture, taking Caterina's hand in a reassuring clasp.

"It'll be okay, Cat. I promise," his sister said.

Mick wished he could make the same pledge, but said nothing as Liliana walked toward him, the glowing blood sample in her hand. "I'm due back at the hospital in a couple of hours. I'm going to try and grab a nap before then."

"I'm sorry I've made it so hard for you," he said, but his sister surprised him by smiling.

"Not hard at all. You've given me a place to stay and a reason to believe in myself again. It gave me the strength to do the right thing."

"Harrison?" he questioned and she confirmed it with a slight dip of her head.

"Harrison and Caterina. I know you'll find the strength to do the right thing as well." She rose up on tiptoe and brushed a sisterly kiss on his cheek before leaving the room.

The right thing, Mick thought, closed the door and approached the bed where Caterina rested, her gaze locked on him as he neared.

Her skin had lost the flush of fever and returned to its creamy hue. Thick curly locks of her nearly black hair, heavy with moisture, rested against the side of her face.

She turned the deep blue of her gaze up to meet his. "No matter what happens at the end, you've done the right thing by me."

At the end, he thought, unsure of anything other than the fact that this would all not end well for someone. Whether it was Edwards or Mad Dog or Caterina or even himself, someone would likely pay a high price at the conclusion of this assignment.

Mick sat on the edge of the recliner and cradled her cheek. Her skin bore a slight chill from the water and was smooth beneath the pad of his finger. So smooth and womanly.

Caterina covered his much larger hand with hers. His

palm was rough. Clearly the hand of a man who worked hard with his hands. A strong hand, she thought as she moved her hand past his wrist and to his forearm. The hair on his arm soft beneath her palm. His body muscled and lean until she reached the edge of the waterproof bandage on his forearm covering the wound he had received battling for her. Another scar to add to those on his body.

It had to be the fever that was making her remember just how that body had felt against hers when he had held her in the pool. How he had kissed her and she him, rousing passion that might be better left unexplored only . . .

"Would you hold me?" She needed the human contact. Needed the affirmation that she was still a woman. A desirable woman, unless she was misreading the signals he was giving off.

"If holding is all you want, I may not be your man," Mick replied and dipped his thumb down to trace the edges of her lips.

"I want more. I want to feel alive again," Caterina said.

She was using him, but it wouldn't be the first time or the last that a woman had done so, Mick thought. Considering he found her damned attractive, weird genes and all, why not give in to the temptation and get it out of his system.

"Move over," he said.

Caterina shifted to the center of the bed and he joined her there, lying on his side and facing her. Their bodies were only inches apart.

"Touch me," she said and pulled away the sheet, exposing the fullness of her breasts with their soft tips.

He ran the pads of his fingers across the tip of one breast. Cupped the weight of it in his hand and rubbed his thumb across the tip until her nipples beaded into stiff nubs. He needed to taste, he thought, and bent his head, licked the one tip while continuing to caress the other nipple with his hand.

She arched her back to give him easier access and cradled the back of his head. Moaned as he teethed the peak of one breast. He soothed that gentle nip with another lick and suckled at her breast while shifting one hand downward, across the flat expanse of her midsection. Past the delicate indent of her navel until his fingers gently brushed between her legs.

She moved closer and threw her thigh up over his, inviting him to her most private core.

Tardily he accepted that invitation, skimming his fingers across her center until the sensitive nub swelled and his fingers dipped lower.

Caterina gasped as he explored her dampness, gripping his shoulders as he eased in first one finger and then another, stretching her in preparation for his possession.

"Mick," she keened, shifting her hips against his hand. Holding his head to her, but wanting to feel the warmth of his body beside her.

He slipped slightly away and she reached for the hem of his shirt. Pulled it over his head while he skimmed the sweatpants down his body, revealing the nakedness beneath the fleece.

She laid her hands on his shoulders once more and took a moment to enjoy all of him that was visible. The articulated and defined muscles of his body. The scars and bruises that spoke of a man familiar with danger and accustomed to violence.

But there was nothing violent about the way he touched

her. About the gentleness of his mouth and hands as he resumed his loving.

She once again granted him access and he used it to full advantage, rousing her passion much as she urged him on, using her hands to stroke him. Playing him much as she might a sonata, each measured beat and pull of her hands giving him pleasure until he, too, was trembling and breathing roughly.

"I can't wait anymore, Cat," he said, rolling her beneath him. His arms braced on either side of her body as he slipped between her legs, but paused before entering her.

"I can't, either, Mick," she replied and dropped one hand so she could encircle him and guide him into her center.

He sucked in a shaky breath as she gasped at his entry, held still as her body accommodated to his size. Thick in girth and perfect in length, he filled her completely.

She was the first to move, raising her knees to grasp his hips. The motion driving him even deeper within.

He met her gaze then, his eyes almost black with desire. A flush across the high cheekbones inherited from some long-ago Aztec descendant. Full lips she wanted to savor.

She cradled the straight, strong line of his jaw and brought her lips to his. Eased her tongue past the seam of his mouth to mimic the motion of their bodies. Her tongue darting against his much like he was drawing her ever closer to release with the pumping of his hips.

His movements grew more hurried and she urged him on with soft cries of pleasure she whispered against his lips, until something suddenly coalesced in the center of her.

The energy gathered into a ball and then exploded throughout her body, pulling him into her and caressing him as her climax overtook her body.

Mick exhaled roughly against her mouth as her soft cry of completion came against his lips and the muscles of her body milked him, pulling and tightening on him as his own release erupted in his body.

He managed to drive into her a few more times, prolonging her climax, but then he dropped down onto her, drained. His body heavy against hers, but she wrapped her arms around him and urged, "Don't leave me yet."

Yet, he realized, glad that she understood the limits of what they had just experienced, but saddened by that as well.

He allowed himself to bask in the pleasure of her soft skin beneath him, and the heat and wet of her center as her body caressed him while he slowly softened within her.

The temperature of her body remained warm, a little more than normal. Thankfully nothing like it had been earlier in the night.

Guilt rose up on so many levels, but he ruthlessly drove it back, justifying what had just happened with one simple truth.

They had both wanted it to happen.

The question was, now that it had, where did they go from here?

CHAPTER 28

Mad Dog hadn't worried about circumventing the security system guarding Mick's office/apartment.

He wanted Mick to know he was on his trail.

Shitty digs, he thought, walking around the one-room office before heading up a back staircase to the loft apartment overlooking part of the U Penn campus and the railway yards for 30th Street Station.

The layout of the loft was basic: living and dining areas, kitchen, bedroom. The furniture, utilitarian—a spartan residence empty of any personal touches.

He rifled through the kitchen cabinets and the drawers of all the furniture, but found nothing of interest. He returned to the office, where there were a few cabinets filled with what appeared to be old case files. No computer anywhere. Too hard to secure, so Mick probably took it with him wherever he went. That's what he would do.

And that's probably where Mick had any of the kind of information that would lead Mad Dog to where his old colleague might be hiding.

There was nothing in the apartment to tip him off.

No bills or mail. Everything probably went to a P.O. box somewhere. No personal papers of any kind.

Begrudgingly Mad Dog admitted that Mick was damned good at what he did, but Mick wouldn't be able to play hide and seek much longer.

Disgusted, Mad Dog plopped onto the leather chair by Mick's desk. As he did so, he noticed the paper shredder sitting on the garbage can beneath the desk.

He tossed off the shredder and pulled out the long, thin paper shreds, placing them on top of the desk. Carefully he began to sift through the pieces and discovered bits of color in all the boring business white.

He pulled those soft pinkish shreds out of the pile. They were of a heavier weight, likely from an envelope. Unfortunately, most of the pieces were too small, except . . .

Mad Dog pulled one larger piece from the pile where the cross-cut shredder had failed to do its job. Printed on the pale pink corner was the start of an address. He rummaged through some more of the colorful shreds and found another few strips that he pieced together.

From one set he got part of a word: Brad.

From another just a "ch."

Not enough yet, he thought, perusing the strip of paper from what had likely been a personal letter. He hadn't realized Mick had any liabilities, but now he had a possible lead to the name of a place where there might be someone of interest to his old colleague.

Someone who would end up dead if Mick didn't hand over Shaw.

He rose from the desk and did another search of Mick's apartment and the office.

Nothing else provided any useful information.

As he was about to leave the office, he noticed the security camera tucked up into one corner of the room where it would provide a view of everything and everyone who entered the space.

He walked up close to the camera, wanting to make sure there was no doubt about who had paid a visit. Smiling into the camera, he slashed his hand across his throat, his message clear.

With that broad, satisfied smile on his face, Mad Dog left behind the mess he had created, certain that the small bit of the address from the envelope would point him in the right direction.

Mick had been in a number of dangerous places, but none more dangerous than this.

In her arms.

He hadn't expected the peace and contentment that had followed the sex. Amazing, satisfying, mind-blowing sex.

Each time had been different and possibly more satisfying than the first.

Because of the danger of remaining in her arms, and possibly finding the strength to do it yet again, he was trying to muster the will to leave. She must have sensed it.

Caterina propped her head on her arm and glanced at Mick as he lay on his back beside her. She had been resting against him, her head pillowed on his chest.

"I'd understand if you want to go," she said and made no motion that contradicted that statement. No touch or caress. No little pout of those full and incredibly mobile lips. Nothing like what he was used to from other women he'd taken to bed.

Which only confused him more and had him about

to protest her statement when the angry buzz of his cell phone alerted him to a security breach.

"Shit," Mick swore as he rolled off the bed, reaching for the cell phone with one hand while grabbing his weapon with the other.

The code buzzing on the cell phone indicated the breach was at his office/apartment and not at one of the perimeter points surrounding the house.

"Stay put," he ordered and rushed to access his laptop so he could find out who had broken into his apartment.

He jerked on his sweatpants and raced out of the room and to his office. With a flick of his finger across the touchpad, the laptop sprang to life to display the feeds from the house, office space, and apartment on the three monitors sitting on the desktop.

The view of the loft area was empty of any intruders, but clearly someone had gone through his things. Clothes and other items littered the floor of the apartment.

He caught a flash of motion from the camera trained on his office. Someone leaving the area? he wondered as Liliana and Caterina walked into the room.

Liliana took one look at his half-naked state and another at Caterina's in his robe and immediately put two and two together. She narrowed her eyes, assessing the situation, but kept silent about it. Instead she focused on the computer screen and asked, "Trouble?"

Caterina walked over to him, tightening the belt on the robe as she did so. She laid a hand on his bare shoulder. That touch alone was enough to awaken need in him.

He slipped behind the protection of the desk and sat down. Worked on recovering the stored video feed to see what had happened and said to the two women, "Someone broke into my place in Philly."

Liliana came to stand beside Caterina. Both of them had a view of the monitors as Mick replayed the video, from the moment Mad Dog had entered the location to the last few minutes when he slashed his hand across his throat.

Liliana tucked her arms tight against her midsection and glanced down at Mick. "Is he serious or is this some kind of game he plays?"

Mick tucked his arms across his chest and leaned back in his chair. "Mad Dog loves to play sick games and he is nothing but serious when he's on an assignment."

Surging back toward his laptop, Mick rewound to the point where Mad Dog had finished piecing together the shreds of paper, captured that screen shot and sent it to the printer. He picked up the photo and stared at it, recalled the pale pink envelope that had come from his mother, together with a letter and family photo. The photo was in his wallet, but the envelope and letter...

Those shreds were the only things in his Philly place that had anything to tie him to anyone outside of his life as a hired gun. He had been so careful to separate his two lives to avoid the violence of one spilling over into the other. Now the smallest trace of his personal life may have changed what might happen next, and not for the good.

He said nothing as he handed the screen shot print to his sister, who examined it and said, "It's just some paper."

"With part of an address, I suspect," he said, and watched as Caterina took the paper from his sister. She perused the photo with seemingly great care and said, "An address for here?"

He shook his head. "It was a letter from our mother, so it would be our parents' address."

Their home was several blocks away, but even just the name of the town was enough to provide Mad Dog with the information he needed to begin his search. A visit to town and some questions to the right locals and Mad Dog would know where to find his parents. And then possibly him.

"It won't take much effort for Mad Dog to pinpoint an exact address. A little longer to connect the dots to us," he warned and held out his hand so Caterina could return the screen shot.

"What do we do now?" Liliana asked.

"We've got a day or two at best before Mad Dog—"

"This Mad Dog is the one you warned me about before," Liliana interjected.

He shot a glance at her and then Caterina, who stood there hugging herself, clearly in defensive mode.

"Yes, this is the man I warned you about. He's quite dangerous. If we can't settle this thing with Edwards soon—"

"I'll turn myself over to the authorities," Caterina jumped in, looking back and forth between him and Liliana. "If the police have me—"

Mick rose and laid a finger on her lips. "There's no place you'll be safe so long as Mad Dog is around."

Caterina eased her hand into his, once again shaking his core with her simple touch. She raised her chin and cocked her head at a thoughtful angle. "I'm not worried about *my* safety. I'm worried about your family. They shouldn't be at risk because of me."

He was about to answer, but Liliana beat him to it. "The Carreras stick together, Cat."

"We don't leave anyone behind," Mick added. His family was as tight as any military unit in which he had ever served. He knew they would band together to protect each other and in this case, to protect her.

Caterina embraced Liliana in a hug and then leaned into Mick, encircling his waist with her arms, the gesture more telling than it should have been.

With Caterina's arms around him, Mick met Liliana's gaze over Caterina's shoulder. He awkwardly returned Caterina's embrace.

Caterina could feel the tension radiating from Mick. Stepping out of his arms, she looked from him to Liliana. She instantly recognized the concern in his sister's eyes. "We had sex. *Just sex*. No commitments. No promises." With that, Caterina fled the room, leaving Mick to avoid Liliana's sisterly stare-down all alone.

He took up a spot at the laptop to start formulating his plan. Liliana stalked right to the edge of his desk and jammed her hands onto her ample hips. "Miguel de la Guadeloupe Roberto Carrera," she began, but he raised his hand in the air to cut off a tirade that sounded too much like one his mother might give.

"It won't happen again."

"It's not that, it's just the wrong time for it to happen," she chided. "She's vulnerable. You're...a bad boy. Dangerous. Women eat that up."

Didn't he know it, only...

He refused to acknowledge that it could be different with Caterina. How could it be, considering the playing field where they were starting their little game?

"I know she needs time to get her head straight. That's why this won't happen again," he repeated, hoping to foreclose any further discussion.

It worked. With an annoyed huff, his sister stomped out of the room.

He turned to the laptop and considered calling Franklin to see if he had found out anything else. Given Franklin's usual mode of operation, however, he knew his old friend would have phoned if he had any additional information to offer.

He didn't even know if Mad Dog would reach out to Franklin, but suspected that when he did, it would be to flush out confirmation of something Mad Dog already suspected—like the address on the envelope.

Late as it was, he had to forewarn his friend about Mad Dog.

He dialed and when Franklin answered, he quickly provided him with an update on Mad Dog's break-in, as well as the details on the Wardwell-Gates Genengineering merger.

Franklin emitted a low whistle and said, "No wonder he has the three of us after Shaw. That's a lot of money to lose if the merger goes south."

"It's the kind of money people kill for, which is why he probably had Wells eliminated."

There was hesitation on the line before his friend said, "You think Edwards did it and not Shaw?"

"I'd put my money on it not being Shaw, wherever she is."

No sense admitting he knew just where Caterina was. That would only complicate things further if Mad Dog went after Franklin.

"I made some progress with the families of those two patients. They think their loved ones died from medical complications relating to their illnesses. I'll keep on digging around, but if it's getting too hot—"

"Pull out. You've got other obligations more important than this assignment. I'm five-by-five with that," Mick offered, wanting to be square with his friend on what he expected.

"I'll be back at you if anything comes up."

Franklin hung up and Mick went back to work. Combined with information from an investigative service or a personal visit to the area, the security of his safe house would be compromised in no time. His family, with the exception of Roberta, who was serving a tour in Iraq, would be vulnerable.

Liliana was already aware, but Mick would remind her in the morning. He would talk to his parents and brother then as well, possibly suggest that they all take a vacation together somewhere for at least a week.

In the meantime, he picked up the phone and dialed Ramon to ask his cousin to see if he could arrange for some additional drivebys past the restaurant and his parents' home. Even though he suspected Liliana wouldn't like it, he mentioned her problems with Harrison also, eliciting a promise from Ramon that a discreet call would be placed to hospital security.

Mick needed to keep his family safe.

And he needed to reaffirm to Caterina that he intended to keep her safe.

CHAPTER 29

Sweet music reached Mick's ears as he neared the closed bedroom door. He assumed Caterina had the stereo turned up to help soothe her, but when he entered, Caterina was in the far corner of the room, eyes closed, playing his younger brother's old beat-up cello. Clearly lost in the music as she played, her body swayed and shifted as her fingers and bow arm stroked emotion from the strings and wood.

"Never sounded that good when Tony played," Mick joked.

Caterina stopped mid-stroke, opened her eyes, and shot him a puzzled look.

"Tony?"

"My younger brother, Antonio. He stopped playing when he got to high school. Didn't think the girls would find it sexy that he was in the orchestra."

That comment dragged a fleeting smile to her lips. "I suppose he became a jock instead."

Mick chuckled and shook his head. "Lettered in lacrosse and was All-State in football, but he had a geek's heart. He's working and going to school part-time to get a bioengineering degree."

Caterina nodded and set aside the cello, carefully leaning it on the chair as she rose and slipped into bed.

She didn't look at him again as he stood at the foot of the bed. She couldn't without revealing the turmoil she was experiencing about her emotions toward him. Emotions she had poured into her music as she played, releasing them into the music until balance had returned.

Of course Mick's entry had dashed her equilibrium once again. As she sat there, distressed about him and the threat to his family, she sensed the change coming over her and watched as the hand lying on the sheet before her assumed the pale blue color of the linens.

No way, she thought, focusing on that transformation and forcing it away by the demand of her will.

"Cat," he said, the tones of his voice uncertain and apologetic as he walked to the side of the bed.

"It's okay, Mick. I totally understand." Not that she did. But it wasn't his fault that she was confused.

He said nothing else. She sensed his continued presence by her side; heard the slight groan of the wood frame on the chair by the bed as he sat down, and the swoosh of fabric sliding against fabric, maybe when he covered himself.

Covered all that wonderful muscle.

She forced that thought from her mind, bringing other images instead of the assorted small scars on his body, the shocking white of the tape on his stitched-up forearm, and the bruises he had earned on this latest assignment. An assignment intended to deal with her existence.

One hundred million dollars on her head.

Quite a bounty.

A difficult temptation to ignore and yet she had no hesitation about Mick's earlier promise.

After resting her head silently on the pillow, she said his name, not sure if he had already fallen asleep.

"Hmm?" he answered sleepily, although she knew just how quickly he became alert.

"You're not the hard-ass you try to be. There's a big soft spot inside that you hide."

No response followed. Before she could question if he had heard her, the rustle of fabric came again. The bed dipped her toward the center and over the corner of her shoulder she caught a glimpse of him as he eased himself next to her. Too quickly for her to protest, his front was pressed to her back and he had thrown his arm across her waist.

"Go to sleep, Cat."

Easier said than done, she thought, but closed her eyes anyway.

Mick lay awake long after the cadence of her breathing announced that she had finally fallen asleep.

He couldn't rest. His mind was too busy working out all the possible permutations of what might happen once Mad Dog figured out where they were.

He had already set some of the gears into motion. Franklin. His cousin Ramon and his police force. Hospital security.

When he thought about the way Mad Dog had tossed his place in Philly, it tore at his gut that he might do the same here.

This was his safe house in more ways than one.

No matter what mission he had been on, from his time in the Army to his life as a hired gun, this place had always been his escape from it all. This home had always been where he could go for comfort and peace.

This mission had threatened that.

He could take Caterina and run. Find a different place to hide.

Or he could take a stand.

Force Mad Dog to bring the fight to him, because the only way Mick would allow his old nemesis to trash this home and hurt his family was if he was dead.

"Mick?" Caterina asked and turned to face him.

He caressed the satiny skin of her cheek. "Didn't mean to wake you."

"You haven't slept yet, have you?"

He shook his head, rubbed his thumb along the elegant ridge of her cheekbone. "Too much to think about."

"This Mad Dog guy has you really worried? It's about more than this assignment, though, isn't it?" Caterina covered his hand with hers, stroking it tenderly. The pressure of her hand light, but disturbing nevertheless.

He met her gaze in the dark of the night. The deep blue of hers interrupted here and there by bits of blue-green glow. A testament to how little time he had to set things right. Something he hadn't been able to do the last time Mad Dog had been involved in his life.

"Three years ago, Franklin, Mad Dog, and I were on a private security detail down in Miami. Should have been an easy gig. Keep an eye on the wife and nine-year-old son of some bigwig politico who had been receiving death threats." He sighed deeply and looked away as he recalled that day, but Caterina would not allow his avoidance.

She cradled his jaw and urged him to face her. "What happened?"

"We had a protocol if we were threatened. Call the police and head to the nearest secure location. Easy enough to do."

Tension radiated from Mick's body. It was what had awakened Caterina from a sound sleep. Beneath her thumb, the vibrating anger in his body communicated his anger. She ran her thumb across the hard line of his lips and urged him to continue with a soft, "It should have been easy, but Mad Dog wasn't on board with that, was he?"

Mick shook his head. Against her face, his hand trembled. "We picked up a tail going over the McArthur Causeway on the way to the politico's home on Star Island. Mad Dog was driving and he could have kept on going to the police station on Washington Avenue in Miami Beach. Instead he pulled into the entrance for Star Island."

A shudder snaked across Mick's body and he closed his eyes as he continued the story. "A guard came out to see what was up. The car behind us opened fire, killing him. Our car was armored, so we were safe for the moment."

Another more violent tremor traveled through his body.

"It got worse," Caterina whispered, and gently stroked his face again, trying to soothe him.

Mick's eyes snapped open, pupils contracted from his distress. "Franklin tried to grab the wheel to get Mad Dog to move forward past the gate, but Mad Dog threw open his door, got out, and returned fire."

Mick sucked in a breath, and then expelled it roughly. "We had no choice but to defend ourselves. In the firestorm that followed, one of the bullets ricocheted off the door, killing the nine-year-old."

"I'm sorry," she said and embraced him.

Mick was stiff in her arms at first, but gradually he relaxed against her. He slipped his arms around her and brought her close, until every inch of their bodies touched.

She was soft. Warm. Too warm.

"You've got a fever again," he whispered by the shell of her ear.

"It comes and goes," she replied with a nonchalant shrug.

She was trying to be strong.

No, correct that. She *was* strong and Mick admired that strength. She was more woman than he had ever encountered.

Rubbing his face against the curls of her hair roused the smells of summer—hints of pine from the woods they had traipsed through earlier, chlorine from the pool.

"We'll make you better, Cat. Trust me."

She laid her hand flat against his chest. "I do trust you, Mick. Like I said, you've got a soft spot."

He had a soft spot all right—a soft spot in his head to maybe think that somehow this would all turn out right. He couldn't afford such softness because it might lead to a misstep, but he also couldn't harden his heart against her. Against the concern she was showing for him and his family. A concern he had never experienced with any of the other women who had spent a minute or two in his life.

Despite that, he forced some command in his voice in an effort to create distance between them. "Go to sleep, Cat. There's a lot to be done tomorrow."

"Good night, Mick," she said, but remained close. Her body pressed to his, the beat of her heart strong beside his, the out-of-sync cadence merging with his until the beats became one.

A dangerous one, he thought for the barest of seconds before he allowed sleep to claim him.

CHAPTER 30

Forewarned was forearmed, Liliana thought, cautious as she exited her car in the hospital parking lot the next morning. She was early for rounds much as she had been on several other occasions, needing to see Carmen Rojas and have her friend take another look at Caterina's blood.

She was walking toward the entrance to the hospital when Harrison exited the building. He sported a white bandage across his nose and two black eyes.

She had done this to him. Despite the many times he had hurt her, Liliana took no joy in seeing his injuries. If anything, she feared such a visible testament to his failure would only create more problems for her.

He hadn't seen her and for a moment she considered going back to her car to wait until he had left, but then decided she'd had enough of being afraid of him.

Picking up her head and straightening her spine, she walked toward the hospital entrance and Harrison.

He noticed her then and came straight toward her.

"What do you want?" she asked as she stopped a good distance away from him, wanting to be beyond his arms' reach.

He looked around, clearly wanting to make sure that

no one would witness their exchange. Then he took a step toward her and whispered, "You got away the other night, but don't think it'll be so easy the next time."

She thought about the bullies in the world and the one thing they all had in common. They were inherently cowards when someone stood up to them.

"There isn't going to be a next time, because if you even come within one foot of me again, I'm going to take the tape of what happened the other night to the police and then the hospital board. Understood?"

His face paled, making the dark bruising beneath his eyes even more stark.

"You wouldn't do that. What would people think about you?"

A month ago or even a week ago, the shame associated with people discovering how he had hurt her might have actually made her reconsider her threat. Even the fear of how it might hurt her career at the hospital no longer held sway with her.

With a harsh laugh, she said, "They would think that I was smart enough to get away from you."

She shoved past him, intent on starting her rounds. Hopeful that Harrison finally got the message that she would no longer serve as his punching bag.

Once she was within the hospital, Liliana headed straight toward the lower levels that housed the labs and other non-patient areas.

Like always, Carmen was at her station in the pathology lab, making Liliana wonder if her friend ever left her spot. As she entered, Carmen shot her a bright smile.

"*Hola, amiga.* What interesting thing do you have for me today?" Carmen said.

"Are you always so cheery about a blood sample?" Liliana chided as she pulled the tube out of her pocket and handed it over.

"Only when it's packed with GFPs and all other kinds of interesting anomalies."

Liliana shook her head and chastised her friend. "*Sabes* that there's a person behind that sample. Someone who's not well."

Carmen remained unremorseful. "It's why I'm down here. No people skills."

"You're underestimating yourself," she said, but Carmen ignored her, removing a drop of blood from the vacutainer and putting it on a slide. She slid a slip glass over the specimen and placed it beneath the microscope.

"Whoa," she replied and immediately looked up at Liliana. "We've got an excessive number of white blood cells present as well as lysis of an assortment of other cells."

Liliana thought about the inhibitor drug and what it might do. Was it the aftereffects that were creating the fever and the need for plasmapheresis after multiple treatments? she wondered.

"Do you think the lysis is a result of the white blood cells or something else?"

"A chemically induced lysis?" Carmen posited out loud and returned to examine the sample under the microscope once again.

After long moments spent staring at the specimen, Carmen backed up and said, "There's a lot of cell damage, plus the leukocytes contain a large percentage of macrophages and basophils."

"As if her body had an allergic reaction and is trying to mop up all the destruction afterward," Liliana noted.

"There may be too much lysis for her body to handle."

Liliana nodded, understanding now the need for the plasmapheresis. Aware that they didn't have much time to undertake the therapy in order to help Caterina. She motioned to the microscope.

"With that sample, could you prepare the cell separator with what was needed to cleanse the patient's blood using plasmapheresis?"

"I could. I will. Just let me know when you need it done," Carmen confirmed, understanding the urgency of the matter.

"You call me when you're ready so I can arrange for the treatment," Liliana said and walked out.

CHAPTER 31

Caterina's fever had returned. The heat of it had warned Mick of her fragility when she had taken hold of his hand earlier that morning before dozing off to a fitful sleep.

He grabbed his cell phone and speed-dialed Liliana as he sat in the chair by the bed, hoping she would have some news about the latest blood sample she had taken. His sister answered almost immediately, but strain colored her tones.

"You okay, *hermanita*?" he asked, worried that something was up with his sister. Something having nothing to do with the trouble in which he had embroiled her.

"Lots of emergencies. There's good news, though," she said, and her voice actually brightened at the end, giving him hope that the earlier strain was from just too much work.

"You were able to get something from the blood sample?" He shot a half-glance at Caterina as she stirred for a moment, but then drifted right back to sleep.

"We did. The bad news is there's too much going on. Lots of white blood cells and too much cell damage."

Mick cursed beneath his breath, but Liliana immediately said, "The good news is we've got a plasmapheresis setup ready and waiting for Caterina. Once we run her blood through the separator, it should relieve some of her symptoms."

He thought about bringing her into the hospital and the risk it presented. Caterina's picture had been in the papers and on television for the last few days. Reaching over, he brushed the back of his hand against her cheek.

Heat blasted from her. Too much heat.

If he didn't risk bringing Caterina into the hospital, she might continue to get worse.

She might die.

His gut tightened at the thought of losing her.

"Where should I bring Cat?"

Mad Dog cursed and tossed aside the bits of the pastel pink envelope. Immediately after his late night break-in, he had spent a few hours searching the Internet, but had made little progress in tracking down where Mick might be.

His first guess had been that the address was from a town somewhere along the Eastern Shore. He'd put his money on the Jersey Shore given its proximity to Mick's home base in Philadelphia. Probably the South Jersey shore.

That guess had left him trying to decipher the name of the town with those few letters. It had taken less than an hour to discover they most likely stood for Bradley Beach, a small shore town near Asbury Park. At least an hour away from South Jersey and Philly.

Whoever had sent Mick the envelope lived in that town. Possibly a member of Mick's family, which would give him some leverage if he could get them and trade them for Shaw.

Mad Dog's cell phone rang. His client, based on the number on the caller ID.

"What are you doing?" his client asked, his words laced with anger and frustration.

"I'm doing what you paid me to do," he said nonchalantly, not about to let some piss-ass scientist boss him around.

"People are asking questions."

"People, huh? Which people?" It was easy to take care of people who asked too many questions.

The other man nearly hissed the name. "Edwards."

Interesting, he thought. "You and your buddy have a falling-out?"

"Carrera and Shaw paid him a visit last night. He's quite dissatisfied. There's a lot at stake here."

Fuck. Not only did Mick have Shaw, she seemed to be cognizant and working with him. Not good.

"I understand what's at stake. I stand to lose as well," Mad Dog reminded the man. He had only received half of his fee up front. Another cool million would only be delivered once he brought Shaw to them.

"We need her soon. The longer the police continue their investigation, the more likely they are to rule her out as a suspect."

"I'm on his trail," Mad Dog lied, frustrated that the clues provided by the envelope had so far yielded no results.

"Hurry it along, Mr. Donnelly. If the police start looking somewhere besides Shaw, everything will be jeopardized."

In other words, they'd stiff him for the rest of the money they owed him. "I'll have Shaw for you within forty-eight hours," he said, determined not to let Mick screw things up.

"Forty-eight hours. If it takes longer—"

"I get it. No cash. For either of us. Like I said, I'll have Shaw for you in forty-eight hours."

Mad Dog hung up as his client continued with his dire warnings about the risk of failure. He hadn't failed on any mission he'd undertaken. Well, none except the one with Franklin and Mick. If they hadn't been such pussies, they could have salvaged that one as well. They had been too worried about collateral damage to handle the problem. He had no such qualms.

He returned to his laptop and his search on the Internet. Plugging in Bradley Beach and Carrera yielded lots of results, from fan sites for Porsches to an assortment of news articles from area papers.

Methodically Mad Dog began to go through the materials, skipping those that seemed less relevant. Finding several articles about an Antonio Carrera and his football exploits.

Unfortunately, many of the articles had been archived or were dead links. The use of the Wayback Machine site yielded the text of the articles, but not the pictures.

Damn, he thought. A picture might have helped him make a stronger connection to Mick if the football player looked anything like his ex-colleague.

What he did realize from the articles was that Antonio appeared to be at least eight or so years younger than Mick.

Additional hunts on the Net yielded another Carrera—a

Liliana Carrera who had been valedictorian of her high school class. Still no picture. This woman was just a few years younger than Mick, and Mad Dog had little doubt that all of them were somehow related.

Tracking down the names of the local high schools, he tried to see if they had old yearbooks up on their Web sites. They didn't.

He had the same result at the local library. Although they had the yearbooks listed in their collection of reference books, the yearbooks were not available online.

Powering down his laptop, Mad Dog decided he needed to do some hands-on investigating.

Later this morning he would take his hunt to the streets. If he could confirm that the Internet hits for the two Carreras were for Mick's relatives and verify that they still lived in the area, he could track down any properties they might own and scope them out.

As he considered everything, he was certain of one thing: Forty-eight hours from now he'd be a million dollars richer.

The smell of the cheap spray-in hair color was strong, but it was all Mick could manage in the short time between the call to Liliana and her announcement that she had arranged for Caterina's much-needed therapy.

He pulled the Jeep up to the back door to the hospital. Liliana was waiting there with a gurney for Caterina. She didn't need it, but with the change of hair color and a blanket strategically obscuring part of Caterina's face, it was possible she wouldn't be noticed as they wheeled her through the hospital corridors.

He only hoped his sister and whoever was helping her wouldn't be punished for their assistance with the therapy.

He helped Caterina to the door and got her settled on the gurney.

"We'll be on the third floor. Room 303," Liliana said. The faster they got the procedure going, the more they lessened the risk of discovery.

Mick leaned down and tucked the blanket up around Caterina's neck, covered part of her face and dropped a swift kiss on her cheek. "I'm going to park the car. I'll just be a few minutes. Hang in there."

Caterina nodded weakly and said, "I'm fine."

She watched him race out the door and met Liliana's concerned gaze.

"So how are you really feeling?" Liliana asked.

"Hot. My joints ache and I have pain here," she said and covered her midsection in the spot right between where her ribs ended.

Liliana eased her hand beneath Caterina's. Pressed slightly, causing Caterina to moan from the pressure.

"It could be your spleen. It probably can't handle all the stress your system is in."

Liliana walked to the foot of the gurney, bent, and pushed with all her might. The gurney slid against the polished hospital floor and then began to roll with her guiding it from behind. The *ding* as they approached the elevator bank was welcome, and they were soon on their way up.

Caterina closed her eyes and tried to ignore the assorted aches and pains in her body and the intense heat. When the gurney rolled to a stop, she opened her eyes.

Liliana was at her side with another young Latina in a light blue scrub suit. "This is Dr. Rojas. She's a fellow doctor and a friend. She can be trusted."

"Thank you," Caterina said and the young woman nodded.

Dr. Rojas walked up to Caterina and held up a syringe connected to a long section of tubing. There was something familiar about it, and in the back of her brain Caterina realized she had seen something similar while in Wardwell's care.

"We need to put one needle in each arm. We'll also be giving you an IV with citrate to avoid coagulation while we're processing your blood. That may interfere with your clotting for the next twenty-four hours, so try to avoid any strenuous activities and watch for excessive bruising."

Caterina nodded and winced as the woman pierced a vein in her arm with the needle. The young doctor walked around and did the same in the other arm. As she did so she commented, "I see you've had this done before, and often, so you know this may take about two hours. Close your eyes and get some rest."

Dr. Rojas patted her arm, the action slightly mechanical and stilted. She slipped a device over Caterina's finger, and a machine a couple of feet away kicked to life.

"Thank you," Caterina said and did as instructed, knowing rest was essential to rebuilding her strength.

Liliana approached her friend and clapped her on the back as she turned on the plasmapheresis unit. "That wasn't so bad now, was it?"

"Dead people are easier to handle," Carmen teased while keeping her eye on the equipment to make sure it was working properly.

"Easier, but not as rewarding, *amiga*."

A knock came at the door and Liliana walked over. She opened it to admit her brother, who scrutinized Caterina as she lay on the gurney, tubes running out of her arms and wires leading to the pulse oximeter that was keeping track of her heartbeat and the oxygen saturation in her blood.

"She'll be okay, Mick. We'll be extracting the remnants of the cell lysis and antibodies plus adding some sterile plasma substitutes to help stabilize her," Liliana said.

Mick glanced at Carmen and held out his hand. "Mick Carrera. Liliana's—"

"Brother," her friend said as she shyly peered up at him. "I've heard a lot about you from Liliana."

As he arched a brow, Carmen quickly confirmed, "All good things."

"*Gracias.* I appreciate you helping us," Mick replied.

Carmen nervously half-glanced at Liliana. "I know Liliana wouldn't ask unless this was an emergency."

"It is. You're helping save her life," Mick said.

Carmen nodded and faced Liliana. "I need to return to the lab, but I'll check back in about an hour."

Her friend left the room and Mick walked over to Liliana and hugged her. *"Gracias, hermanita."*

Liliana returned the embrace, and then went to where Caterina was resting on the gurney. She laid her hand over Caterina's, waking her.

"How are you feeling?"

Caterina offered up a weak smile. "A little dizzy and my fingertips are numb."

Liliana squeezed her hand. "That's normal, but I'm going to check your blood pressure just in case."

Mick came to Caterina's side and laced his fingers with

hers. The smile Caterina offered him was brighter and there was a look in her eyes that Liliana couldn't fail to notice.

Caterina was in love with her brother, she thought as she wheeled over the blood pressure machine. As she wrapped the cuff around Caterina's arm, she half-looked at her brother as he stood by the gurney.

She couldn't miss the look in his eyes, either.

Mick had feelings for Caterina. She couldn't say love feelings because she wasn't sure she'd ever seen her brother truly in love. But she was sure that was more than a we're-having-great-sex kind of look.

Which was so not good, Liliana thought as the blood pressure machine kicked to life, inflating the cuff and then shuddering and deflating it to calculate the blood pressure. As much as she liked Caterina, and as much as she'd love for her brother to settle down, nothing would be easy about this relationship.

"Your pressure is on the low side of normal, which is typical for this treatment. It'll stabilize in a few hours," Liliana said, inclined her head, and nodded to get her brother to meet her at the far side of the room.

Mick reluctantly left Caterina, and the anxious look on his face only confirmed Liliana's earlier observation.

"She's okay, right?" he whispered.

Okay was not a word Liliana could use considering Caterina's condition. She didn't want to shatter her brother's illusions, but he seemed to need a reality check. "She'll be better. For a little while. Until she'll need another dose of the inhibitor drug and this starts all over again. And then when you run out of the inhibitor drug…"

Mick tensed beside her. "Sounds like you're warning me off, *hermanita*."

"Just being realistic 'cause I know you, bro. You brought home strays and saved the day, but this is a situation where you may not be able to make it better."

A muscle twitched along the hard line of Mick's jaw as he clenched his teeth. "Duly noted. When can I take her home?"

Liliana glanced at her watch. "To be most effective, I'd like to let this run for at least another hour and a half."

"You're on duty, right?" he said and she couldn't fail to grasp his real meaning.

"You want me gone," she said, wondering if it was because he was angry with her about her comments.

Mick must have sensed her concern because he explained his request. "The less you're involved here, the better."

It might be a little too late to curtail her involvement, but Liliana understood his apprehension. "Call me on the cell if you need me. Otherwise I'll be back to help you get Caterina home."

He hugged her hard and whispered, "Don't worry about me, Liliana. I know what I'm doing."

She embraced him and as always, marveled at the sense of safety and strength she felt in his arms. He had always been the protector in the family. Always the hero who had come through for them.

It was why he deserved some happiness in his life.

She pulled away from him and looked at Caterina as she lay on the gurney. She knew there might not be a happy ending there.

She only hoped her brother was wise enough to realize it as well, before it was too late.

CHAPTER 32

Mick had managed to get Caterina home in the late morning with little fanfare.

She now lay tucked in bed, resting. Calls to Ramon and Franklin had yielded only the reassurance that nothing was happening. Yet.

He dialed his parents' number and his mother answered.

"*Hola, mi'jito.* How is your *amiga*?"

"She's doing fine, *mami.*" He hesitated, unsure of just how to broach his request, but then plowed ahead. "I need to ask a favor, *mami.*"

"Of course, *mi'jito.* What can I do? A nice *sopa de pollo*? Or maybe some *arroz con leche* to sit easy on her stomach," she offered.

He smiled. His mother always thought the world's problems could be cured with the right dish of food. "Actually, *mami*, I need you, *papi*, and Tony to close the restaurant for a few days. Maybe take a vacation somewhere. I'll pay for it."

"Close the restaurant?" Her disbelief escalated with each word, as if he had just asked her to shut down the Pentagon.

"It's important, *mami*, or I wouldn't ask."

"*Pero, mi'jito*, we can't just shut down. What about our employees and our customers? What about Tony's classes—"

"You take vacations, *mami*. You visited *abuelita* last year, remember?" he chided, wishing that his mother wasn't turning such a simple request into a battle. He didn't want to tell her the real reason for the request. That would only create more of a problem.

A long silence filled the line before his mother said, "Is it that important, *mi'jo*?"

"It is and don't ask me why. *Por favor*. Just close up as soon as you can and—"

"We'll do it, but if you need us—"

"If I need you, I'll call, *mami*," he finished, eager to have them out of harm's way.

"*Mi'jo...cuida tu corazon*."

"Don't worry about my heart. It'll be fine," he said and bid his mother goodbye again.

He leaned back in his chair, considered both his mother's and Liliana's warnings. Decided to ignore them. He didn't know what was happening with Caterina, but he knew he had to see it to its conclusion.

He flew out of the chair and went to the guest room.

Caterina was curled up on her side, seemingly asleep, but as Mick took the first step into the room, she opened her eyes. He sat on the edge of the chair, his elbows resting on his knees. Fingers laced together as his hands hung loosely before him.

"How are you feeling?" he asked.

"Much better."

In truth, he probably hadn't needed to ask. The skin on

her face no longer had the flushed fever look and her voice was strong.

"I heard what Liliana said to you. She's right, you know. This may be a lose-lose situation."

Anger rose sharply in him. "You didn't strike me as a quitter."

She sat up, holding the sheet against her body to hide her nakedness. "Just being realistic, Mick."

He leaned forward and cupped her cheek. The skin was smooth, the temperature of it sleep-warm. He met her gaze and caressed the line of her cheek with the pad of his thumb. "Why don't you let me decide what's realistic?"

Caterina laughed harshly and shook her head. "I never liked it when my dad made decisions for me. What makes you think—"

He leaned forward and silenced her with a kiss. Kept on kissing her until she dropped her hold on the sheet and brought her hands up to his shoulders.

By the time they broke apart, they were both breathing heavily.

Mick laid his forehead against hers and said, "That's what makes me think this is worth a try. This feeling that I can't just ignore."

When his gaze met hers, the blue of her eyes was as dark as the ocean at night and shimmering with unshed tears.

"Come to bed. You need to rest," she said.

He nodded and toed off his shoes, but slipped in beside her fully clothed, unwilling to waste even a moment before he was next to her.

Enveloping her in his arms, he pulled her tight to him until every inch of their bodies was pressed together. Her heart beat against his, strong and steady. Her head was tucked beneath his chin, the silk of her hair soft beneath his cheek. The warmth of her breath spilled against his throat.

A sense of homecoming he had not experienced with any other woman calmed his warrior's restless soul. Peace filled his heart.

Much as he had battled for country and family, he knew as he held her that he would fight for her.

For them.

And this was one battle he did not intend to lose.

Caterina woke him with the gentle whisper of her lips against his. Invited him to join with her.

"Are you sure?" Mick asked, his voice husky from sleep.

"I'm sure," she replied. So that there would be no doubt about it, she grabbed the hem of the T-shirt he wore and made short work of pulling it off his body.

She pressed against him, warm skin against skin. The hard tips of her breasts brushing the smooth flesh of his chest as they kissed over and over. Beside the soft flatness of her belly, his erection jerked to life and began to harden.

Laying her hand over him, she caressed the shape of him beneath the denim and he groaned into her mouth, reached down and undid his jeans.

The hard length of him sprang forward and she encircled him with one hand, stroking him. Urging him onward as he cupped her breasts and teased her nipples with his hands, drawing a pleased sigh from her.

"Make love to me," he said and sat up against the headboard. He urged her over him with the gentle grasp of her hips and she needed no further invitation.

She held onto Mick's shoulders and sank down onto him, gasping as the length and width of him filled her. As the comfort of his arms surrounded her and drew her near until she was tight against his chest.

She couldn't move, overwhelmed as she was by the sense of unity in his arms. With her possession of him.

She sucked in another rough breath and trembled in his arms, but his body echoed the movement with a sympathetic shudder.

"When I'm with you... it's like my soul is filled with music," she said. He cradled her face in his hands and tenderly brushed his lips across hers before moving them to her cheeks and then to her forehead.

"It's special for me, too," he whispered, the words so soft she thought she might have imagined them until she met his gaze and it confirmed his sentiment.

"Very special," she responded, earning a smile from him which she kissed, memorizing the feel of it against her lips as a talisman for what would be the hard days to come.

He returned the kiss and then she moved on him, offering herself up to him. Accepting what he offered in return.

As a climax ripped through her and pulled him along to his own release, she held him close and realized there was no lose-lose in his arms.

Caterina vowed to battle beside him so that she might have more time to spend with him. She'd waited too long to find something as fulfilling as this was with him and she wasn't about to give it up now without a fight.

CHAPTER 33

Forty hours to go, Mad Dog thought as he drove east on the expressway. Bradley Beach was less than two hours away from the hotel in Philly where he had set up his base camp. The town wasn't far off the Garden State Parkway. It consisted of a quaint Main Street lined with bakeries, restaurants, and the occasional ice cream parlor.

The library was a few blocks off Main in a redbrick building on a well-maintained plot of land. The walk to the large wooden doors situated beneath an ornate portico was lined with deep green low-growing plants. He parked around the corner from the library on a quiet residential street, walked to the library, and entered.

A perky young teenager manned the checkout desk inside. He didn't approach at first, scoping out the interior of the library and the number of patrons within.

You never knew when you'd have to start shooting.

Satisfied that no one presented an immediate threat, he approached the teen, eliciting a cheery reaction from her.

"May I help you?" she asked as she stamped a date onto a card and slipped it into a sleeve in a book that she returned to the patron by the desk.

"I have an old friend in the area, but can't remember

how to spell his last name, so I can get an address for him. I know he attended the local high school and I was hoping you would have some yearbooks I could search."

"What year was he? Maybe I know him?" she said, but Mad Dog shook his head.

"He's a lot older, but he had a younger brother not much older than you—Antonio Carrera," he advised, and the young girl's tweezed eyebrows narrowed as she mulled over the name.

"Sounds familiar, but I can't say I know him. Maybe Bill would, though. He's been around forever."

She walked to a wall at the back of the desk area and then around behind it. He heard the murmur of voices and seconds later the young woman returned with an older man in tow who had an ex-military look.

He wore a dark blue security guard's uniform and was brushing off some crumbs from it, probably because the young girl had interrupted him during a break.

The man could be a problem, he thought, but kept a neutral look on his face.

The security guard eyeballed him up and down before asking, "What can I do for you?"

"Looking for an old Army buddy. Last name is Carrera."

Mad Dog noticed the *Semper Fi* tattoo on the older man's forearm. The ex-Marine squinted at him and then shot him a curious look once again. "You're not from around here, are you?"

"No, sir," he answered with military precision. "From the Boston area, sir. Just came to win some money down in Atlantic City, but figured I'd drop by to see my friend."

Seemingly satisfied with the answer, the grizzled

ex-Marine motioned with a gnarled finger toward the back of the library.

"Phone books, yearbooks, and Little League directories are all in the reference area. You might find what you need back there."

He thanked the man and headed to the back, where another helpful librarian handed him a couple of yearbooks based on the dates Mad Dog had found for Antonio Carrera. He hit paydirt in the second yearbook, which had a picture of Antonio in his suit and tie. The young man was a dead ringer for his old friend Mick. Probably a younger brother.

As he flipped through the pages of the yearbook, he realized that Antonio had been on not only the lacrosse and football teams, but also the baseball team.

Assuming that the younger Carrera might have played on a Little League team, he asked the librarian for the directories, but as she was handing them over she said, "I'm assuming you found your friend in the yearbook."

"I did. I was hoping to track down his address," he said, since his searches on the Internet the night before had not yielded any phone listings for the Carreras.

"Do you know what year your friend played?" she said.

"Actually, I found his brother in the yearbook— Antonio Carrera," he replied, and a broad smile erupted on the librarian's face.

"You should have mentioned his name to me earlier. I can tell you where you can find Tony," the librarian said.

Mad Dog smiled.

At noon on the nose Edwards dialed the number Carrera had given him. The mercenary answered on the second ring and his voice projected into the room via the speaker-phone.

"Dr. Edwards."

Edwards glanced at Ricardo Morales. The other scientist sat across from him, his face expressionless as Edwards said, "Mad Dog was here to see Ricardo Morales. He's a geneticist with our company."

A long pause followed his statement before Carrera said, "A geneticist? You expect me to believe that this scientist is the one responsible for—"

"He's been working with Wells for at least a decade. I suspect the two of them developed the plan to experiment on the terminal patients. After all, who would miss them?"

"You son of a bitch—"

"Not me, Mr. Carrera. As I said, it was Wells and Morales," he urged.

"Where is Morales now?"

Edwards smiled and looked across at Morales as he said, "Long gone, along with the remaining patients in the program."

Patients and a genetic engineering process that might be worth a great deal more than the one hundred million and options he stood to gain from the Gates deal. Of course, if Mad Dog did the job for which Morales had hired him, Edwards could have his cake and eat it, too.

"I'd get a lawyer, Dr. Edwards, because you're not going to be able to hide behind Wells and Morales for long," Carrera warned and the line went dead.

Edwards calmly pressed the button to shut off the speakerphone. "We have to eliminate Carrera, Ricardo."

Morales shrugged. "I'll put my money on Mad Dog successfully completing that assignment."

"You did put your money on it," he reminded the geneticist.

The other man laughed and said, "Luckily there's a lot more where that came from. My partners are quite excited about the possibilities for the process."

Edwards could well imagine that—genetically enhanced warriors and assassins would fetch a high price.

"What if Mad Dog fails?" Edwards asked, picking up a gold pen from his desk and nervously tipping it over and over again on his blotter.

"There's Santiago and now Bradford. Either one can tear apart Shaw or her would-be hero."

"If we can get to Carrera and Shaw before they reach the authorities," Edwards replied, dropping the gold pen to the desk's surface.

"And what if they do reach the police? Shaw's time is limited even with treatment and from what I understand her protector's reputation is dubious at best."

Not all that dubious, Edwards thought, but didn't say. If the house of cards started to collapse, he wanted to be able to extricate himself before it fell in on him. "We need a contingency plan that isn't all death and destruction."

"Not to worry. There's enough money in a Swiss account if we need to disappear, and my friends have promised a great deal more based on what they've seen," Morales replied. He rose from his chair, smoothing the lines of his expensive silk suit as he did so.

He looked more like a drug lord than a geneticist, Edwards thought with distaste.

"Let's hope that won't be necessary," Edwards said.

*   *   *

It had been easier than Mad Dog could have imagined.

No need for any extensive searches, since the librarian had immediately recognized the Carrera name. Antonio was the youngest in the family and worked at a Mexican restaurant owned by his parents. It was apparently a local institution.

The librarian had also confirmed that Mick was the eldest and that there were two younger sisters—one serving in Iraq, the other a local doctor. The very helpful librarian had even provided the name of the hospital where the one sister worked.

Mad Dog had done some reconnoitering in the late afternoon, only to discover that a family emergency had resulted in an unanticipated closure of the restaurant earlier in the day. Luckily one of the workers had failed to get the message and had been loitering at the door when he arrived.

Twenty bucks later, the worker had confirmed that the eldest Carrera son—Mick—was probably in the area. The man had no idea where Mick lived, but had overheard one of the parents speaking about Mick recently and that his mother had left with a large delivery of food days earlier. Since she didn't normally make deliveries, the worker had assumed the food was for a family member.

Armed with that information, Mad Dog had gone back to his car and powered up his laptop and broadband card. An hour later, he had the address for the hospital where Dr. Liliana Carrera worked and a photo of her from a brochure the hospital had made up for a recent gala.

Dr. Carrera was a pretty woman. Attractive enough to do. He might even keep her for some fun after using her as bait to draw in her brother and Shaw.

The thought of doing both the Carrera woman and Shaw made him hard. It was a shame that they'd soon both be dead.

By early evening Mad Dog had a solid lay of the land and an escape route in case things went sour. Last, but not least, he had done some additional investigations and decided where to take Dr. Carrera and Shaw for his entertainment and after, where to dispose of their bodies.

Now all that was left was to put his plan into action.

Liliana had heard the relief in Mick's voice when she had called earlier. The treatment had worked and Caterina was feeling better. Their parents and younger brother, Tony, had closed the restaurant and driven off to a much-needed vacation to visit family in Chicago.

These developments had imbued her with a second round of energy. Enough to let her finish the last few hours of her shift with a spring in her step.

The only troubling aspect of her shift had been the occasional sightings of Harrison, who seemed to have gone into stalker mode. However, looking at the bright side of things, at least stalker mode meant he was keeping his distance.

As Mick had warned her to be vigilant, she carefully scoped out the hospital parking lot before heading to her car. In the early morning hours, there was little activity and the path to her vehicle was well-lit and empty.

With a relieved sigh, she gripped her keys firmly. As

she hurried to her car, a big SUV came screeching through the parking lot and jerked to a stop in front of the entrance to the emergency room.

The driver's-side door flew open, and a man came around the front of the car.

His shirtfront was covered in blood and as he noticed her, he rushed over and said, "You've got to help me. My son had an accident."

She'd seen parents like this before, eyes wild with concern, so she let him guide her back to the SUV.

"Calm down, sir," she said and walked beside him to the back of the car, intent on helping them into the emergency room where someone could take care of them.

"He was partying with some friends and hit his head. There's so much blood," the man said, his actions jerky. Voice tight with emotion.

At the back of the SUV, he pulled open one of the doors and said, "He's back here. I'm afraid to move him."

Liliana brushed past the agitated man to get a look at his son, but the rear of the car was empty.

Before she could turn to face the man, a sharp sting came against her arm, and suddenly all her body functions seemed to be scrambled. She battled the sensation, realizing that this might be the man Mick had warned her about.

He was on her immediately, encircling her in his arms. Even in her weakened state, she tried to fight him, rocking back and forth to loosen his grip on her. Slamming her heel into his instep and earning a pained grunt.

Another sharp blast came, this time at the side of her neck. Her body bucked from the force of it and her knees gave way, nearly upending both of them. Yet she continued to struggle, knowing that one of the hospital security guards could only be yards away at the entrance to the emergency room.

Her assailant cursed at her continued resistance and pounded her body against the back door of the SUV as her vision began to fade.

Then another jolt of electricity surged through her system and plunged her into blackness.

The chirp of his phone roused Mick from the peaceful bliss of her arms. Not an alarm, but a phone call; he knew from the ring.

Franklin's number flashed on the cell phone screen.

"What's up?" Mick said sleepily, easing an arm around Caterina's back to keep her close.

She sighed and laid her thigh over his legs, tucked herself tighter against his side, still half-asleep.

"Got some news from a friend down in the Camden PD that you might want to hear."

Instantly alert, he tried to keep his body neutral, but Caterina must have sensed the change, since she sat up so she could watch his face.

With the peace shattered, he sat up in bed also, but once again wrapped his arm around her to urge her to his side. "Good news, I hope."

"Maybe," Franklin said and filled Mick in on all that he had gotten from his police department informant.

"Thanks. Let me know if anything else comes of it," he said and hung up.

"Something important?" Caterina asked, glancing up at him, her eyes wide and trusting.

He nodded and filled her in on the news from Franklin. "The lab boys down in Camden were able to get DNA samples from two different people off the stake that killed Wells."

"Two?" she asked, scrunching up her brows as she said it. "I remembered two men fighting before I found Dr. Wells. It could be their DNA, so that's good, right?"

He knew what she hoped—some evidence would be found that would clear her of any wrongdoing. He hated to shatter her hope.

"The lab boys didn't know what to make of the DNA samples. Too many irregularities, which led them to believe the samples were either corrupt or contaminated and therefore unreliable."

Her shoulders slumped and she seemed to disappear right before his eyes. In a way she had, since her upset triggered another response, this one more immediate than the others before them.

She realized it almost instantly and held up her hands, examining their blue state against the blue of the sheets. "Corrupt like me. Contaminated like I am."

He took hold of her hand and cradled her cheek. Gently urged her face upward. "It's flesh and bone. Nothing more. It's not who you are inside."

She sucked in an uncertain breath, her body trembling beneath his touch, and suddenly she was back to normal and in control.

"Science sinned against me. Violated my flesh and bone. This isn't what I am, only... When body and soul unite, what will I be?"

"There's got to be a way to handle this," he said, trying to calm her.

"There is no way to stop it, Mick. We can't stop whatever is going on in my body."

Surprise filled him that she was talking about a "we" even as worry took root. It was only a matter of time . before they would have to administer the inhibitor drug again. Have her suffer through the fevers before undergoing another round of plasmapheresis to cleanse her blood.

But she was right that it wouldn't stop what was happening in her body. With each cycle of replication, the experimental gene fragments implanted themselves more firmly in her native DNA.

He wouldn't wonder about that. About what would be the eventual outcome of the constant battle raging between the cells that made her human and those implanted in her by Wardwell.

Instead he pulled her close and whispered, "*We* will handle this. *We* will find out what to do."

She nodded, a small smile coming to her lips with his words and he bent his head and kissed her.

Another chirp of his cell phone registered as he opened his mouth against hers, only this time he sprang into action, grabbing his Glock from the nightstand drawer and racing to his office.

Caterina followed behind and arrived just in time to see what had tripped the first of the warning alarms.

The video feed on his laptop showed a small bag sitting on the path to his front door.

"What is it?" she asked.

"Don't know," he said and rewound the stored video to show the bag flying through the air from a passing car. A big black SUV was racing away. The video also showed that Liliana's car was not parked in front of the house as it should have been.

Mick replied, "Liliana should have been home from her shift by now."

He bolted from the room and Caterina followed. In the guest bedroom he had already put on his jeans. She grabbed a robe, slipped it on as she followed him down the stairs. Neither of them stated the obvious—Liliana wasn't in Mick's bedroom nor was she anywhere on the main floor of the house.

Mick disarmed the alarm, but before he walked out, he pointed to a round red button on the wall opposite the door. "If anything happens with that bag on the path, you lock up and hit that panic button."

Then he tucked his gun into the waistband of his jeans, walked down the path, and picked up the bag.

CHAPTER 34

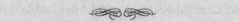

Nothing happened. At least not right away.

Caterina watched as Mick opened the bag and then seemed to crumple before her eyes. His shoulders sagged and his head dropped down. He turned and slowly walked back up the path, the bag in his hands. When he entered, he shut the door and reset the alarm calmly, but tension vibrated throughout his body.

"Mick, what happened?" she asked and laid a hand on his arm.

He reached into what appeared to be a plain brown paper bag and extracted a set of keys, a cell phone, and a note.

She didn't need to guess whose keys, and the cell phone looked familiar. The message on the note was simple but dangerous: *Wait for my call.*

"Liliana—" she began, but Mick went into action, bolting up the stairs to his office.

By the time Caterina caught up to him, he had rewound the video before the moment when the bag had flown out of the SUV. He finally stopped the rewind and played the video.

At first there was nothing, but then the SUV came into

view. It slowed before the house and the passenger side window lowered, allowing them a glimpse of Mad Dog.

Mick gazed up at her, anguish on every line of his face. She wrapped her arms around his shoulders and pulled him close. Cradled his head against her and laid her head against his.

"We'll handle this. We'll figure out what to do," she said, echoing his earlier words and taking solace in his reply.

"We will."

Liliana woke to incomplete darkness and the odors of wet dirt and mildew.

Forcing herself to concentrate only intensified the steady throb in the middle of her skull, but she fought it back. Slowly the shadows took shape. Walls made of either stone or cement were wet with seeping water that puddled here and there on cracked floors littered with sand and debris. Somewhere ahead of her there appeared to be a tunnel of some kind that leaked in indistinct light, allowing her the limited glimpses of where she was being held.

From the tunnel also came the susurrus of distant waves and the occasional raucous cry of a seagull.

She was somewhere near the ocean.

But where?

She racked her brain for an idea of where there might be tunnels or sufficient mounds of earth to create a holding pen such as the one she was in.

The Highlands? Cheesequake? Sandy Hook? she wondered. A figure emerged from the shadows, his silhouette limned by the light from the tunnel.

"About time you woke up," he said with some irritation and approached her.

She guessed him to be a couple of inches over six feet, as tall as Mick, but not as lean. Mid-thirties with a face which bore signs of a hard life. A noticeable scar at the edge of his lip and another that cut across one brow. A number of bruises, as well as a relatively fresh scrape, across one cheek.

"Mick kicked your ass good, didn't he?" Liliana said.

He slapped her hard across the face, rocking her head to rebound against the high back of the chair on which she sat. Warmth trickled down the side of her mouth and the coppery taste of blood filled her mouth, but she couldn't do much about wiping it away. Her hands were duct-taped to the arms of the chair. She tried to move her legs, but it was impossible. The pressure at her ankles confirmed he had bound her there as well.

"Mouthy for someone in your position," he said, and she detected a nasally tone in his speech. A New Englander, she guessed, not that such information was useful. So she asked him, "And what position would that be?"

"Soon to be dead meat, but not before we have some fun."

He crouched before her and the minimal light in the room glinted off something very shiny and very sharp.

She controlled the urge to flinch as he brought a long, thin knife close to her chest. He eased it beneath the edges of her shirtfront and with a quick flick of his wrist, cut off a button.

She stared straight ahead, refusing to acknowledge his actions, but it was impossible not to feel the release of the fabric as each button came loose and her shirtfront parted.

The damp air chilled her skin as he pulled apart the edges of her shirt. The knife blade was even colder as he slid it beneath the straps of her bra and sliced through them.

"Beautiful," he said as he dragged down the bra to expose her breasts.

She focused her gaze on the wall in front of her, but couldn't control the shudder that racked her body as the chill in the air and coolness of the knife's metal registered.

"Cold?" he asked and shifted the knife across her skin, but made no other motion to touch her.

"You're a sick bastard," she said through gritted teeth.

He leaned close to her, a twisted smile on his face.

"Sweetheart, we haven't even gotten started."

Mick knew Mad Dog well enough to know he would run to ground somewhere nearby, unwilling to risk having Liliana out in public for too long. Which meant there were only a few places he might have found to hide out. Somewhere back near Wardwell in the Pine Barrens. Maybe even where Edwards and his partner had taken the remaining gene therapy patients.

There were some other hiding areas by the Twin Lights in the Highlands, but more possible locations in Fort Hancock. Even with the many battery areas which had been opened for public tours, there remained a large number of tunnels and ammo storage areas in which to hide. Unfortunately, they were the more dilapidated areas and risky to navigate due to their deteriorating conditions.

But that was where he might go if he had to hide someone for any length of time.

Liliana's cell phone sat on the desk before him. Silent.

Mad Dog was nothing if not predictable. He'd call and offer Liliana in exchange for Caterina. Make him bring Caterina to him and then try to take them all out so he could walk away without leaving behind any witnesses. Collect whatever bounty Edwards and his partners had placed on Caterina's head.

Too bad he intended to mess up Mad Dog's plans.

He picked up his cell phone and dialed Edwards. Annoyance filled the other man's voice as he answered.

"What now, Mr. Carrera? I already gave you—"

"Mad Dog grabbed my sister."

An exasperated sigh sounded across the line. "As I told you before, I have nothing to do with this Mad Dog fellow."

Mick didn't believe that for a moment. "You better pray I find my sister safe and sound, Dr. Edwards."

He didn't wait for Edwards's reply.

When he looked up, Caterina was at the door, worry etched onto her features. "Have you heard anything?"

He shook his head, concern gnawing at him. Mad Dog treated his captives like a cat with a mouse. He liked to play with them first. His gut tightened at the thought of what Mad Dog might be doing with his sister, driving him to his feet.

"I need to find them. I can't just sit here and do nothing."

"Mad Dog said to wait for his call. I'm sure—"

"He's probably hurting her. That's his M.O.," Mick said, driving an agitated hand through his hair as he paced before her.

Caterina walked to his side and laid a hand on his arm. "He's got the advantage right now."

"I think I know where he is," he said.

"And what will you do? Go off half-cocked? Even if you're willing to risk your life, what about Liliana? What if Mad Dog has involved anyone else?"

Mick thought about what Mad Dog might be doing to Liliana, but then forced aside such thoughts. He had to keep emotion out of it to stay logical and in control.

"You're right, Cat. Mad Dog will call when he has everything just like he wants it."

Caterina embraced him. "I'm sorry. I know this is all my fault."

He shifted away from her and took hold of her arms, his touch gentle as he attempted to reassure her. "This is not your fault at all."

She tapped the center of her chest with her fingers. "He wants *me*. Just *me*. I'm willing to go to save Liliana."

He wagged his head in chastisement. "Do you really think Mad Dog or his bosses are content to let any of us live?"

With a sad shake of her head, she said, "No. There's too much money involved to allow that."

He dug his hand into her hair and cradled the back of her head. "Trust me. I suspect where he might have taken her."

"Where?" she asked, but Mick shook his head.

"Fort Hancock probably. Right now we sit tight until we hear from Mad Dog. If I'm right, we'll wait until it's dark to go to him. I need cover to approach and have any hope of saving Liliana. Then I'll head there."

"We'll go together," she insisted.

"No," he replied curtly. "The tunnels are risky even during the day. At dark they're treacherous and I need to have the benefit of surprise on my side."

Liliana's cell phone chimed, the ring tone overly loud and excessively cheerful.

As Mick answered, he hit the speakerphone button so Caterina could also hear what Mad Dog had to say.

"You there, Carrera?" Mad Dog asked.

Mick kept his tone neutral as he asked, "Where is she, Mad Dog?"

"I've got someone who wants to say hello," the other man said, but silence followed for long seconds before the muffled noise of what sounded like a slap pierced the quiet.

Mad Dog warned, "Speak up, bitch," before the sound of another louder slap filled the line.

Mick clenched his fists and Caterina covered his hand with hers, offering support while they waited.

Finally Liliana weakly said, "I'm okay, Mick."

Mad Dog's harsh chuckle followed. "Bitch is stubborn. She's just making it harder for herself."

"You're a dead man, Mad Dog—"

"Let's get this over with, Carrera. You know what I want. Shaw in exchange for your sister."

Mick met Caterina's gaze. Determination filled her gaze as he said to Mad Dog, "When? Where?"

"Midnight at Fort Hancock. Tunnel off the second set of battery buildings. Follow what's left of the paths for the old Nike missile tracks until you reach the ammo storage area. We'll be waiting for you."

Before Mick could say another word, the line went dead.

Caterina squeezed his hand gently and asked, "Do you think he's telling the truth?"

"About where he is? It's where I thought he would go to hide," he admitted, but quickly added, "But he doesn't plan on making an exchange. He'll probably lay out a trap or two somewhere along the tunnels to take us out long before we reach Liliana."

She shuddered against him and her color paled. "I want to go with you." Mick twined his fingers with hers and seemed to be considering her request. Finally he said, "I suspect you won't be left behind no matter what I say. So I guess we need to be ready for whatever Mad Dog throws at us."

"What about Liliana? Will he—"

"Kill her? Not until he's sure we're out of the way. She's his insurance."

Caterina leaned against him. Against his rock-solid strength. He picked up his hand and splayed it across her back, urging her even closer.

She wanted to apologize again for all the trouble she had brought him and his family, but understood that he didn't hold her responsible. It didn't make it any easier to consider that his sister might die because of her. That either of them might die later that night.

Because of what Edwards and his people had done.

Because of plain old greed.

Caterina looked up at him. "We can't let Edwards get away with this. Someone needs to know what he did. Someone has to find the other patients who were being treated. Some of them were my friends."

As Mick met her gaze, he must have realized what she was thinking—that if they both died tonight, their secrets died with them. The sins Edwards and the others had committed would go unpunished.

With a certainty she couldn't muster, he said, "You and I are going to see to it that Edwards is punished and the other patients are set free. I promise you that."

From what Caterina knew of him, she knew he meant to keep his word, but with a man like Mad Dog to fight...

"How can you be so certain?"

A cheerless smile crept onto his features and he cradled her cheek, a slight tremble in his hand. "Because I'd die before seeing any more hurt come to you or Liliana."

With a nod, she burrowed against him, hoping that was one promise he wouldn't have to keep.

CHAPTER 35

Edwards sat staring at the phone long minutes after the call from Carrera.

If he had been a praying man, he might have done as Carrera had suggested and start asking a higher authority for some answer to the problems with which he was faced.

But he wasn't a religious man, although some might have said he worshipped at the temple of science.

Leaning back in his chair, he tapped a finger against his lips, pondering how it was that this had become so complicated. How it had gone from being a brilliant scientific idea to the serial violations and terminations of various patients and Rudy Wells?

Of course Wells had always been the weakest link in the whole complicated chain, he thought. From the beginning Wells had shown more compassion for the patients than was healthy. As a scientist one had to disassociate oneself from the experiment, and Wells had failed miserably, getting too emotionally involved.

Wells's humanity had been his downfall.

Morales had seen that weakness in Wells immediately. He had expressed his concerns to Edwards when their partner had started to get balky about the introduction of the additional DNA strands into the patients' therapies.

In truth, Edwards had been more interested in the science of what would occur than any possible financial gain. It had been Morales who had seen the economic potential of the ultimate genetically modified organism—a human GMO altered for whatever your need and under total control.

Too bad Morales had complicated everything by having Wells killed before the completion of the Gates Genengineering merger, and now by hiring a psycho to take care of Shaw.

Morales needed to know what was going on. He picked up the phone and dialed, but the call went to voice mail.

"Call me," was all he said.

Edwards set the phone back in its cradle and once again considered what Carrera had told him. If Mad Dog succeeded, there would be no more worries, but he had hired Carrera because of his reputation for success.

He couldn't take a chance that this was the one time Carrera would fail.

Swiveling his chair to face his computer, Edwards accessed his assorted accounts as well as those of Wardwell and reviewed the various financial records. Then he began transferring money to a number of his private overseas accounts. He was in the process of shifting cash to one of the banks when he realized there was already a rather large sum of money in the account. More money than he recalled being there.

He was about to access the transaction log when his phone rang. He would have ignored it, but the caller ID indicated it was Morales.

With a quick glance at his watch that showed that nearly an hour had gone by, he said, "It's about time you called."

Morales chuckled, clearly unfazed by his anger. Never a good sign when an underling didn't respect you, Edwards thought. "Well? Where were you?" he insisted.

"Transferring one of our GMOs."

Transferring one of the patients? "What are you talking about?"

"Someone needed a way to deliver a bomb into a secure facility. Shaw's genetic twin was the answer to their problem," Morales advised. He spoke as calmly as if he were ordering take-out.

"You sold one of the patients?" Edwards asked in disbelief, even though he had come to understand that was the ultimate goal of his partnership with Morales.

"Check your account. I deposited half of the payment there this morning."

He didn't need to check. He now had his answer about the extra money. Morales had put the other woman who had been implanted with the same gene fragments as Shaw on the market. A woman who had been much more malleable, both mentally and physically, than the prickly cellist.

"What if she's discovered? What if—"

"It's a one-way mission. The bomb will take care of her no matter what."

Several million for a disposable GMO.

More than Edwards had expected, but there was still the problem of Mad Dog.

"Your mercenary has taken Carrera's sister hostage. The body count may get too high on this project."

Morales laughed once again, much more wickedly than before.

"I wouldn't worry, Raymond. I've got it all under control."

Morales hung up. The second time someone had hung up on him that day.

He didn't much care for it. Didn't much care for Morales calling him by his given name. It was downright disrespectful, and he intended to set Morales straight about it.

But first he had to finish transferring funds. After that, he would make sure to gather everything he needed to protect himself regardless of whether Carrera or Mad Dog was victorious.

Edwards had seen what Morales had done to Wells.

He had no doubt the little pimp would do the same to him unless he had some insurance.

Mick had spent hours preparing both of them for that night's mission, reviewing dozens of photos of the site from both amateurs who had visited on tours to images stored in the private archives of the military. Aerial shots had provided an overall picture of the layout of the assorted batteries and buildings comprising Fort Hancock, as well as the roads and parking areas on Sandy Hook.

He had even hacked into one site to secure more detailed diagrams of the tunnels and mechanisms that had formed part of the Nike missile system, a frontline defense deployed during the Cold War but made obsolete by the development of ICBMs. The Nike missiles hadn't been fast enough to take down the newer, faster weapons, which had resulted in their decommission.

Mick and Caterina must have scrutinized the schematics and maps for what seemed like the hundredth time when he shot a quick glance at his watch and said, "It's time you got some rest."

In truth she was tired and hungry, but they still had several hours to go until their assignation with Mad Dog.

"I'll go make us a bite to eat," she said and left him behind in his office, understanding he needed some time alone. As well as Mick had tried to prepare her, Caterina knew there were things he had kept to himself. Things he had to deal with in order to be ready for tonight's mission.

The pickings in the refrigerator were slim. She quickly made two turkey sandwiches and took them upstairs. They ate together and yet apart. Each bite mechanical because they were both thinking of other things.

Of what the night might bring.

When they finished their sandwiches, Mick thanked Caterina and woodenly repeated his earlier instruction. "You should go get some sleep."

She returned to the guest room but was too wired to rest.

In the corner, leaning against the wall, was the cello. As it had always been for her, the music was the salve to her soul as she sat down and began to play, her fingers shifting smoothly along the strings. Her bow stroking alive deep rich tones from the cast-off instrument. She didn't know how long she played, only that when she was done, her heart raced, her bow arm ached a bit, and the back of her neck was damp with sweat.

As Caterina laid the hand with the bow on her knee and took in a deep breath, she realized Mick was standing at the door to the room. Arms across his chest. A predator's look in his gaze. When he took a step toward her, her heartbeat skipped and then accelerated when he kneeled before her and took hold of the bow and cello. Gently he moved them aside. Took the place of the cello between her legs.

Mick clutched her face between his hands, the action in rough contrast to his earlier approach. The look on his face more fierce. She understood.

There would be no gentleness in this taking. This was the warrior needing what might possibly be a last taste of life before facing death.

She grabbed hold of his wrists, her grip tight as she demanded he release her. He did and she shifted forward in the chair. Urged him forward until they were face-to-face and she became the aggressor.

She kissed him hard, accepting the reason for what would follow. Absolving him of guilt for any lack of tenderness because frankly, she wasn't sure she could be gentle herself. She needed his loving too much to reaffirm the reality of life.

He answered her, opening his mouth and accepting the rough thrust of her tongue. Digging his fingers into her scalp to imprison her head as the kiss deepened until every breath they took was one. Until they were both shaking and she needed to feel the heat of his body beside her.

Inside her.

She yanked at his clothes as he did hers. Separated from him only long enough to remove them. Then he was kneeling before her again, cradled by the softness of her thighs. The jut of his erection pressed to her midsection.

She encircled him and stroked the length of him, but he surprised her by brushing away her hand and bending to suckle the tips of her breasts. She cradled his head, holding him close. Raising her hips to invite him to enter, but he tantalized her by shifting downward.

He trailed his mouth along the center of her body. Dipped his tongue into her navel before continuing lower until she had no doubt about his destination.

She bucked up off the chair as he grasped her thighs and found the center of her with his mouth. Tongued the nub between her legs until it swelled and became more sensitized. Brought his one hand to caress that nub as he kissed her nether lips and then tasted her. Eased his tongue within her center.

Moaning, she gripped him tighter with her knees and caressed the back of his head as he pleasured her. Gasped as the pressure built inside of her, needing more. Needing the hard wide length of him buried within her.

"I want you, Mick," she said, placing her hands on his broad shoulders to compel him upward.

He complied, shifting forward to take her mouth with his as he filled her and then held still.

His arms wrapped around her waist, eliminating any space between their bodies. His kisses were flavored with her taste beneath the more demanding essence of his masculinity.

Then he began to move. His strokes sure. Growing more forceful and faster until the chair groaned and bucked beneath them.

He tightened his hold on her and with one powerful thrust, rose from his knees.

She wrapped her legs around him as he turned and took the step or two to bring her to the edge of the bed.

They fell upon it. Upon each other.

Their movements almost frantic as they sought release. Fought for that final acknowledgment of life.

But what of love? she wondered.

Was there anything of love between them at that moment?

There was so much doubt. So much fear for anything lasting to possibly be forged by this union.

She drove those saddening thoughts away and focused instead on the strength of Mick's body as he moved. As he took them both to the edge before the free fall came and they collapsed in each other's arms.

He was heavy against her, growing limp within her when he said, "I'm sorry. I didn't mean—"

Caterina silenced him with the barest touch of her finger against his lips.

"Don't apologize. I wanted this. I *needed* this."

The soft strands of his hair tickled her breasts as he nodded and said, *"Te quiero."*

He shocked her with his words. Smiling, she urged him upward to place a gentle kiss on his lips as he slipped out of her. "I love you, too."

As he gazed down at her, a hesitant grin blossomed on his lips. "Glad to hear that."

CHAPTER 36

Mad Dog would expect them to come down either Hartshorne Drive or one of the multipurpose paths running beside that main road. He might also be familiar with the black Jeep Mick drove.

A stop to see his cousin Ramon to advise him of what had happened, as well as to swap out cars, took care of one of the problems. Ramon's Safari Wrangler with its desert sand paint job would be hard to pick out, especially since Mick planned to drive it along the water's edge.

Based on his review of the area details and Mad Dog's instructions, Mick guessed that the other man had Liliana in one of the old ammo areas between the Nike radar site and the gun batteries toward the northernmost part of the national park. If Mad Dog positioned himself along the top floors of any one of the remaining battery buildings or close to the rise for the lighthouse, he would have a clean line of fire toward the path and road.

As Mick drove past the ranger station, he cut the lights on the Wrangler and pulled the car off the road and onto the sand.

He stopped it for a moment to make sure Caterina was ready.

She was buckled into the passenger seat beside him, once again dressed all in black. Her upper body appeared bulky from the Kevlar vest beneath the sweater.

"Are you ready?" he asked.

Caterina nodded and he reminded her, "Keep your head down and stay behind me. If things go south—"

"I've got your back no matter what," she reassured and Mick had no doubt about it. She had proven her strength of character time and time again.

Her strength was why he loved her.

With a curt nod, Mick sent the Jeep careening along the hard-packed sand close to the waterline. It might have been a fun ride under different circumstances, with the moon bright above them and the occasional refreshing spray of water kicked up by the tires as they cut through the water at the shore's edge.

Caterina hung tight to the handle along the roll bar as the car bounced from side to side as they hit a dip in the sand.

They made it past the radar site, but Mick feared they were too close to Atlantic Drive as they neared Gunnison Beach.

He trained his gaze toward the lighthouse as they approached and breathed a sigh of relief as they passed without incident. Ahead of him, the half-moon's light illuminated the shadows of the older buildings and battery guns. To their right, beyond the water's edge, lay the glittering lights of New York City's boroughs.

Mick stopped just short of North Beach where the walking trails would lead them to the old proving grounds and batteries.

The first *ping* sounded against the Jeep a second later.

"Get down," Mick said and forced Caterina's head below the edge of the windshield, which cracked in one corner as a second bullet struck the Jeep. He hit the gas and the vehicle lurched forward until, with a sharp turn, he nearly buried it in the side of a high row of dunes, which provided cover from Mad Dog's sniper fire.

"You okay?" Mick asked as he undid his seat belt.

"Fine," Caterina answered. She quickly crept from the car toward the protection of the dune.

He went to the back of the Jeep and removed his M16 assault rifle and satchel. At the dune's edge, he slipped on his night vision goggles and peered above the rim of the dune, using thick tufts of marsh grass for cover.

A bullet plowed into the sand a few feet away. A good sign. Mad Dog had lost sight of them, but the shot had exposed Mad Dog's position at the top ledge of one of the crumbling battery buildings. A chain-link fence with posted trespassing warnings lined the perimeter of the building.

From this angle Mick couldn't get off a killing shot. Plus, he suspected Liliana was hidden well below ground in one of the old ammo storage areas. If he and Caterina could swing around the edge of the dunes and enter one of the farthest battery buildings, Mad Dog would likely fall back to where he held Liliana captive, counting on the traps he had presumably set to take out Mick and Caterina.

Mick crawled back down to where Caterina was hunkered at the bottom of the dune and swung the rifle strap over his shoulder. In the barest of whispers, he explained their next moves. "At the end of this dune there's a chain-link fence. We need to get past it and into the nearest building."

He returned to the Jeep and pulled a small bolt cutter from the back. With that in hand, he crept along the dune's edge to the first accessible section of fence. To distract Mad Dog, he picked up a large clamshell and tossed it back toward where he had grounded the Jeep. The clamshell landed with a noisy clatter on the hood of the Jeep.

Mad Dog opened fire much as Mick had expected, giving him the opportunity to cut through the bottom section of the chain-link and pry it up and out of their way. Unfortunately, the jangle of the metal fence alerted Mad Dog to their real location.

Mad Dog shot in their direction, but not before Mick had gotten a clear look to confirm where they should enter the crumbling battery building. Rifle in hand, he crouched down close to the high dune. "I'm going to give you cover. When I start firing, run straight ahead. You'll see a rusty metal door that's hanging half-open. Go through that doorway and wait for me. Understood?"

"Understood," she said. At his nod, she slipped around him to wait at the dune's edge.

"On three," he said and counted down.

On three Mick stood up and opened fire on Mad Dog's position. Caterina charged ahead, straight for the opening.

Bullets struck the ground behind her, sending up bits of dirt. She reached the door unharmed, too quick for Mad Dog to hit.

Ducking back behind the safety of the dune, Mick took a deep breath before he began his way through the fence. He would be exposed for a few moments while he tried to fit through the opening, but there was no other choice.

Mick ducked through the opening and came up firing, but not before he felt a stinging burn high up on his arm.

He ignored the heat that said he'd been hit and plowed forward to the door and past its rusty exterior to where Caterina waited for him within.

"Thank God," she said as he joined her. She laid a hand on his arm but pulled it away immediately.

Caterina looked down at her hand, wet with his blood. "He shot you."

"A scratch," he said, and meant it. The bullet had only grazed his arm.

Sensibly, she didn't argue with him. There was no turning back, so it made no sense to waste time in such a fashion.

Mick examined the interior of the building. The white-washed cement walls were damp in spots, rust-stained in others, and showing extreme signs of decay. If the tunnels were in similar condition, they would be treacherous in and of themselves. Plus he had no doubt Mad Dog would have rigged at least one booby trap in the tunnels near where he held Liliana.

"Keep close behind me. Watch where I step. Do the same."

At her assent, he headed to the rusty stairs leading to the battery tunnel.

Fuck. He had underestimated Carrera, Mad Dog thought as he picked his way across the crumbling roof to the climbing gear he had used to get up there in the first place. The interior of the building had been too uncertain to navigate.

He rappelled down the side of the building and onto the weed-choked ground. The area was littered with bits of rubble from the disintegrating structures. He crouched down, picking his way back to the rear entrance and the tunnel where he had stowed Carrera's sister.

Morales was waiting for him by the entrance, a sly smile on his face. When he approached, Morales said, "You understand what you need to do."

As if he hadn't understood all along. Not to mention that he didn't much care for people interfering in his plans. "I get it, but I don't like your kind of insurance."

Morales clucked and shook his head. "Santiago understands what to do and when. You'll thank me for the help when this is all over and you're two million dollars richer."

Only the pay raise made Mad Dog willing to tolerate Morales's interference. "I'd make myself scarce, Dr. Morales. It's going to get hairy around here."

"I believe I'll do as you suggest," the other man said, heading toward the public parking lot a short distance away from the battery buildings.

Eager for the fight, Mad Dog made sure he had a full load in his rifle and ducked into the tunnel to finish the job.

CHAPTER 37

The stairs leading up the wall barely held Mick's weight. The rungs on the opposite side leading down into the tunnel had disintegrated beyond use. He sat on the ledge of the wall and waited for Caterina to top the rise. "I'll help you down."

When she was settled on the ledge of the wall he turned and, using his upper-body strength, lowered himself down before dropping the last few feet to the ground.

Caterina was a fast learner, copying his move and falling to the floor with little need of his assistance, reminding him of the strength that Edwards's experimentation had produced in her.

"Show-off," he teased.

"I have a good teacher," she said and offered up a hopeful smile.

Mick gestured to the wide vaulted tunnel before them. "Remember, step where I step. Mad Dog probably laid some traps."

Caterina nodded and Mick cautiously entered the passageway, keeping his eyes open for signs of tracks that might lead him toward Liliana, or for any trip wires or other traps. He moved carefully but not slowly, since each second of delay at this point could risk his sister's life. Caterina was sure-footed behind him, following his lead and orders like any good soldier.

When their tunnel met with another one, Mick held up his hand and Caterina stopped behind him. Ahead of them along the tunnel floor were tracks in the sand and dirt that had drifted in through the gaps in the walls.

Mick flipped up the night vision goggles he had donned and resorted to using the flashlight from his belt. Sweeping the flashlight back and forth along the floor, he noted signs that someone had been dragged down the corridor, as well as occasional spots darkening the ground.

"Is that—"

"Blood," he finished for Caterina. A chill sweat erupted on his body at the thought of Liliana being hurt, but he reined in his reaction.

Calm and logic had to be in control.

He bent for a closer examination of the tracks, and something gnawed at him. These tracks were deep. Deeper than he expected given Liliana's weight.

Keeping that point in mind, he rose and entered the second tunnel, carefully following the trail left behind in the dirt and sand.

He had not gone more than twenty feet or so when he caught the glint of something close to the ground. He held up his hand and Caterina paused behind him. Crouching down, he gingerly reached out and encountered the recognizable bit of metal—a trip wire strung across the width of the tunnel at ankle level.

Peering beyond the trap, he saw that the area appeared clear. The drag marks continued onward as far as he could see in the darkness within the passage. Another fifteen ahead, there was more water along the tunnel floor, seeping in through breaks in the wall. A large chunk of the ceiling had collapsed and lay strewn along the ground. The tracks seemed to sweep around that debris.

Mick glanced over his shoulder at Caterina and pointed to the booby trap. "There's a trip wire here. Be careful as you cross."

She confirmed his instruction with a nod and he rose, stepped high over the trip wire. Moved ahead just enough for Caterina to clear the booby trap as well.

At the puddle of water and spill of debris, he hesitated again, searching for another snare, but the area was clear. He picked his way past the rubble, treading carefully. Knowing that each step brought him closer to saving a woman he loved and possibly losing a woman he loved.

He couldn't live with either choice.

The momentary distraction of that thought cost him.

The floor gave way beneath his foot a second before totally collapsing. He grabbed at the air and one hand found temporary purchase along the lip of the cement floor. His body slammed against the side of the wall in the hole into which he had fallen.

He picked up his other hand, reaching for the floor, struggling to keep from plummeting the rest of the way down, and encountered Caterina's hand.

She grabbed hold of him, her grip strong.

"You okay?" she asked as she poked her head over the edge of the hole. She was lying on her stomach along the floor.

"Could be better," he admitted and risked a glance downward. The drop to the ground was at least another ten feet. Too far to fall without injury, although the water at the bottom might cushion his drop.

He was about to ask her if she could help him up when she slowly began to pull him upward.

As she did so, he got a better hold with his other hand. Working together, they lifted him out of the hole.

"Forgot how strong you were," he admitted once he was back on the ground and sitting beside her.

"Another trap?" she asked, and leaned over the edge of the hollow to look downward.

Mick shook his head and joined her at the edge, peering into the deep well, examining its circumference and depth before it occurred to him what it was.

"It's an old Nike missile silo," he said and glanced upward where a round metal hatch sat above the cavity, confirming his impression. Water dripped in from around the edges of what had likely been a gun battery during World War II.

"I should have been more careful," he said aloud, angry with himself, but she laid her hand over his, the hand that had just saved him, now comforting.

"You've been careful, but you can count on me to help."

He could. She was level-headed. Strong, as she had just proven. Not to mention the camo thing.

"I won't forget that again, Cat. When it comes down to the fight—"

"I'll be there," she reassured with a gentle squeeze of his hand.

"Roger. Let's head out," he said and rose, careful to skirt the edges of the missile silo. Even more vigilant as they neared the end of the tunnel and the rusted metal door, which he assumed would lead to the ammo storage area where Liliana was being held.

Mick paused at the door and signaled Caterina to take a spot by the opposite wall. Dropping into a crouch, he pushed the door open a bit with the muzzle of his rifle. It groaned from the movement, and the sound produced an immediate response.

Rapid-fire gunshots, probably from an AK-47, pinged against the metal doors, driving him back from the opening.

Mick dropped to the ground, proceeding hand over hand toward the opening again. The door had remained partially open, and as he remained behind its protection he peered within the ammo room. Even in the dim light he perceived a figure strapped to a chair in the center of the space.

Dead center.

Another burst of gunfire sounded against the metal door and ricocheted back into the room, driving him back to consider how to breach the area safely.

Mick judged the barrage of bullets to have come from the right side of the room.

He couldn't enter without exposing himself or Liliana to danger.

Looking up toward Caterina, he said, "No matter what, stay put."

Before she could respond, he crawled back toward the opening and called out, "This isn't much fun, is it, Mad Dog?"

Mad Dog answered with another volley from the AK.

He cursed beneath his breath, but forged ahead with his plan. "Getting soft on me, Mad Dog? Too scared for a little *mano-a-mano* again? Might be more interesting than just wasting ammo."

The scuff of a foot on cement sounded loudly in the room. "Scared, Carrera? *Mano-a-mano* it is," Mad Dog said.

A shadow became visible, falling against Liliana's feet as she sat in the chair. A clatter followed as a clip for an AK hit the floor beside the chair.

Mick rose from the ground, but remained behind the protection of the door. Releasing the clip on the M16, he tossed it close to the chair as well.

"Now this is going to be fun," Mad Dog said and stepped into Mick's line of sight. He had no doubt the other man had at least another gun somewhere on his body, but for now, the AK was useless. To further prove it, Mad Dog dropped it to the ground by the chair.

Mick rose and slipped the strap for the rifle over his head. He settled the rifle against the door close to where Caterina stood and removed his satchel. He placed it beside the rifle and pointed to it, hoping she would remember there was a spare clip inside the bag.

With a last glance at her, Mick entered the ammo room and faced Mad Dog as he stood several feet away from Liliana, who was strapped to a chair in the shadows. Despite the lack of light there, Mick could see dark stains on the front of her shirt and the way her head lolled back at an awkward angle.

Fear gripped him, followed by anger.

Killing anger.

"You promised to let her go if I brought you Shaw," Mick said, fists clenched at his side.

Mad Dog chuckled and shook his head. "So where is Shaw?"

"She's outside, waiting in the tunnel for the exchange."

Mad Dog laughed again, louder than before. "Perfect. I'm going to have fun letting you watch what I do to your two ladies."

Somehow Mick tempered his killing anger, reserving it for when the time was right because he intended to exterminate Mad Dog today. It had been a long time coming, but this vendetta would end this night.

"Bring it on," Mick said.

CHAPTER 38

Mad Dog copied Mick's stance, hands held up loosely, feet braced slightly apart. Ready for any attack or defense.

They approached each other, anticipating each other's movements. Feinting and challenging until Mad Dog finally attacked, shooting out with a drop kick that Mick blocked with his arm.

Mick dropped back, bouncing on the balls of his feet. Waiting for another attack as he played his own version of rope-a-dope, understanding Mad Dog well. Mad Dog thought himself invincible. Never a good trait.

Mad Dog charged him time and time again, unleashing flurries of kicks and punches, which Mick repeatedly blocked, waiting for his moment. His arms and legs ached from Mad Dog's blows, but the pain was minor compared to how Mad Dog would feel when Mick finally engaged him.

Mick ducked a drop kick, but Mad Dog surprised him by following up with a flying roundhouse kick that caught him across the side of the head. Staggering for a moment, he intentionally let down his guard, inviting Mad Dog closer.

The other man accepted, charging in for the kill.

*   *   *

Mick had told her to stay put, but Caterina couldn't keep on listening to the sounds of battle within the room, unaware of whether Mick was winning or losing.

As she neared the door, she stepped on the satchel by her foot and realized why he had left it behind.

She bent, opened the bag, and removed the clip. Forced herself to remember how Mick had loaded the gun and locked the clip home.

As she walked to the door, the white of her hand against the rifle stock shocked her. It was the white of the tunnel walls. Prompted by her fear for Mick, she had gone all camo.

It was what might make a difference in today's outcome.

Caterina placed the rifle down as she quickly disrobed, even down to removing the Kevlar vest Mick had insisted she don.

Her body had become the same mottled white as the walls. As she entered the room, rifle in hand, neither of the two men registered her entry.

As Cat watched, Mick delivered an uppercut to the other man's midsection, doubling him over, then following up with another blow that lifted Mad Dog's body from the ground with its force. Made a sickening crunch as bones broke.

With Mad Dog doubled over, Mick brought his elbow down across the back of the man's neck.

Mad Dog crumpled to the ground, his body limp at Mick's feet.

Mick slowly stood upright, bloodied fists clenched at his sides as he glanced down at his opponent. His body heaved as he sucked in breaths heavy from his physical exertions.

Believing the battle concluded, she dropped the rifle, drawing Mick's attention, although he peered with confusion toward where she stood, obviously not seeing her.

Heavy pounding footsteps sounded as something big lumbered from a far tunnel and then across the room. A large man plowed into Mick, sending him crashing into the opposite wall with a bone-rattling blow.

Mick's head rebounded against the wall and as he sagged to the ground, a trail of blood marked his fall.

Caterina drew in a shocked breath, drawing the attention of the one man left standing.

Santiago.

She remembered him now from the medical facility. Remembered him fighting with another man the night Wells had been murdered.

Santiago searched out her sound and she reached down and picked up the rifle once again. She shifted quickly toward the shadows, wanting to maintain the element of surprise, since she knew she wasn't much of a match for the hulking man.

As she did so, Mad Dog stirred, coming to his knees as he shook his head, as if to toss off his dizziness.

Mad Dog snared Santiago's attention. The big man plodded over and stood there, waiting for Mad Dog to rise.

Once he was upright, Mad Dog stared past the tattooed brute to where Mick sat unconscious against the far wall.

Mad Dog put his hands on his hips and chastised the huge man. "You did good to follow Morales's instruction and wait. I just hope you didn't kill him, big guy. That would spoil all the fun."

Shit, Caterina thought, tightening her grip on the rifle. Hoping she wouldn't have to use it because...

Santiago surged forward and grabbed Mad Dog around the neck. Snapped it with one swift twist.

Mad Dog fell to the ground, only this time he wouldn't be getting up. His head rested at an unnatural angle against the floor as his sightless eyes stared toward her.

A moan came from across the room. Mick was beginning to stir.

Santiago noticed immediately.

The big man took a step toward Mick, clearly intending to finish him off, but Caterina couldn't let that happen.

She pounded the wall with the butt of the rifle, drawing Santiago's attention away from Mick.

The massive man turned in her direction, immensely muscled arms open wide to draw someone into their deadly embrace. The broad width of his chest provided a huge target. The proverbial side of a barn.

She drew up the rifle and aimed, pulled the trigger.

The first bullet struck Santiago high up on one shoulder, but the unexpected kick of the rifle made the next few shots go wide of that very large expanse of chest.

The bullet did as much damage as a BB might. Santiago lurched in her direction, but Caterina raced deeper into the shadows so she could prepare to shoot again. Her body color changed as she ran, providing her cover, but as she cut across the room, she stepped into something wet and slippery.

Her feet flew out from under her and she landed hard, just a few feet away from the chair holding Liliana.

Santiago rounded the back of the chair and stopped short, searching the area for her.

Caterina held her breath, waiting for him to charge.

Trying to figure out what to do next. Hoping she could get the rifle up in time to get off another round.

From across the room came the scuffle of a footstep and a pained breath.

Mick was on his feet, the wall behind him the one thing that seemed to be keeping him upright.

Santiago turned in that direction and laughed the large loud laugh of a lunatic. Echoing eerily throughout the room until another, smaller sound intruded.

A soft pop. No louder than a soda can opening. Followed by a second pop that finally silenced Santiago's insane humor.

The colossal man landed barely a yard away from her, shaking the ground with the force of his impact, a neat round hole in the middle of his forehead.

Caterina scrambled to her feet and over to where Mick slowly sagged back down the wall. She kneeled beside him and reined herself in, regaining the normal human tones of her skin.

"Must be in heaven 'cuz I see an angel," Mick said, wincing since it seemed every breath cost him great effort. The deep rattle that came from his chest caused her heart to constrict with fear, as did his slightly unfocused gaze and the blood on the wall behind his head.

"We need to get you to a hospital."

A limp and ungraceful nod confirmed that Mick understood, but somehow he managed to say, "Liliana."

"Give me a second to dress." Caterina left him the rifle just in case and quickly retrieved her clothes, along with his satchel.

She returned to Mick's side and eased his arm around her shoulders, helped him to his feet, but she sensed what it cost him. Mick leaned on her heavily and his breath rasped in his chest, each inhalation clearly paining him.

With heavy plodding steps they approached the chair to which Liliana was strapped, but as they neared the figure in the shadows, fear increased with every step.

The large amount of blood behind the chair became apparent, as did the awkward angle of the person's head.

But as they took another step, they stopped short, realizing the person was much larger than Liliana and was wearing a dark khaki shirt with olive green pants.

"It's a park ranger. She's not here," Caterina said, glancing up at Mick only to see the despair nearly overcome him before he controlled his emotions.

"She's here. I know it. He'd want to keep her close," he answered and applied light pressure on her arm to guide her in the direction of the tunnel from where Santiago had emerged.

"To use her as bait again?" she asked, worried at the way he leaned on her, barely able to remain upright.

"He'd ... want ... play ... with her." It was a sacrifice for him to speak. With each word came a fearsome rattle from deep in his chest.

Caterina didn't ask any more, providing him with the strength he needed to take each painful step down the hall until they came to another rusted door.

Mick leaned against the wall heavily and took out his gun. His hand shook as he did so. As their gazes met, Caterina understood.

"Let me have it. I promise not to miss this time," she said.

He didn't argue, handing her the Glock.

Caterina approached the entrance. The door was ajar and a spill of low light fell into the tunnel. Gingerly she opened the rusty door, which creaked with the movement.

She waited, thinking the noise might have given away her presence, but nothing happened.

Pushing the door wider, she copied what she had seen Mick do earlier, staying low as she peered within to scope out the room.

In the center, someone was strapped to a chair, head of dark hair slumped down toward her chest. Fear crept over Cat and as it did so, the strange halo sight took over, outlining the figure in the chair with an aura and filling it with colors—the colors of warmth and life, she realized.

As she glanced all around the room, she could sense no one else was there and entered, the halo sight receding as she did so.

"Liliana?" she asked as she approached and the person's head lifted up.

A mumbled sound escaped the prisoner and Caterina took another step closer, realizing that this time they'd found Mick's sister.

Caterina rushed over and kneeled before her. Carefully removed the duct tape over Liliana's mouth. Tried to avoid the sight of Liliana's naked breasts and the bruises on her face as she said, "Are you okay?"

"Never better if you and Mick are here," Liliana said and glanced toward the door, as if expecting her brother to enter.

"He's hurt bad," Caterina advised and looked around for some way to cut the tape binding Liliana to the chair. A short distance away a long knife rested by the door and she grabbed it, made short work of the bindings.

Liliana rose stiffly and tied her shirtfront together,

trying to hide her condition. While she did so, she asked, "What happened?"

"A park ranger is dead, along with Mad Dog and another of the gene therapy patients." As Caterina spoke, she urged Liliana to follow her and they hurried back to Mick's side.

As they rushed through the door, they spotted Mick slumped against the wall. His labored breathing was louder than before and a sickly pallor had replaced the healthy tones of his skin.

Liliana kneeled before her brother and gently eased his head up. He opened his eyes and looked at her, but Caterina could see his gaze was unfocused.

"*Hermanita*. You're safe," he said and coughed, bringing up rich red blood.

Liliana nodded and gently swiped away the blood along the side of his mouth. "I'm okay and you're going to be okay as well, Mick."

Together they helped him to his feet, but as her gaze met Liliana's, Caterina realized how concerned Mick's sister was. How serious his sister was about Mick's injuries.

Carefully they picked their way back, avoiding the pit of the missile silo. Gingerly walking over the trip wire.

From some distance away, Mick managed to advise Caterina on how to trip the booby trap to protect anyone who might enter the tunnel. The small explosion that followed brought down part of the tunnel wall. It would have trapped them beneath the debris if they had tripped it on the way in.

With the area now safe, they moved as quickly as they could back toward the Jeep and laid Mick in the small jump seat area, Liliana kneeling beside him.

Caterina took the wheel, aware that she had to get him medical help.

Liliana braced Mick's body, trying to keep him steady. She was certain he had broken a rib or two and punctured a lung. She wanted to avoid doing any more damage by the errant motion of the Jeep. He seemed weaker with each passing moment, but he held onto consciousness somehow as Caterina drove up off the beach and onto the nearby public road, obviously aware that Mick couldn't handle a jostling ride along the surf's edge.

"Hold on, *Miguelito*. We'll get you help soon," Liliana said, feeling his pain as if it were her own. Aware that he had once again sacrificed himself for her.

"I'm okay," Mick said, registering the mixture of guilt and concern in his sister's voice. Not wanting her to feel responsible for what had happened.

But even on the smoother public road, every movement brought pain and Mick gritted his teeth to contain the agony. His broken ribs were grating together with every bump. His labored breath and the blood he coughed up once again confirmed to him that one of his ribs had damaged his lung. His ears were ringing and he realized he had a concussion, maybe even a skull fracture.

He was done for sure, Mick thought as he fumbled to extract his cell phone from his pocket. Somehow he managed to hand it to Liliana as his fingers began to go numb. His extremities were cold from shock and the blood filling his lung, drowning him and making each breath laborious.

But the mission was also done. And it had been a success because both Caterina and Liliana were safe.

"I'm going home," Mick said to his sister, satisfied that he had completed the mission he had been meant to do.

Feeling freer than he ever had as he allowed himself to slip into the darkness calling him.

Liliana watched helplessly as Mick lost consciousness. Tears complicated making the phone call, obscuring her vision, but she somehow speed-dialed Ramon. Fighting back tears, she explained where to find Mad Dog and the others.

"Where are you now?" Ramon asked.

"Hartshorne. Heading to the Highlands," she said and shot a glance at Caterina as she drove.

"I'm going to give you directions to the hospital," Liliana yelled to Caterina against the road noise as she took a quick look at her brother before returning her attention to Ramon.

"Meet us there, Ramon. But I need a promise from you."

Her cousin hesitated. "I can't make any promises, Lil. Bring them in and we'll figure out what to do."

She shot another glance at Caterina, who seemed to have overheard a snippet of the conversation.

"I don't care who's looking for me. We're going to the hospital," Caterina shouted back over the din from the wind whipping into the open vehicle.

Somehow Liliana had never had a doubt that's what Caterina would say, because Caterina loved Mick. Liliana had never been more certain of anything else in her life.

"We're on our way, Ramon," she said, hung up the phone and took Mick's limp hand in hers, praying that it wasn't too late.

Liliana had no doubt her brother cared for Caterina as well, and hoped the two of them would have time to be able to share that love.

CHAPTER 39

A steady throb behind his eyeballs kept pace with the repetitive electronic beep nearby. Mick cracked open his eyes and a gentle familiar touch on his hand told him he was not alone.

"Cat?" he asked, and suddenly she was standing above him, her beautiful face filling his vision.

"I'm here, Mick," Caterina said.

He tried to smile, but his lips were dry and pulled with the motion. Caterina quickly offered up some ice chips to wet his lips and parched throat.

"Thank you." Turning his head, he realized he was in a hospital bed with an assortment of tubes and wires attached to his body. He tried to move, but he felt stiff and moving was painful. "How long have I been here?"

"A little over a day, love," she said and offered him some more ice chips, but he shook his head, which only created an intense well of pain in the middle of his skull.

"Easy, Mick. You have a hairline skull fracture and concussion. Several broken ribs and a punctured lung. You almost didn't make it."

He was thankful that's all it was, because he remembered feeling as if a Mack truck had run him down. But the pain was mitigated by the knowledge that he had found his sister.

"Liliana," he said, not realizing he had said it out loud until Caterina replied.

"She had to leave a few hours ago to do her rounds, but she'll be back."

"How are you?" he asked and closed his eyes, the light in the room too bright to his concussion-sensitized sight.

Caterina ran a cool hand across the side of his face and said, "I'm fine. When we brought you to the hospital your cousin Ramon was waiting for us. I explained what happened—"

"He called in the Feds," Mick jumped in, recalling the dead park ranger.

"As well as the local and Camden PDs," he heard and opened his eyes to see Ramon strolling in, wearing his summer khakis, his sheriff's hat in hand.

Ramon came to stand by the railing of his bed and smiled at Caterina. "Glad to see you decided to join us, *primo*."

"What's going on?" he asked his cousin.

Ramon's lips tightened into a thin line before he said, "Feds are coordinating with the locals, since it seems the MO for the park ranger's murder is the same as for Wells. There's also a DNA match to the goon you plugged between the eyes."

"Santiago," Caterina said and the name struck a discord with his cousin.

"Rob Santiago, the cop killer. Seems they reduced his sentence if he agreed to participate in the Wardwell study."

"Son of a bitch," Mick cursed and glanced at Caterina. "You saved my life. You and Lil."

She twined her fingers with his. "I couldn't lose you."

Mick tightened his hold on her hand and faced Ramon once again. "Cat didn't kill Wells. We've got—"

"Caterina's been released on my recognizance, but I suspect they'll be dropping all charges shortly," Ramon advised.

Mick's major mission had been accomplished, but something still gnawed at his gut. "Did you get Edwards and Morales?"

Ramon looked away, unable to hold his gaze, and Mick repeated, "Did you, Ramon?"

His cousin jiggled his hat up and down in his hand before finally meeting his gaze. "Edwards and Morales have disappeared, along with the remaining four patients in the gene therapy program. They'll need lots of space and equipment. It'll make it hard for them to hide for long."

Mick thought about how much money Edwards had paid him and Franklin. How much they must have offered Mad Dog to eliminate all of them. With that much money . . .

"Those families need closure. Someone's got to find the missing patients."

Caterina echoed Mick's sentiment. "Someone will."

Ramon nodded. "Definitely. And soon. Trust me."

Mick glanced at Caterina and knew she understood. After Ramon excused himself, he squeezed her hand and said, "I'm glad you'll be cleared of any charges."

A confused look crossed her face. "That's sounding a bit too much like a brush-off."

Mick shrugged. A big mistake as pain lanced through his side, but he bit back a groan and said, "You and Liliana are safe now. You'll be able to go back to your regular life."

"What if I don't want to?"

Now it was his turn to be confused. "Your music is your life."

Caterina nodded and pulled her hair back, trained those stunning blue eyes on his face. "Music is a big *part* of my life, but I've found something else I want in my life. Something that makes it complete."

Mick's heartbeat did a funky beat that registered on the monitors, drawing Caterina's attention to the machines. "You okay? Should I get a doctor?"

"Actually, if I'm the something else you want, I think you should go get a priest."

Caterina narrowed her eyes and examined his face.

"A priest?" she repeated.

Mick allowed a slow grin to spread across his face as he said, "Well, I've either died and should get last rites or I need to make this relationship more permanent before you change your mind."

Caterina chuckled and shook her head, sending her long dark locks shifting with the motion. "Not what I would call a romantic proposal."

"I love you, Cat. Heart and soul. Flesh and bone. Every part of me is yours, *querida*."

Caterina stood and bent over him, her lips barely an inch from his. "I love you, Mick. You are the music of my heart and I never want to be without you."

She closed the distance and kissed him, her lips warm and mobile against his. The intensity of the kiss growing until a cough sounded from the doorway, yanking Caterina away from him.

Caterina jerked upright and turned, but slipped her hand back into Mick's.

His mother stood at the door bracketed by two men who could only be his father and brother, since the resemblance was so strong. Liliana had called them as soon as they knew Mick was out of the woods, but it had taken some time for them to return home from Chicago.

Obviously they'd arrived and, from the worry etched on his mother's face, hearing the news about Mick's injuries had clearly taken a toll on her.

"Mariel," Caterina said and walked toward the woman, took her hands in hers, and offered a reassuring squeeze. "He's feeling better than he looks."

"Good, because he looks like shit," said the man she surmised to be his younger brother.

"*Mi'jito*, watch your language. Caterina, this is Antonio—"

"Tony will do," he said, a broad welcoming smile on his face. "Are you Mick's girl?"

Mick's girl, she thought and glanced over her shoulder at Mick before returning her attention to his family.

"Actually I'm Mick's fiancée; that is, if you approve," Caterina said and watched as surprise flickered across the three faces.

His father finally mastered that shock and spoke up. "Welcome to the family, *mi'jita*."

EPILOGUE

One month later

The summer sun beat down mercilessly, and not even the tinted windows on the SUV could fight its assault. The heat in the interior of the vehicle had been steadily rising as Morales sat there waiting for them. Slowly baking while the three of them were probably off somewhere cool.

He drove his thoughts away from the heat. Ignored the trickle of sweat down the side of his face as he told himself that they were bound to arrive soon.

It would be time for Ms. Shaw to have another plasmapheresis treatment, and a crisp hundred paid to one of the orderlies had confirmed that she would be arriving today.

As a black Jeep pulled into the parking lot for the hospital, Morales tracked its passage to an empty spot at the far side of the lot. Held his breath as he waited for the occupants to emerge and was not disappointed.

Caterina Shaw slipped from the vehicle, along with a handsome Latino man. Carrera, he supposed, since he had never encountered the man in person.

The couple met at the back of the Jeep and embraced. Shared a kiss before joining hands and walking together toward the door to the hospital.

As they neared the entrance, the automatic doors swooshed open and a young woman exited the building. Petite. Wearing a lab coat and badge that identified her as one of the hospital personnel. Her dark good looks, so similar to the man with Shaw, identified her as family.

Beneath the canopy of the hospital's entrance, the three embraced, happiness and love radiating from one and all.

Sickening, Morales thought, tapping his fingers on the steering wheel. Itching to rush out and grab Shaw. Finish what he had started.

But not today, he thought as the clueless trio walked into the hospital together, believing themselves safe. Believing that the nightmare was over for them, only...

Morales started the engine, cranked up the air-conditioning and drove away, his smile as chilly as the air coming from the vents of the SUV as he thought, *It's only just begun.*

Turn the page
for a sneak peek at
the next exciting story in
Caridad Piñeiro's sinfully
good new series . . .
Stronger Than Sin

CHAPTER 1

The scientist enjoyed the rage even more than the control he possessed over his captive.

In truth, Jesse Bradford enjoyed the violence as well. It let him vent his frustration at being imprisoned. Allowed him to release his anger over the deadly mutation his body was undergoing thanks to Morales's science experiment.

Jesse pounded the heavy bag with such force that a seam on the side began to split. Another blow with his rock-hard fists opened the tear even farther.

Morales egged him on. "That's it, Bradford. Destroy it," the scientist urged as he stood, a cattle prod in hand, just outside the cage that held Jesse.

Jesse remembered the sting of that device. He had a deadened and hard piece of what had formerly been flesh along his rib cage where the good doctor had stuck him months earlier.

Jesse had been punished for interfering as another patient had murdered Morales's colleague—Dr. Rudy Wells. Wells had seen the error of his ways, and Jesse had hoped then that Wells would be able to stop the experimentation and torture being visited on him and the other patients.

Now Wells was dead and Jesse was still a captive. Others also; he knew from their screams during the long days and even more interminable nights.

At Jesse's delay, Morales picked up the prod and stepped closer. Exhorted him once again: "Destroy it."

Jesse needed no further instruction. He walked up to the heavy bag, encircled it in his muscled arms, and, imagining that it was his captor, squeezed until the bag compressed in his arms, straining the seams, which parted farther from the pressure. He dug his fingers into the gaps and yanked, ripping the bag open and spewing its innards along the floor of the cage.

Releasing the mangled bits of bag, Jesse stepped away, but as he did so he noticed Morales's new assistant entering the warehouse that had been converted into the laboratory and prison where he and the others were now being kept.

The man swaggered over to Morales, his odd gait and the spiky strands of his bright blond hair giving him the appearance of a bantam rooster. His diminutive stature and jerky motions only added to that impression.

"Did you get her, Jack?" Morales said as his assistant neared.

"She's in the SUV," Jack replied.

"Then bring her in," Morales chastised.

The rooster crowed. "She's no lightweight. I'll need some help with her."

Morales immediately turned to Jesse. "Help Jack."

Jesse would, knowing the punishment for refusal—the prod and an assortment of drugs that made his brain scream in his skull. At his nod, Morales approached and unlocked the door. Motioned for him to follow Jack. As

Jesse did so, Morales stayed close enough to employ the dreaded prod.

As Jack opened the door to the warehouse, Jesse noticed the large black SUV sitting close by. Jack used the remote and the back door slowly lifted open, revealing the body of the woman within.

No lightweight, Jesse's thoughts echoed, noticing the lush rounded curves of a real woman.

"Get to it, Bradford," Jack instructed, pulling his shoulders back and twitching his head in the direction of the unconscious female.

Jesse bent toward her and as he did, he got a better look at her face.

Stunning, he thought.

High cheekbones and full lips. Finely arched brows of a deep cocoa color, much like her shoulder-length hair.

A familiar face, he realized when he finally had her in his arms and lifted her from the back of the SUV.

"Take her inside," Morales commanded.

Jesse walked into the warehouse with her, wondering why she had been taken. From the elegant evening gown she wore, he knew she wasn't one of the homeless that Morales had begun to bring in for the experiments.

Which made him wonder who she was and why Morales had decided to kidnap her.

Once again he examined her features, trying to place where he might have met her. Too many women had come and gone in his life, a byproduct of the fame and fortune that came from being a successful professional athlete. There had always been more than one groupie hanging out at the arena to satisfy his physical needs.

Only after the fame and fortune had been taken from

him had he realized just what an empty existence it had been. How stupid he had been not to appreciate the company of a woman as beautiful as this one, he thought, following Morales's silent command to place her on the stainless steel table in the center of the lab portion of the warehouse.

The surface of the table was cold. He placed her on it and waited.

Chill metal, hard and unyielding, registered against Liliana Carrera's back, exposed by the low cut of her gown. The sensation slowly roused her from the stupor that had overtaken her.

She tried to open her eyelids, but the strong lights above her were sharply bright, creating a knot of pain in the center of her skull. Guardedly she cracked her eyelids open against the glare, her vision blurry at first.

Liliana tried to make sense of what was happening as consciousness returned. The last thing she remembered was standing backstage, listening to the closing notes of the concerto her brother's newlywed wife was performing. Then a prick had registered at the side of her neck and blackness had claimed her just seconds later.

She had been drugged.

Now she was on an examination table.

As Liliana finally opened her eyes, squinting against the harsh light, she saw that a man stood beside her. A very large and tall man, she could tell from his fuzzy outline, until her vision finally sharpened and she could make out his details.

He had a mop of wavy dark brown hair and pale blue

eyes. She had seen him before somewhere, but her brain was still too muddled to remember where.

"I know you," she muttered, struggling to place him.

At her acknowledgment, a broad joyful smile erupted on his handsome face, but before he could comment or say anything else, someone stepped beside him.

Chill fear gripped her hard, driving the last of the fuzziness from her brain.

"Morales, you son of a bitch," she said, recognizing the scientist who had arranged to have her kidnapped months earlier.

"So nice to see you again, Dr. Carrera," the man said with a sly smile before he held up a cattle prod and slipped it between her and the large man. Applied light pressure to urge the giant away from the table.

"Tie her up," Morales instructed before she could say anything else.

Another man raced from the shadows to do Morales's bidding, although not fast enough.

Liliana slipped half off the table before the man corralled her against its surface. She rolled from right to left to avoid him, punched and scratched while trying to escape Morales's goon as he attempted to place leather restraints around her wrists and ankles. She even managed to land a solid kick that had the much smaller man reeling away from the table.

With that action, the giant who had stood beside her earlier reacted unexpectedly.

Jesse burst forward with the speed that had made him famous on the football field, tackling Jack. If the woman escaped, she might be able to lead someone back to this place. They might all finally be freed from their torture.

His interference allowed the woman to slip from the surface of the table and head on unsteady feet toward the door of the warehouse.

Morales muttered a curse and raced around the table and up and over the tangle of Jesse and Jack to chase the woman. He caught up to her with the cattle prod and brought her down with one blast.

Jack elbowed Jesse in the ribs, attempting to get free, not that the puny man could really inflict much punishment on him. With a rabbit punch to the back of Jack's head, he knocked him unconscious and charged after Morales, fists clenched at his sides, a mix of desperation and hope forcing him to act. Making him pray that the woman would awaken and make her escape before Morales could neutralize him.

"You're not being a good boy, Jesse," Morales said as Jesse insinuated himself between the doctor and the prone body of the woman. Morales raised the cattle prod defensively, although Jesse's only desire at the moment was for the woman to get free.

"Let her go," Jesse said and expectantly held his breath as the woman moaned and rolled onto her side, slowly regaining consciousness once more.

"You know I can't do that," Morales said, his voice deceptively calm. Seemingly unconcerned with the woman as she somehow awkwardly managed to get to her knees.

"Let her go," Jesse warned again and took a step toward the scientist, hiding his fear at what the prod would do to him. Planning for how to get Morales to strike him where it would do the least damage—in the stone-cold area Morales's last attack had created.

The scientist raised the prod and jabbed it in Jesse's direction like a fencer executing a lunge.

Jesse avoided the dangerous tip, feinting to one side. Shifting and turning to avoid the device as Morales attacked again and again. The longer Jesse delayed the scientist, the greater the odds the woman would escape.

Their dance turned them around so that Jesse could see that she had begun to crawl unsteadily toward the exit of the warehouse.

However, Jesse's moment of joy was short-lived as the tip of the prod grazed his upper bicep, unleashing a torrent of pain as the electrical shock traveled across his nerve endings.

He called out in agony and crumpled to one knee. As Morales prodded him again, the rage the scientist had somehow created with his virulent combination of genes awoke, creating a burning pit in his gut. Sending adrenaline racing through his body.

"No-o-o-o!" he screamed, so long and so hard that the woman paused in her flight and turned wary eyes in his direction.

"Run!" he hollered, wanting her to keep on going. Wanting her to escape.

Morales jabbed the prod toward him again, and Jesse managed to turn. Absorbed the blow against the bony deadness along his rib cage.

The pause in the pain provided Jesse with the opportunity he needed.

He snatched the offensive device from Morales's hands. Smiled at the look of fear that stole over the scientist's face.

The woman was now on her feet, weaving like a drunken sailor as she neared the exit.

"Faster!" he called out, urging her on. Praying for her success.

The pain of the barbs in Jesse's side registered only a second before another jolt of electricity surged through him.

His body jerked, dancing on the ends of the wires connected to the Taser Jack held. Long moments passed before Jesse could no longer bear the pain and crumpled to his knees. But as he fell, he realized the woman was now just a few feet away from the door, which made the pain worthwhile.

As dizzying circles of black danced before his eyes and the smell of his burning flesh reached his nostrils, Jesse exhorted her once again.

"Run."

THE DISH

Where authors give you the inside scoop!

♥ ♥ ♥ ♥ ♥ ♥ ♥ ♥ ♥ ♥ ♥ ♥ ♥ ♥ ♥ ♥

From the desk of Lisa Dale

Dear Reader,

Do you believe in love at first sight? I do. The moment I set foot in Burlington, Vermont, two summers ago, I knew I was wildly, head-over-heels, never-to-recover in love with Vermont.

It was a no-brainer to set IT HAPPENED ONE NIGHT (on sale now) on the beautiful shores of Lake Champlain. Lana Biel longs to leave her family's Vermont wildflower farm so she can travel and see the world. And her sister Karin wants nothing more than to put down roots and conceive the child she and her husband just can't seem to have. When a lighthearted fling with a mountain biker leaves Lana expecting, she finds herself tumbling headlong into motherhood while her sister Karin can only look on.

For help, Lana turns to Eli Ward, a professional meteorite hunter and her best friend for the last ten years. But Eli's keeping secrets that could turn their friendship on its head. As the Vermont seasons change and the flowers in the wildflower meadows begin to fade, Lana must make some meaningful decisions about her family, her friendships, her love life, and her dreams.

Many of my girlfriends are new moms—and what a lifestyle change motherhood brings! At some point I think all women must wrestle with the question, *Can* we have it all? The kids, the job, the freedom, *and* the man of our dreams? Lana lives for her future and pins all her hopes on traveling the world. But what happens when fate has other plans?

I hope you'll read about Lana, Karin, and Eli's journey as they discover the courage within. Please check out my website at www.LisaDaleBooks.com. I love to hear from readers and hope you'll be in touch.

Happy reading!

Lisa Dale

From the desk of Caridad Piñeiro

Dear Reader,

I have a confession to make—I'm a science geek.

I've always been fascinated with how things work, and so it was no surprise that I decided to major in science when I went to Villanova. It was probably more of a surprise that I did a switch after college to pursue a career in law and then decided to return to my first love—writing.

What wasn't a surprise with my writing is that over the years my love of science and how things work has always managed to make it into my various novels. Whether they were paranormals, romance, or suspense, the science geek in me always found a way to research and try something new in each novel.

Of course, this is more true for SINS OF THE FLESH (on sale now) than for any of my other novels. With SINS OF THE FLESH (and the rest of the upcoming books in the SINS series), I let the science nerd out of the closet and delved into some of my favorite subjects in college—genetics, immunology, and biology. I also got to use some of the interesting developments that have been going on over the years since I graduated.

Interesting things like the GFPs (green fluorescent proteins) that make Caterina glow—the ones whose creators were acknowledged with the 2008 Nobel Prize in chemistry. Did you know that scientists have developed cats that glow in the dark? GFPs let them trace and mark where genes are going!

There are lots of other factual instances in SINS OF THE FLESH based on new developments in gene therapy as well as my own musings on where splicing human and nonhuman genes may take us in the future.

Tossed in with all that science are some of the things that I love most when I write—a determined heroine who is not afraid to fight her own battles and a hero who is strong enough to embrace the love of family and a special woman.

Mix all those parts together and I hope you will find yourself hooked on the world I've created for the SINS series!

Wishing you all the best and much edge-of-seat reading,

www.caridad.com

Want to know more about romances at Grand Central Publishing and Forever? Get the scoop online!

GRAND CENTRAL PUBLISHING'S ROMANCE HOMEPAGE

Visit us at www.hachettebookgroup.com/romance for all the latest news, reviews, and chapter excerpts!

NEW AND UPCOMING TITLES

Each month we feature our new titles and reader favorites.

CONTESTS AND GIVEAWAYS

We give away galleys, autographed copies, and all kinds of fun stuff.

AUTHOR INFO

You'll find bios, articles, and links to personal websites for all your favorite authors—and so much more!

THE BUZZ

Sign up for our monthly romance newsletter, and be the first to read all about it!